Acclaim for Alexander Fedderly's

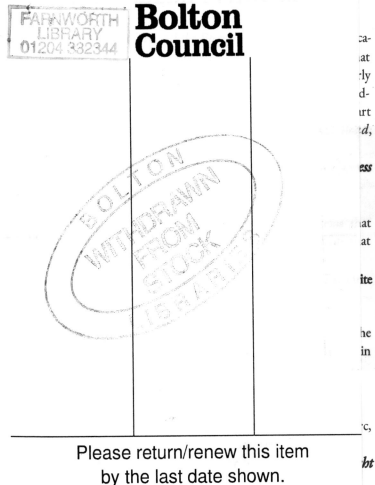

Bolton
Council

ca-
at
ly
d-
urt
d,

ess

at
at

ite

he
in

c,

ht

Please return/renew this item
by the last date shown.
Books can also be renewed at
www.bolt

to
id

– Jeff Beesler, auth

ALL THE EMPTY HOUSES

A NOVEL

ALEXANDER FEDDERLY

Alexander J. Fedderly
Atlanta, GA

First Edition, March 2022

Publisher's Cataloging-in-Publication data

Names: Fedderly, Alexander, author.
Title: All the empty houses / Alexander Fedderly.
Description: Atlanta, GA: Alexander J. Fedderly, 2022.
Identifiers: LCCN: 2022902492 | ISBN: 979-8-9856689-0-2 (paperback) |
979-8-9856689-1-9 (ebook)
Subjects: LCSH Survival--Fiction. | Survivalism--Fiction. | Preparedness--Fiction. |
Science fiction. | Dystopias. | Apocalyptic fiction. | BISAC FICTION / Science Fiction /
Apocalyptic & Post-Apocalyptic | FICTION / Science Fiction / Action & Adventure |
FICTION / Disaster | FICTION / Dystopian
Classification: LCC PS3606.E328 A55 2022 | DDC 813.6--dc23

@alex_fedderly

This book is dedicated to my wife, Beth
& my mother, Karen,
&
to my friends & family who helped make its writing possible.
It takes a village.

ALL THE EMPTY HOUSES

Pour accomplir de grandes choses il ne suffit pas d'agir, il faut rêver; il ne suffit pas de calculer, il faut croire.

To accomplish great things we must not only act, but also dream; not only plan, but also believe.

Anatole France

THE BUNKER

Christopher Michael James inched toward the station on the corner in his beat-up pickup, the needle on the dash bearing down on empty. Knotted around the pumps up ahead, the lines for gas spilled off the lot and stretched back onto the road. Gridlock. He jammed his palm into the horn with a sigh. "Not again," he said, waving his arm out the window in disgust.

He was home from the Sandbox for good, honorably discharged to 1st CivDiv. Back in the real world, a place with strange annoyances like city traffic. But he was a soldier and damn proud of it, and he didn't plan on getting soft. He was still a young man. His duty to God and country had been fulfilled, but the heart of a warrior still thumped in his chest. Military training had chiseled his body. The desert honed his senses. Nothing would take away that edge, not even the civvies replacing his fatigues.

"You've got to be kidding me."

Drivers were getting out of their cars, pacing on the road, talking into their cell phones. Some leaned over their doors, dejected stares on their faces, helpless until the tangle around the pumps cleared.

"What a fucking mess." He glanced at the gauge on the dash and laid on the horn again. "Let's go," he yelled out the window from the back of the line, tension building in his gut.

He had been searching for gas for nearly two weeks, most of the time he'd been stateside, but there was hardly any to be found in the entire Atlanta metro area. Just as he had been settling into an apartment in Marietta, Hurricane Ike was gathering strength in the Gulf, disrupting the distribution of gasoline throughout the South. After a panic-buying spree, every pump was bone dry. Day after day, he watched the news for reports of open stations and would hop in the truck the second he saw one. By the time he arrived, there would be plastic bags wrapped around the handles of the pumps and "No Gas" signs taped over the credit card slots. The needle inched closer to empty with each unsuccessful trip.

"Back from that shithole country only to deal with this," he muttered, shaking his head. "You'd think *this* was the third world. Can't get a simple tank of gas."

He turned off the engine and sank into the seat with a huff. Nothing to do but wait. He stared through the windshield at the snarl of traffic and the anxious drivers on the road.

Though he couldn't quite put his finger on it, the world had changed since he had enlisted—a subtle shift—and he could feel it now that he was out. Maybe it was the new smartphones glued to everyone's hands or e-commerce with two-day shipping on any product imaginable. Maybe it was everyone and their mother broadcasting their lives on social media. Everything so immediate, so *connected*.

He winced whenever he felt it, and the feeling gnawed and nagged. It was like seeing a flash of lightning and counting the seconds until the thunderclap, only the thunder never came. The suspense chewed up his insides.

The gas shortage intensified the gnawing, nagging feeling in this strange new world. Sitting in the truck, stuck in the snarl, his mind raced with questions.

What would happen if the connections holding society together break? I mean *really* break. What if something happens, some event that prevents people from working, and supply chains are interrupted? Wouldn't fruit and vegetables rot in fields without ships and trucks to transport them to supermarkets? Wouldn't the toilet paper run out? What if the internet goes down and water stops flowing from treatment plants? What if the power grid goes down and the lights go out? What if the next gas crisis isn't just a temporary inconvenience?

The thunder would crash eventually. But when?

He crawled closer to the pumps as the sun dipped beneath the horizon and darkness crept over the scene at the gas station. Even with a hapless worker directing traffic, it was a nightmare weaving through the tightly knotted cars in the cramped lot. He tapped the wheel in a nervous, disjointed rhythm until it was finally his turn at a pump.

He exhaled as he slipped his card into the slot and pressed the button for Regular. $4.09 per gallon. Double what it had been only a few days before. He yanked the handle from its holder and jammed the nozzle into the car, then pressed the trigger and flicked the hold, letting the gasoline flow automatically.

He stood by his truck under the station's canopy, fluorescent lights buzzing overhead. Other frazzled drivers filled their tanks with the precious fuel they had always taken for granted, some exchanging knowing, wide-eyed glances across the pumps or shaking their heads in mutual disbelief. Lines of cars still stretched out onto the road.

The pump whirred.

He stared off into the darkening sky.

Horns blared on the other side of the station. He turned around. A man shook his fist through his window and spat curses at the car in front of him. The woman driving the car ahead of the man's rolled down her window and cursed back.

"This place is a powder keg," Christopher said under his breath. "Wouldn't take much for it to blow."

It wouldn't take much. The thought charged through him.

If something sparked that powder keg, it would be war. Not a war like the one he had just fought in the desert, between armies and insurgent networks, but one between ordinary people—civilians. A war between accountants and soccer moms, teachers and waiters, janitors and corporate middle-managers. Neighbor against neighbor, fighting in the aisles of their local grocery stores and at gas stations just like the one where he stood. A mad dash for everything taken for granted. A final gasp for air as the floodwaters rise.

The pump clicked off as the seed of an idea took hold. He slapped the top of his pickup and nodded to himself. A decision had been made.

He had been neck-deep in the shit and made it through, alive and in one piece, and now that he was outside, as soldiers say, he for damn sure planned on staying that way. *Alive.* He would not be trampled in some pathetic stampede over a pack of toilet paper or the last gallon at the pump. No fucking way. On that day, when the shit hits the fan, he would be ready.

He would prepare.

As his parents used to say, Christopher was an all-American boy, blue-eyed and fair-skinned with light-brown hair. He was tall and muscular—strong enough to lift the back end of a car off the ground—but also lean and athletic. He snickered at the guys on *American Ninja Warrior* who thought they were hot shit. "I'd put all those candyasses in their place," he'd say, and his Army buddies would tell him he should try out for the show. He'd probably win, he told them, but he wasn't gonna prance around for the cameras like a cheap dancing clown.

His parents were dead. His brother, too. But he was a good ol' Georgia boy, and Georgia was what he knew. When Iraq was done with him, he came home to Cobb County. After a year in Marietta, he ditched the apartment for a house in Smyrna, just down the road from where he had grown up. His military savings covered the down payment.

The house was modest and plain, flanked by others equally as cookie-cutter, along a picturesque suburban street. With its beige vinyl siding, brown shutters, and white trim, it drew no attention to itself, blending anonymously into the suburban landscape, and that was all right with him.

The only unusual feature of the property was its backyard, which was deceptively large due to the placement of the house in front of a short hill that flattened out into a wide yard under the shadow of a tall, sturdy hickory tree in the center. The plateau on top of the hill was secluded, hidden from the spying eyes of neighbors by tall evergreen trees that lined the perimeter. A short fence lay just beyond the tree line. The privacy of the yard gave him a feeling of comfort and safety. It was calming and peaceful and was the major selling point of the house.

He settled into the suburban house, and his old friends from high school would come by to visit. His buddies from the Army kept in touch on Facebook. The ones who were left, anyway.

He got a job not far from home as an assistant manager at a big-box home improvement store. The employee discount helped make up for the salary he might have made in an office job downtown, not that he'd want to get caught up in that rat race anyway.

He began stocking up on supplies from the store and non-perishable foods from the supermarket across the street. Just a few things, at first. Tools. Batteries. Cans of soup.

One day, a pretty girl with long blonde hair pulled back in a simple ponytail came into the store looking for a light bulb. She introduced herself as Amy, and after spending half an hour asking him questions about energy efficiency, wattage, and the difference between soft white and daylight, he finally got the hint and asked her out.

They were a bit of an odd couple. He was tall and built like a tank. She was barely pushing five-two and was skinny enough that a stiff wind might upend her. He was Southern, born and raised, and she was a transplant from the North. He was a former soldier and an outdoorsman, and she screamed at the sight of spiders. But, for whatever reason, it worked.

Amy moved into his house and adopted him into her circle of friends. Every Wednesday, the gang got together and played trivia at a smoky bar downtown. The couple would laugh and have fun, then, half-drunk and smelling of cigarettes, they would go home and make love.

For most of a year, they lived together effortlessly. Amy stayed out of his business, never pressing him to talk about the war or pressuring him to get a "real job" like some of his friends had suggested. But every so often, when he came home with another load of non-perishable food and survival supplies, he would catch her staring at him, a quizzical expression on her face, her eyes searching him like she was trying to pierce his flesh and see inside. He could sense the distance growing between them but said nothing to ease her trepidation.

His hoarding of food and supplies increased. The surplus piled up in the garage until a breaking point was reached.

"I don't understand. Why do you need all this stuff? It's creepy!" she shouted.

"It's not up for debate," he snapped back. "This is my house. If it bothers you that much, you can leave."

She did.

Once she was gone, he pushed Amy out of his mind and dove deep into internet forums on prepping and survivalism, reading posts like "How to Start a Home Garden" and "Can We Trust the News Media?" late into the night. He bought survival handbooks and think pieces by writers like Rand, Kelton, Weaver, Hayek, and Mill.

His prepping intensified and became more methodical, growing from a hobby to a full-blown way of life. He traded in his old pickup truck for a Nissan Xterra SUV —better equipped for survival situations. He installed shelves in the garage for the growing stockpile, and, before long, they were meticulously organized and packed with labeled bins. Soon the garage wasn't enough. He bought two storage sheds and put them in his secluded, oversized backyard, up over the hill at the furthest edge of his property, well out of sight from any casual passersby on the street.

He made room for the SUV in the garage, clearing out one side and relocating the goods to the sheds. The first shed was for foodstuffs—cans of soup and baked beans, jars of peanut butter, boxes of oatmeal, buckets of rice and salt, and a wide assortment of nuts and granola, as well as canned vegetables and meats—and the other was for tools and gear: shovels, hammers, saws, a cordless drill set, and a motorless push lawnmower. Over time, he added propane cooking supplies, lanterns, flashlights, plywood, rope, and a large stock of nails, screws, and other assorted small parts. He started stocking up on gasoline, adding stabilizer and storing it in five-gallon cans, which he kept in the garage and the tool shed.

He watched the news obsessively. Not because he trusted the self-righteous windbags on the air, but purely to keep tabs on global events and monitor trends. The local stations showed a steady stream of robberies, home invasions, and murders, usually accompanied by pictures of black or Hispanic suspects. He began buying weapons: a Glock 17 9mm, a bolt-action Remington 700 SPS, a Colt M4 Carbine similar to his military issue but without the happy switch. Later, he added a chest rig for extra mags.

The national news revealed increasing turmoil, both home and abroad. A spontaneous uprising in Paris. Famine in South Sudan. Anti-capitalist protests on Wall Street. Night after night, the rips at society's seams grew larger. He added night-vision goggles and a gas mask to his stockpile and stored five-gallon jugs of water in the attic.

He stopped replying to messages from his Army buddies. Eventually, the messages stopped coming. His old high school friends stopped swinging by the house. Amy's group of friends had long become ghosts.

Christopher went to work, shopped for supplies, and organized his stores of food and surplus. Slowly, he boiled in the stew of internet forums and the news. "Animals," he would say to himself as the TV flickered in the dark. "Just a bunch of fucking animals."

The world was going fucking crazy. The systems running things were too fragile. Resources were too decentralized, supply chains too brittle. With the right spark, it would all come crashing down.

That day was getting closer, he was sure of it. It was so obvious, how could people not see?

He barely slept, and it showed. He ignored the concerned looks from coworkers, who had begun to keep their distance. Once a week, he would roam the store after his shift and fill a shopping cart with products. While he was in the checkout line, a coworker once asked what the stuff in his cart was for. "None of your damn business," he grunted as he swiped his credit card. That was the last time anyone asked.

He rationalized his social alienation. It was necessary. Other people would only slow him down, hold him back, distract him. So what if they thought he was a paranoid crank or a deranged obsessive-compulsive? He didn't need anyone else. In isolation, away from short-sighted judgments of others, he could focus, he could plan, he could prepare, and he took comfort in knowing that when The End Of The World As We Know It eventually came, *he* would turn out to be the sane and rational one. *He* would get the last laugh while the unprepared world eats itself alive. *He* would survive.

He assembled a greenhouse on the east side of his backyard. It had an aluminum frame and resin-coated fiberglass windows. He stocked it with pots, bags of soil, and a large supply of heirloom seeds for a variety of vegetables, ready to be planted.

Off the side of one of the supply sheds, he installed a gutter that drained into a water collection tank. He added hundreds of water purification tablets to his stockpile.

His neighbors looked on from their windows, peeking through their blinds as a backhoe rolled into his backyard to dig the pit for his grandest endeavor. The bunker, as he would call it, was made from a shipping container. He had it buried in his backyard, centered behind his house just beyond the lip of the hill. He built a hatch into the top and installed a ladder leading down into his new doomsday shelter. Once the ventilation system was installed, he furnished the container with a small mattress, a table and chair, a composting toilet, and shelves to store all the essentials of daily life: clothes, food, water, and kitchen utensils. He placed a bookshelf in the corner and filled it with the survival literature he had collected, along with novels and other books recommended on his survival forums.

He dug a small pit in the southeast corner of the yard and constructed a wooden outhouse over it. On the side of the outhouse, he installed a gravity shower; a pouch filled with water hung overhead.

Into the tall hickory tree in the center of the yard, he built a tree stand between two sturdy branches; a wooden platform to stand on, a railing to keep from falling, and a ladder to reach it. From the platform, he could see over the evergreens, into the backyards of his neighbors, across the street, and down the road in each direction.

He planted another row of evergreens along the ridge at the top of the hill, completing the circuit of privacy trees around the perimeter, enclosing the entire upper portion of the yard. From the street, no one would suspect there was anything behind the evergreens at the top of the hill.

The final piece of his backyard survival retreat: a single apple tree seedling, which he planted on the east side of the yard between the greenhouse and the outhouse.

A year passed. Then another, and another.

He kept going to work at the store and kept coming home to haunt his lonely house. He kept a detailed inventory of his stores and rotated out his expiring rations to make room for fresh goods. He went on solitary hunting trips to hone his skills and keep his senses sharp. He made emergency checklists and ran drills. He bought silver and gold coins, a few pieces at a time. He kept watching the news, noting the latest signs of unrest.

And he waited. He waited for the day his efforts would pay off, his sacrifices justified. He waited for vindication.

Sometimes, when he would sit at the table in his kitchen, he would stare through the back window to the row of evergreens along the ridge and imagine himself holed up in his underground bunker, living off his hoarded bounty, guarding his territory from the outside world.

A decade after his homecoming to Georgia, he waited.

Season after season, the apple seedling grew thicker, taller, and stronger, spreading its roots deep into the soil. Christopher waited for it to bear fruit.

The newscaster tugged at his tie and shuffled the stack of paper on the anchor desk as he regretfully informed the audience this would be the station's final broadcast until further notice. He wished good luck to the people of America and everyone around the world, then the screen cut to color bars and a high-pitched tone.

"This is it," Christopher said as he rose from the couch, alone in his living room. "It's finally happening."

He turned to the window. The line of evergreens waited at the top of the hill, sitting still in the clear February air. The sun lingered low in the cloudless sky, bathing the atmosphere in a warm orange glow. It was peaceful, almost serene—a moment of calm he allowed himself to enjoy. The storm was coming.

"It'll be a new world when the sun comes up tomorrow," he said to himself in the darkening room. "Five-thousand years of civilization snuffed out in the blink of an eye."

The bars on the TV screen splashed colors on the white walls and the piercing tone filled the room. The sound gradually moved from the background to the foreground of his awareness.

He turned away from the window and picked up the remote. Adrenaline surged through his veins and a dark half-smile formed at the corner of his mouth as he clicked off the TV.

He went to a window at the front of the house, twisted the blinds shut, then pushed his finger between two slats and pressed his eye to the opening.

Across the street, his neighbors were rushing back and forth from their wide-open front door to the car in their driveway, stuffing it with household items one armful at a time. The man came out of the house lugging a stack of photo albums. The album on top slipped off the stack and crashed onto the pavement, then the rest toppled from his arms when he bent down to pick it up. The woman came out with pillows and blankets stuffed under her arms while the man gathered the albums and tossed them into the trunk. When the car could fit no more, the woman snapped their baby into a car seat while the man urged her to hurry from the driver's seat. She slammed the back door shut and flung herself onto the passenger seat. The tires squealed as the car lurched backward down the driveway and entered the street, then a horn blared and brakes screeched as another car, racing down the street, swerved to avoid it.

He smirked at the near collision. "It's too late," he whispered to the glass. "Can't run from what's coming."

He went to the window on the west side of his house, flicking off the light as he entered the room, and peeked through the blinds to see his next-door neighbors looking through their window. Unlike him, they hadn't turned off the light. They held each other in their arms as they watched the commotion outside. A car's engine roared as it streaked down the suburban street. Somewhere in the distance, gunfire popped.

"Time to get moving," he said, and he took his finger out of the blinds.

His pulse quickened as he flew from room to room, turning off the lights and drawing the blinds over each window, exhilarated. The scientists and liberals who demanded the lockdowns might have been idiots, unaware they were snapping the supply chains like twigs, but the how and why of it didn't matter now. This was the thunderclap, the moment he had been anticipating. His years of preparation were about to pay off.

As he ran up the stairs to check the windows on the upper level, he thought of all the people who had doubted him, saw him as a dangerous lunatic, and disappeared from his life. His old high school friends, all "grown up" with wives and kids. His coworkers, who kept their eyes on the floor when he passed. Even Amy, sweet Amy, who he thought accepted him for who he was. Without secure shelter, without food and supplies, without an emergency plan, they would soon be dead. Every last one of them.

Who's crazy now? The world is on fire and there's nowhere to go.

The run on supermarkets had been the last story breathlessly reported on the news. When the paltry stock in people's pantries and refrigerators began to run out, their need for food overrode their fear of the virus. Mobs descended on the already bare supermarkets and left them in flaming ruins. The panic on the streets was broadcast live around the world, amplifying it, and the thin veneer of civilization shattered. There was no stopping the avalanche once it was set in motion.

He moved quickly, aware that the most important seconds of his life were ticking away.

With the second-story windows secured, he ran back down the stairs and through the hall and opened the door to the garage, flipping on the overhead fluorescent lights once he was inside. He went to the gun safe against the wall and dialed in the combination. The garage lights flickered as he opened the safe. "Move, soldier," he said to himself, "the lights won't be on much longer."

A thin duffle bag lay neatly folded at the bottom of the safe. He grabbed it and spread it out on the cold concrete floor. First, he pulled the M4 from the safe, then the Remington, and placed them in the bag along with the chest rig and all the boxes of ammunition. He zipped the duffle closed, then pulled the Glock and a holster from the safe and strapped the pistol to his side.

He lugged the bag into the house, setting it down just inside the door, then went back into the garage and peeked through the window of the SUV, checking the gas gauge. The tank was only half full. If things went sideways and he needed to make a run for it he'd need more than that. Several gas cans were lined up in a row along the opposite wall. He grabbed one and filled the tank, tossed the empty aside, then opened the SUV's back hatch and loaded two full gas cans into the trunk.

Before speed-walking back into the house, he went to a bin of batteries and fished out a double-A. He hustled down the hall to the front of the house and loaded the fresh battery into the wireless magnetic alarm on the door.

He started a pile by the sliding glass door in the kitchen. First, the duffle filled with guns and ammo, then he went upstairs to his bedroom, pulled down two large suitcases prepacked with clothing and protective gear from the top shelf in his closet, and added them to the pile downstairs. Next, he added his bug-out bag to the pile; an army green cargo backpack filled to the brim with everything needed for a quick getaway, including rations of water, high-calorie survival bars, flares and matches, ponchos, a first-aid kit, a multi-tool, rope, personal hygiene supplies, and even a small tent.

The last item added to the pile by the door was his box of gold and silver coins. In the short term, anyone coming near his territory would be treated as a hostile threat, but years down the road, if there was anyone else left, he might need something of value to trade with, and Uncle Sam's money would sure as shit be worthless.

The lights flickered again, then slowly dimmed before kicking back on.

"Power plants are shutting down," he said, looking up at the kitchen light. "Welcome to the new Dark Ages."

He walked through the kitchen and back out into the garage and found the red knob next to the water heater. He turned it slowly to the right until it would turn no farther, shutting off the water supply to the house, then he went across the garage to the circuit breaker. He opened the panel and flipped all the circuits off with the palm of his hand. The buzzing, flickering fluorescent lights above him cut off.

He closed the breaker's door and stood in the darkness.

All the work he had done. All the money he had spent. All the sacrifices he had made. All the studying and planning. It had all led to this moment, shutting off the power once and for all.

Alone in the dark, he considered the millions who were about to have their lives cut short. He told himself he felt bad for them. He told himself that he didn't *want* this to happen. It was a tragedy on a global scale, there was no doubt about it. But he brushed these thoughts aside. It was simply the way of life, the way it always had been, hidden just beneath the manners of civilization. Now the harsh reality of human nature was bubbling up to the surface. A new age of history was dawning, and it would be everyone's individual responsibility to deal with it.

We're all on our own now. The strong and the prepared will survive, and the rest won't. That's all there is to it.

Gunfire peppered the air again, closer than before. "Get moving," he whispered to himself, then he felt his way through the dark garage back into the house and through the kitchen to the back door. He pressed his face to the glass. The sun had sunk beneath the horizon and the moon was rising in the clear evening sky, casting a silvery glow over the evergreens.

Christopher slid the door open then picked up all he could carry. Under the cover of darkness, he walked into the yard, up the hill, then crossed through the row of evergreens. He dropped the load behind the tree line then went back for the rest.

Once he transferred the gear outside, he opened the hatch to the bunker and descended the ladder with an armful of supplies, then went back to the surface for another load. As he began his second descent, a loud cracking sound came from the house next door, followed by screams and gunfire.

Christopher slid down the ladder into the bunker, his heart beating with excitement. Another gunshot echoed through the crisp winter air above.

"Shit, that's close."

He stood in his hidden bunker, a clear sky of stars and the moon's pale light faintly illuminating the interior through the open hatch. He smiled.

"Home free."

Two more gunshots thudded like hammer strokes.

He stepped back onto the ladder and reached for the hatch. He gripped the handle and pulled it partially closed, then stopped. Frozen in place, he waited, listening.

Another shot, then silence. He gritted his teeth.

"You're not gonna hide down here like a little bitch while shit's going down up there. Get your ass topside."

He hopped off the ladder, rattling the steel floor, then clicked on a lantern, filling the bunker with white light. He unzipped the duffle bag, pulled out the night-vision goggles, and secured them on his head.

"Stay calm, Chris. Don't be fucking stupid. You worked too hard for this."

He strapped on the chest rig and loaded it with spare mags, then he pulled the M4 from the bag, relishing its familiar weight in his hands.

"Don't give away your position, and don't start any shit."

He slapped a magazine into the rifle and chambered a round.

"But be ready to finish it."

Armed with the M4, the Glock holstered at his side, and the goggles on his head, he climbed back up the ladder and slowly opened the hatch, careful not to make a sound. At the top of the ladder, he clicked on the night vision then stepped onto the grass. He charged to the tree line on the ridge with the speed and stealth of a soldier, regulating his breathing as he moved.

The temperature was dropping fast but the cold didn't faze him. The atmosphere was on fire with a glow only he could see, charged with electricity only he could feel, the way a child feels on Christmas morning. This was Day One, and he was born anew.

He paced the tree line at the top of the hill until he found a good spot along the ridge toward the west side of the yard, then he got down on the ground and pressed between two evergreens. Secured against a trunk, he was hidden from sight but had a clear view of his neighbors' house to the west, where he guessed the shooters were from the echo of the gunfire. With his thumb, he clicked the semi-automatic rifle from Safe to Fire. And he waited, still.

"Come on out, shitstains," he whispered, his hot breath misting into the air, sights trained on the gap between the houses.

A gust of wind tumbled through the evergreens. He raised his head.

This is stupid, he thought. If I have to fire, I'd need to kill them all. Anyone gets away and I've given up my position. They'll come back with reinforcements.

"I need to move," he whispered, and he bolted upright with the twitch of muscle memory. He flung himself down the hill and circled to the east side of his house, then leaned against its vinyl siding with the M4 cradled in his hands.

The neighborhood was still with an eerie, pregnant pause, as if the houses themselves held their breath.

Anyone left around here is shitting themselves after all these shots. But this ain't over yet.

He was standing still, his back against the house, straining his ears when he detected a low rumble, barely audible beneath the brisk night breeze and the steady hum of central air units. An engine? He peeked around the corner to the west through his night-vision lenses. Nobody was visible on foot in the green images, but a light-colored van was idling along the curb in front of his neighbors' house.

The nearby streetlamp flickered for a moment then went out, along with the few remaining house lights peppered down the block. The whir of the air units cut off. A deflating quiet fell over the neighborhood as the houses exhaled their dying breaths, leaving their corpses lying silent and still. The night became oddly dark despite the brightness of the moon. The low rumble of the van swelled in the air. In the distance, a dog barked. A faraway scream echoed off the siding of the still, silent houses.

There was a clattering in the house next door and what sounded like a man's anguished moan. The van's headlights turned on, flooding the road with light. The front door of the neighbor's house swung open and an intruder stood in the doorway. "Come on!" the man shouted back into the house. "Grab everything and let's go, then let's hit the next house." The van's driver-side door opened and the driver stepped out and went around to the back end. He opened the rear doors and yelled, "What's the hold up?" to the man at the front of the house.

Gotta take 'em now. My house is next.

With the three intruders separated—one inside the house, one at the front door, one at the van—this was the moment to strike.

Don't hesitate.

With military precision, he stepped out from behind his house and made a beeline for the road, closing on the target with quick, silent strides. When he reached the street, his boots tapped against the asphalt and the driver stuck his head around the side of the van. Christopher pulled the trigger and the M4's muzzle flashed. The man fell back into the street. The sound of the shot sliced through the silence and echoed through the neighborhood.

The man in the house's doorway ducked as he fumbled for his weapon. "Shit!" Christopher came around the rear of the van and pivoted toward the house, firing three quick shots in stride as he moved up the driveway. The startled man crashed against the door and fell into the foyer.

Christopher sprinted to the front of the house. When he reached its brick facade, he crouched beside a shrub and waited. He could hear someone pacing inside, hysterically repeating, "What the fuck? What the fuck?"

"I've got you, punk," Christopher yelled.

The man in the house fell silent. The pacing stopped.

"Trying to figure out what to do, aren't you?" he whispered. "Will you make a run for it out the front door, or try to sneak out the back?"

After a few moments of silence, he got his answer. A quick series of steps thudded through the house, then the man bounded through the front door and leapt over the stoop, firing a handgun wildly into the darkness while he flew through the air. Christopher, seeing clearly through the night-vision lenses, aimed and fired a single shot from his crouched position by the brick facade. The man yelped as his foot touched down on the walkway, and he tumbled forward into the dead grass in the front yard. Christopher rose and fired two shots, and the man lay sprawled on the grass. Keeping his rifle trained on the target, he approached and kicked the man's gun away, then stood over him as he coughed up a mouthful of blood.

Up close, the man could barely be called a man at all. He was young, probably no older than nineteen or twenty.

"Sorry, son. Nothing personal."

He aimed the rifle at the young man's head and coolly ended his suffering with a single pull of the trigger. The sound of the shot tore through the dark and silent neighborhood then evaporated into the winter chill.

Christopher stepped through the open doorway of his neighbors' house and over the body lying in the foyer. He nudged the young man with his boot, making sure the threat was eliminated. A packed suitcase rested on the floor beside the body.

M4 at the ready, he crossed into the living room. The couch was overturned, and the television lay broken beside its stand. A large bookcase was on its side, and picture frames, books, and jar candles littered the carpeted floor. Fresh blood was splattered on the walls and the carpet. He followed the trail through his night-vision lenses until he found the body of a middle-aged woman sprawled awkwardly across the brick base of the fireplace. He crouched and turned her head toward him and recognized the face of his neighbor. Only an hour or so before, she had been standing at the window in the arms of her husband. It occurred to him he didn't know their names.

He let the woman's head slump back the way he had found it, then he stood and walked into the kitchen. A camping lantern lay shattered on the tile floor in front of the island in the center of the room. As he walked toward the island, there was a horrible groan, then a man's voice, weak and raspy, said, "I can hear you there." He lifted the rifle, wrapped his finger around the trigger, and stepped carefully around the island. Legs outstretched, the husband sat on the floor, propped up against a cabinet. His eyes were closed, and he gripped a large kitchen knife in his hand. His shirt was soaked with blood.

"Don't come any closer," said the wounded man, raising the knife in the dark. "Take a step back."

He approached slowly, ignoring the empty commands, and crouched down, matching eye levels with the man, who breathed slow, wheezing breaths.

"The men who attacked you are gone," Christopher said. "Your wife is dead."

The man inhaled sharply and raised his head, and a confused, anguished expression washed over him. A tear dripped down his face, mixing with blood. He squeezed his eyes tightly shut and exhaled, gathering himself. "Who were those boys?" he asked with a groan. "They looked like... kids."

"Nobody," Christopher said. "My guess, just some punks trying to steal supplies at the last minute, now that everything's shut down out there."

The man coughed and blood dripped from his mouth. "But why us? Why my Betty?"

"It's everyone for themselves now. Haven't you been paying attention to what's been going on these last few weeks?"

"I didn't think— I didn't expect... this."

"You should have been more prepared. At least those dead boys out there were trying to do something."

The bleeding man grimaced. "You killed them?"

"They won't be bothering anyone anymore."

"Who— Who are you?"

"I live next door."

"You could have stopped this. You could have protected us."

Christopher smirked. "That's not my job."

"I've seen you," the man said, struggling to get the words out. "Sneaking around. Building things. Putting up those trees."

"Yeah," he replied coldly, sensing the judgment in the man's voice. "And I'm going to be alive tomorrow."

The man let go of the kitchen knife and it clattered on the tile floor. He shook his head. "Shooting each other over cans of soup. What— What kind of life is that?"

"At least I'll be around to find out."

The light drained from man's eyes, his voice fading. "I'd rather join my Betty," he said in a whisper. "At least... we had each other."

The man took a final, wheezing breath, then released the air from his lungs with a long sigh as his head dropped lifelessly to the side.

Christopher rose to his full height and stood over the man. "Nice to meet you... neighbor."

He walked back through the ravaged house, exited through the front door, and hurried across the yard to the still running van. He climbed into the driver's seat and parked it around the block, out of sight from his property. As he jogged back, he tossed the keys into a bush. Tires squealed and an engine roared somewhere in the distance. Farther away, the faint popping of gunfire hung in the night air.

Careful not to be seen, he dragged the five bodies into the backyard of his neighbors' house. He gathered the guns and suitcases of goods left behind by the intruders and slipped quietly away, through the evergreen tree line and down into the safety of the bunker. The next night, or maybe the night after—once the worst of it had blown over—he would go back to bury the bodies.

Christopher woke early in the morning, kicked off the sheets, and swung his legs over the side of the mattress. The foldable steel frame creaked under his weight. He reached for the solar-powered lantern on the end table and clicked on the light. Its flat, white light illuminated the northwest corner of the converted shipping container. He picked up the lantern and hung it from a hook in the ceiling. Shadows shifted on the corrugated walls as the light swayed.

It was March, and the bunker was chilly and dark despite the lantern. The lone light source hanging from the ceiling only emphasized the cold darkness of the metal box. Though he had grown up in the heat of the southern sun, he didn't mind the cold or the dark. It was him against the world, and these discomforts only served as a reminder that he was winning.

He dropped to the floor and did his morning exercises — alternating sets of sit-ups and push-ups, followed by leg lifts and bicycle kicks — then he stood and flexed in the mirror hung next to the storage shelves.

Chest heaving, he crossed another day off the calendar beside the mirror. He went to the water dispenser in the corner and poured himself a cup from the five-gallon jug. Sipping from the cup, he turned slowly in place. Cold and dark but, for the forty-fourth day, it was home.

For the first week, he had kept a low profile, staying underground except to water the plants in the greenhouse and for daily security checks. There was the occasional sound of a car or the bark of a dog, but activity dropped off sharply as the days wore on.

By the end of the third week, there was only silence. No cars. No dogs. No gunfire in the distance. There was only the sound of bare branches clattering in the wind and the occasional song of a sparrow or a warbler, migrated from the North.

His plan had been executed without a hitch. The wave of apocalypse had washed over the land, and he had survived, undetected in his backyard survival retreat, hidden in plain sight.

He took his morning piss in the composting toilet at the east end of the bunker, then he reached for the folded card table in its usual place, leaned against the wall next to the bookcase. He unfolded its legs and set up the table in the center of the chilly room, then dragged over a chair. He cooked himself breakfast—a pot of oatmeal with brown sugar—on a portable propane stovetop. He scraped the warm mush into a bowl, sat at the table, and ate in the solitude of his underground hideaway. Only the sound of the metal spoon clanking against the ceramic bowl broke the silence in the bunker.

He took a multivitamin after he ate, then brushed his teeth and spat the toothpaste into the toilet. He dressed in a pair of blue jeans, a wool button-down shirt over a white undershirt, and a light windbreaker. He opened the weapons locker and armed himself with the Glock, which he holstered. He slung the Remington rifle over his shoulder and a pair of binoculars around his neck.

Dressed, armed, and ready for the day, he looked through a periscope installed in the ceiling. He turned slowly, peering through the skinny, black device, scanning clockwise across the yard. The greenhouse. The apple tree. The outhouse. The hickory. The food and supply sheds. All clear.

He climbed the ladder, pushed open the hatch, and emerged from the dark of the hidden bunker into his secluded backyard. The rising sun bathed the grounds in a golden light. He stood on the brown grass, turned his face into the warmth, and took in a deep breath of the late-winter air.

The rifle over his shoulder, he paced the perimeter, checking the fence line behind the evergreens along the west, south, and east sides of the property. He looked for breaks or any sign of intrusion and surveyed the neighboring properties as he went. He checked the locks on the doors of the supply sheds. He made sure the greenhouse hadn't been tampered with overnight. Pressing through the evergreens, he stood on the ridge overlooking the lower portion of the backyard. His house stood empty and undisturbed. Nothing out of place.

He came back through the evergreens, crossed the yard to the hickory, then climbed the ladder to the surveillance platform. His corner of the world lay beneath him. The houses on the block were quiet. How many still had people inside, quietly hunkered down, trying to survive on whatever they had in their pantries? It had only been a few weeks. There could still be a few families down there, desperately hanging on.

He pressed the binoculars to his eyes and glassed the landscape below. His view was unobstructed since the trees were still bare, and the air was quiet without leaves to rustle in its breeze. The only sound was the creaking of wood when he shifted his weight on the platform. He turned to the east. A gray cat confidently crossed the street then disappeared under a bush.

As he stood high in the morning air, he remembered how he used to hear the train as it crossed through town a few miles away. First, a whistle in the distance, then a low rumble that seemed to emanate from deep within the earth itself, beneath all other sounds—a vibration that swelled until it dominated the atmosphere for a few moments before sinking back beneath the earth. A twinge of sadness passed through him. He would never hear that sound again.

He turned to the west. The lenses lingered on five bare patches of dirt in a neat row in his neighbors' backyard. Grass would cover the shallow graves in the spring.

He glassed the block one last time, scanning the yards and windows of every house within range. No discernible threats. He climbed down from the platform and put the rifle back in the bunker. The Glock remained holstered at his side.

He returned to the yard with a book under his arm and checked the water collection tank. Only a quarter full. He would have to use it sparingly until the next rainfall. He filled a bottle from the tap and went to the greenhouse to water the plants. The muggy air was a drastic change from the chill outside. He unzipped his jacket then poured a small amount of water into each pot. With a spray bottle, he spritzed the growing leaves and vines. It wouldn't be long before some of the new plants began producing.

Without fresh produce, he sat in a lawn chair under the hickory and munched on a granola bar while reading his copy of

Atlas Shrugged. As the hours passed, he worked his way through the pages, sipping occasionally from a canteen.

He came to the end of a chapter and looked up from the book. A crisp breeze blew through the yard, and he inhaled the liberating air deep into his lungs. He surveyed his territory and smiled to himself. He was alive, and he was free, untouched by the mayhem unleashed only weeks before. A self-sufficient kingdom of one, he would outlast everyone.

As he sat in his yard, with plenty of food and a book in hand, he knew he had chosen the correct survival strategy, though the Get Out Of Dodge approach—establishing a survival retreat somewhere out in the wilderness—had been tempting. Had he gone that route, he would have found a plot of land for an off-the-grid cabin, stocked it with food and supplies, but maintained his primary residence in town until the Shit Hit The Fan. Intuitively, it made sense to set up away from civilization, and the idea was appealing in an almost romantic way. A lone mountain man, roughing it in the wild, truly free. An attractive image, but too much could go wrong. The distance involved posed a serious risk, traveling in the open under volatile and unpredictable circumstances. It would do him no good to have the perfect survival retreat set up in the wild if he couldn't reach it safely when the time came.

One way around that problem, which he had considered, was to set up a wilderness retreat and live there full-time. This would allow him to hone his skills and learn the wild territory. When the climactic day eventually came, he would be there at the retreat, ready and prepared, eliminating the need for dangerous travel. But this, too, posed problems. It would be harder to prep in isolation, away from civilization. The constant travel into town for food and supplies would be a hassle, and there was the problem of income. His military savings weren't enough to live on indefinitely, and having to commute long hours into town for work, separating him from his retreat during the day, would defeat the purpose of prepping in a remote area.

But even if, somehow, he could have successfully set up camp in the wilderness, there was another problem to consider: the Golden Horde. Once the desperate masses exhausted their options in the population centers, they would inevitably flee to the countryside in search of food and shelter. Maybe his cabin wouldn't be stumbled upon by a horde of starving people, but it wasn't worth taking the chance.

The smart move—the plan he eventually settled on—was to set up his survival retreat in town, right under the nose of society. It took the best aspect of each strategy and rolled them into one perfect plan. Prepping in town, he could maintain employment with a short commute, he would have easy access to supplies, and when the Shit Hit The Fan, he would already be at this retreat. Plus, the desperate hordes from the population centers would be moving away rather than toward him, minimizing the chances of people stumbling upon his hidden lair. As long as he could get through those first hours unscathed, he'd be home free.

As he sat in his chair, secluded in his backyard sanctuary, home free was exactly how he felt.

The sun sank in the sky, casting streaks of marigold and rose through the clouds. He used the outhouse, then stripped off his clothes and bathed under the gravity shower, taking only a half ration of water from the collection tank. He toweled off and dressed, then retrieved the Remington rifle and binoculars from the bunker for his evening surveillance. Under the colorful glow of the atmosphere, he climbed the ladder to the platform in the hickory.

The cool air was peaceful and calm as he scanned his street and the yards and windows of the nearby houses. A stillness had settled over the neighborhood. Everything was as it had been that morning. No sign of activity.

A chilly breeze blew gently through the tree and he steadied himself on the railing. He turned to the west. The sun slipped beneath the horizon and the sky bled crimson and sangria. He let the binoculars fall to his chest so he could take in the natural splendor through his own eyes.

The sound of a motor rose in the east, quietly, at first, like the soft buzz of a bumblebee.

Christopher stood still, lost in the tapestry of color, as the last moments of the day slipped away.

The distant hum of the motor grew until it echoed off the facades of nearby houses and filled the air, yanking Christopher away from the majesty of the blood-red sunset. He swung the rifle off his shoulder and got into firing position on the platform, resting the long-range rifle's barrel on the railing. Aiming to the east, his finger hovered just off the trigger while he adjusted the scope with the other hand. He placed the crosshairs on the street just as a red pickup came into view in the golden hour twilight.

The truck crept deliberately over the road, no more than ten or fifteen miles per hour. He centered the crosshairs on the driver's head as the vehicle crawled westward.

Hair pulled back in a ponytail. A woman.

"What are you doing out here all alone?" he said as the driver shifted in her seat and looked from side to side, scanning the neighborhood through the cabin's windows.

He placed his finger on the trigger and, matching the truck's slow pace, led the target's head just slightly with the crosshairs. He took a deep breath and held the air in his lungs.

One look. Just *one* look I don't like...

The red pickup crossed in front of his house, out of view from the platform. He pivoted the rifle to the west side of the house and waited for the vehicle to reappear.

"Come on, little lady," he whispered through his teeth, "move along."

The truck came back into view on the other side of his house, and he reacquired the target through the scope. He put pressure on the trigger. The woman was looking straight ahead. The pickup's speed remained slow and constant before crossing out of sight in front of the next house. Its motor grumbled as it pressed forward until it rounded the bend to the north, and the sound faded.

He took his finger off the trigger and released the breath he had been holding. "Who the fuck are you?"

He slung the rifle over his shoulder, hurried down the ladder, then jogged across the yard. After passing through the evergreens and going down the hill, he hid behind the back corner of the house. He faced northward with a view of the street.

The road was clear. The sound of the motor was gone.

Twilight's cobalt glow was fading fast. His heart thumped in his ears. He took a slow breath to calm himself and narrowed his eyes, squinting into the growing darkness. Resting his hand on his holstered pistol, he waited for the pickup to come around for another pass.

"Where'd you go off to?" he said under his breath. "Where'd you come from?"

Night fell over the neighborhood. The red pickup didn't return. In the darkness, he climbed the hill and crossed through the evergreens, back to his hidden refuge.

Adrenaline still coursing through him, he paced the perimeter of the yard. The pickup was gone—for the time being, anyway—but its appearance swirled a galaxy of questions.

Who was the woman driving the truck? Didn't look like she was in a hurry, did it? Why was she driving so slow, like she was surveying the area? What was she looking for? Is my cover blown already? Shit. What do you know about her? What conclusions can you draw? She was alone. Traveling light. She must be holed up somewhere close. But on her own? Or part of a group? Either way, she must have food and supplies. Was she a scout? Should I have taken her out when I had the chance?

"You probably weren't seen," he tried to reassure himself, muttering as he paced. "She kept on driving. If you had taken her out, someone might have come looking for her."

Once he had calmed himself, he went underground and noted the sighting of the truck on the calendar, then he warmed a can of beans on the propane stove and ate straight from the pot. He tried to distract himself with his book, but the red pickup weighed on his mind more heavily than the quest to discover the identity of John Galt. His eyes kept drifting off the page and he would catch himself staring blankly at the corrugated metal wall.

Now he knew there was at least one other survivor in the area. Even if he hadn't been spotted, she was a threat. He would have to be careful.

Christopher set his loaded Glock on the end table and turned off the lantern. Still dressed in his clothes and boots, he lay sleeplessly over the sheets, staring into the darkness.

On a late April morning, Christopher exercised and crossed another day off the calendar. Six weeks and no sign of the red truck or the woman driving it. Maybe she wasn't a scout. Maybe she actually was a random lone survivor, just passing through or looking for a safe place to stay for the night. Regardless, with each passing day, he grew more confident that he hadn't been spotted and settled back into his routines.

He marked the passage of time, one day after the next, with an X on the calendar. He prepared his meals. He kept in shape. He watered the crops in the greenhouse and maintained the grounds behind his evergreen walls. He managed his inventory of food and supplies. He kept a watchful eye over the surrounding area. He read his books. From time to time, he ventured down the hill to his house to retrieve a fresh jug of water from the attic. In the evenings, he would bathe under the gravity shower, then, clean and refreshed, he would climb up to the platform in the tall hickory, just as much to enjoy the view and the air as to survey the neighborhood. Each night, he slept in the safety of his underground bunker.

He was careful. Disciplined. He hardly ever made a sound, and he enjoyed the silence of solitude. His stores were meticulously rationed. He could carry on like this for years, there was no doubt in his mind.

He sat under the shade of the hickory in jeans and a Henley shirt, munching on a slice of fresh cantaloupe, reading a worn-out paperback edition of *Starship Troopers*. The winter chill had been replaced by a refreshing spring breeze. He basked in the cool, clean air while he contemplated how much better society would have been if military veterans were the only people allowed to vote. Might've been able to avoid this whole mess.

He clapped the book shut then raised his head. The greenhouse's glass was getting dingy. He rose from the chair and stretched.

"Time to go to work."

He unlocked the supply shed and returned to the yard with a ladder, a bucket, and cleaning supplies. He stopped at the water collection tank and filled the bucket before lugging the awkward load toward the greenhouse. He tucked a sponge and bottle of soap under his armpit, then laced one arm through the ladder and held the heavy bucket with the other hand. He marched across the yard with short, heavy steps.

The water sloshed in the plastic bucket as he stomped over the grass. The ladder pressed against his shoulder blade. Midway across the yard, he lifted his eyes from the ground to the greenhouse. The bucket's handle ate into his fingers. Grimacing, he quickened his pace and urged himself on. Just a few more steps.

Then his toe snagged a divot in the yard and suddenly he was falling. The bucket slipped from his grasp. Water sprayed his face as the weight of the ladder pushed him forward and he tumbled over the bucket. Something popped loudly as he hit the ground.

Christopher slowly opened his eyes. His face was pressed against something rough and sticky. A blurry shape towered over him. He rolled onto his back. A navy sky was sprinkled with dusk's first stars. He groaned as he straightened his neck and wiped blades of grass from his cheek. The greenhouse came into focus.

"What the fuck happened?" he asked aloud, wincing as he touched his forehead and found a swollen welt on the brow above his left eye. When he took his hand away, his fingers glistened with half-dried blood.

He dropped his head to the side. The ladder and bucket lay beside him on the grass, and suddenly the accident rushed into his mind. Panic shot through him. He jolted upright and felt for the pistol at his side, realizing he had been exposed, out in the open, for hours. His hand found the weapon secured safely in its holster. A wave of relief passed through him.

Vision blurry and head pounding, he hobbled dizzily to his feet. A sharp pain shot through his left knee. He yelped, then tried to swallow the sound. His stomach lurched and he vomited on the grass.

Hunched over, face covered in blood, knee pulsing with pain, he wiped his mouth with the back of his hand. He stood upright and turned to the greenhouse. It sat there, unwavering, still in need of cleaning. "So stupid," he said, and he spat, clearing the remaining vomit from his mouth.

He turned toward the hatch and, finding he couldn't put much weight on his right leg either, tried not to cry out in pain as he took a step. His ankle was stiff, and it burned as he stepped gingerly across the yard.

"Just great," he grumbled. "Two bum legs."

He limped with each pathetic step. First, his left leg, knee threatening to buckle beneath him, then his right, swollen ankle searing. At least there was no one to witness the pitiful display. Crawling would be more dignified.

Like an old, crippled man, he reached the hatch and bent down to pull it open, then carefully lowered himself inside the bunker, using his arms to bear most of his weight on the ladder.

He winced and groaned as he clicked on a lantern and shuffled to the supply shelf. Without ice to keep the swelling down, ibuprofen would have to do. He cracked the seal from a bottle and slapped a few pills in his mouth, swallowing them down without water, then he rummaged through the first-aid supplies and pulled out a roll of medical tape.

"So fucking stupid," he said. He shook his head in disgust as he crumpled into the chair by the bookcase to wrap his injured joints. "Probable concussion. *Definitely* a sprained ankle. And this damn knee." He gritted his teeth, pulling the wrap tight around the swelling. "Maybe a torn meniscus. Hopefully nothing worse than that." He let the leg drop and the impact vibrated the steel floor like a tuning fork. The sound lingered in the air. "Or I'm fucked."

Christopher took another large dose of ibuprofen then unwrapped his ankle. It was bruised like a storm cloud and swollen like a balloon. He rewrapped the joint with fresh tape then covered the foot with a thick sock. He examined his head wound in the mirror. It would be an impressively ugly mess, if there had been anyone around to impress.

He modified his morning exercise, keeping his weight off his swollen ankle during the push-ups. His knee twinged when he flipped to his back and bent his legs to do a set of sit-ups.

Shit. Don't push it.

He crossed a day off the calendar and noted the injury in the previous day's square. He ate breakfast, got dressed, then tried to put his boots on. He groaned, trying to force the swollen foot into the boot. Eventually gave up, opting instead for a pair of tennis shoes. He loosened the laces and slid his foot inside.

He scanned the yard through the periscope then, rifle slung over his back, climbed the ladder to the hatch, straining his arms to keep as much weight off his legs as possible.

He stepped into the yard. The ladder and bucket were still lying in the grass. The greenhouse's windows were still dingy. He touched the welt on his forehead and scowled, replaying the fall in his mind.

"Fucking stupid."

He turned his gaze to the bright blue sky. A sharp pain stung his eyes and his ears began to ring. Dizzy and disoriented, he pressed his eyes shut for a moment, then concentrated on the ground to center himself.

He fought back the urge to vomit as he hobbled to the shed, his vision shifting in and out of focus. His hand shook as he tried to dial the combination into the lock. On his third attempt, he unlocked the door and stepped inside. He located a cheap Ace knee brace in a bin and dangled it in front of his face. It was no more than a tight elastic band.

"Better than nothing, I guess."

He returned to the yard to retrieve the ladder and bucket then dragged them back to the shed, one agonizing step at a time. After tossing them inside, not caring where they landed, he secured the lock on the door.

He put his hands on his knees to catch his breath then, after a moment, turned to the hickory. The tree split in two and the blurry images circled each other. The platform seemed ten times higher than usual as his left knee and right ankle pulsed with pain. He sighed.

"No surveillance today. Pathetic."

He slipped the thin brace into his pocket and hobbled back to the bunker, defeated, unable to put weight on either leg. The ground spun wildly as he reached to open the hatch and he vomited where he stood. He spat and panted and tried to gather himself before working his way down the ladder into the bunker.

He moaned, helpless, and shuffled listlessly back to bed. He shut off the lantern, relieving his eyes, and curled up under the blankets in the corner of his metallic cell.

As he lay in the dark, his head spinning, his stomach weak, the joints in his legs pulsing, he thought of Amy for the first time since Day One. She had always reminded him to schedule doctor's appointments and pushed him to go to the dentist when he complained of a toothache. He always resisted, of course, choosing instead to suppress the pain and soldier on.

He pictured the way she would snuggle up to him in bed, pressing her body into his like she couldn't get close enough. He could almost feel her warm breath on the back of his neck.

What gruesome fate had she met at the end of the world?

Christopher sat on the bed, his back against the wall, a copy of *Animal Farm* open on his lap. The bunker's atmosphere was hot and oppressive. He was crawling out of his skin, restless. He reached the end of a paragraph but his eyes had glazed over the words. He started over, but soon found himself staring into the corner of the room. Exasperated, he snapped the book closed. The sound echoed off the corrugated steel.

His injured legs were spread out over the mattress, mocking him. Three days he had been stuck underground. Waiting, endlessly waiting.

He changed the wraps on his legs each day. He did his best to keep up with his exercise. He cooked cans of soup or beans when he was hungry. He stayed hydrated. He paged through his collection of survival handbooks for the thousandth time. He waited for the swelling in his joints to come down and the pain in his head to subside. He slept in the dark.

Enough. I need to get topside. Today.

He tossed the book aside, hobbled to the periscope, and pressed his eye to the lens.

Rain. Miserable fucking rain. Of course.

His injured legs pulsed. The hatch beckoned.

"Fuck it. I'll get wet."

He threw on long pants and a rain jacket and armed himself with the Glock and Remington. His heart thumped in his chest as he pulled himself gingerly up the ladder.

There were a million reasons he should stay inside, and he knew them all. Chief among them, he'd be at a physical disadvantage in a confrontation with a hostile. And not only that, he could aggravate his injuries, setting back the recovery process. His body needed rest and time to heal. It wasn't worth the risk. But hiding underground day after day was such a bitch move. The thought of cowering in the dark for one more second made him want to fucking puke.

Man up, Chris.

He pushed open the hatch and climbed into the soggy yard.

A light rain pitter-pattered on the trees' young leaves. A gray mist hung in the air. He took a few slow steps and his boots squished into the grass. His ankle radiated with pain as he walked and his knee was weak and unstable, even with the thin brace.

Crutches. That's what he needed.

"How did I not think of that?" he said, shaking his head. He used the butt of the rifle as a walking stick as he made his way to the supply shed. He would have to improvise.

He unlocked the door and stepped inside, then fumbled around for something that could double as a crutch. Nothing. He would have to make his own.

He didn't mind. Though mad at himself for failing to stock crutches, this was a perfect excuse to use some of the tools and supplies he had meticulously organized. He redeemed himself with the thought.

He turned on a lantern, closed the door, and got to work on some plywood. An hour later, he opened the door and stepped into the yard with two makeshift crutches tucked under his arms and the rifle slung over his back. He walked a few feet, getting used to their feel.

Uncomfortable, but serviceable. Later he could wrap a shirt or a towel around the ends for some padding, but they would do for now.

He crutched the perimeter of the yard, performing his usual security check. The gentle rain misted as he sloshed through the muddy grass. He pressed through the evergreens intermittently, scanning the adjoining properties beyond the fence. The neighborhood was quiet and still and the soft tapping of rainwater somehow heightened its silence and stillness, more like a foggy everglade or tranquil rainforest than a suburban ghost town.

He made his way to the east side of the yard and approached the fence through the evergreens. Mist hung over the neighbors' yard like a veil. He scanned from left to right. Patio furniture, a children's swing set, overgrown azaleas along the house, strands of English ivy snaking over the fence.

He stood against the fence with his crutches under his arms. Nature would begin reclaiming the world in the summer. He nodded. Area clear.

Backing through the evergreens, a sound caught his ear—a soft snap. He froze, then held his breath. Raindrops tapped gently against his jacket. He exhaled slowly and stepped forward to the fence. Squinting through the fog, he retraced his neighbors' yard. There it was. Behind the veil, a deer stood in the furthest corner, chewing on a patch of fresh weeds along the fence. The mist lifted on a breath of air. It was a white-tail. A doe. The animal moved its head with quiet grace, and he stood transfixed by its elegance in the rain.

He reminded himself to breathe and leaned the crutches softly against the chain-link fence, then slowly took the rifle from his shoulder. Without taking his eyes off the doe, he steadied the weapon on the fence and put his eye to the scope's lens. The shot would be loud, but the opportunity to bag fresh venison this close to home was worth the risk. He slowly pushed a round into the chamber with the bolt.

The doe lifted its head and looked straight at him. He followed the animal's head through the scope and placed the crosshairs on its forehead, between her black eyes, piercing through the mist. She looked at him, frozen in place, and he held his breath as time stood still. His finger tightened around the trigger. Slowly, slowly.

The sound of the shot echoed off the siding of the empty houses in the neighborhood then dissipated into the misty air as the doe dropped to the ground.

He stood still, head cocked to the side, listening for any reaction to the gunfire. The rain tapped against the leaves in the trees and trickled gently through the downspouts of gutters. Fog drifted by like a whisper. No shouts in the distance. No motors bearing down.

He inhaled deeply. There was work to do.

He crutched to the supply shed, then came back with a tarp and exited the yard through the evergreens on the ridge. He worked his way down the hill with the crutches, keeping his right foot off the ground and as much weight off his left leg as possible. The wood bore into his armpits and he grimaced until he reached the lower yard, then he hobbled around the fence to the neighbors' property.

He approached the doe slowly. A mess of pink and red oozed from the creature's broken face onto the rain-soaked grass. He stood over the carcass. "Better than dying slow," he said, just above a whisper.

Christopher again turned his head and listened for any un-natural sound. When he was satisfied by the silence, he unfolded the plastic tarp and laid it on the grass beside the doe. He guessed she was about one-hundred and fifteen pounds. A piece of cake under normal circumstances, but it would be difficult to move her with a tender ankle and a bum knee. He tossed the crutches aside and got down on the ground behind the carcass. He ran his hand across her torso, feeling her ribs through her light-brown fur. She was still warm. "I deserved a lucky break after what happened the other day," he said to the doe, stroking her fur. "Not your lucky day though, was it?"

He took a deep breath and heaved the deer onto the tarp, and he winced as pain shot through his knee. Pushing through it, he centered the carcass on the tarp and groaned as he got to his feet. He picked up his crutches and tossed one onto the tarp beside the doe, then he grabbed the tarp by the corner, stuck the other crutch under his right arm, and yanked.

The rain-slick grass was both helpful and a hindrance. The tarp slid easily over the wet grass, but getting a firm foothold as he pulled was difficult. He jammed the crutch into the soggy turf for leverage and jerked the tarp forward in fits and starts. One great lurch at a time, he pulled the doe through the neighbors' yard, around the fence, through his side yard, and up the hill. The wet evergreens sprayed his face as he passed through with the animal in tow.

Safely back in his yard, he doubled over, heaving and gasping for air. His ankle throbbed. Searing pain shot through his knee.

Rest. He needed to lie down and rest his burning legs. It was a mistake to be out of bed at all, let alone doing hard labor in this dreary, miserable rain. But there was no turning back. The animal needed to be field dressed to preserve the meat. He gave the bloody doe a side-eyed glare and stood up, regaining his breath.

"Okay. Let's do this."

He grabbed the tarp and dragged the carcass to the back of the yard near the outhouse, straining his weary legs, then hobbled to the supply shed for a knife and a bundle of rope.

When he returned, the animal's mangled face greeted him, and he flashed back to the moment when their eyes met, just before he pulled the trigger. Those eyes. Those midnight black eyes, piercing through the mist. It was like she knew it was the end and chose to meet it gracefully, still and at peace. He couldn't shake the image. The gray, murky sky hung over him and he turned his face into the rain. He closed his eyes and let the drops splash against his skin. What would his final moment be? When it comes, would he meet it with the same graceful poise, the same sense of peace and calm, the same dignified acceptance?

He opened his eyes and knelt to turn the deer onto its back, then searched the yard for objects large and heavy enough to keep it propped in place. He found two stones behind the sheds and placed them under the shoulders and used a fallen branch from the hickory to place beside the hip.

Once the carcass was secure, he picked up the knife and took a deep breath, steeling himself, then plunged the blade into the pelvis, down to the bone. From there, he slit the skin to the jawbone. He peeled back the hide, then cut along the same line, but deeper, through the muscle. The animal's organs bubbled out from its underside and he was struck by a pungent smell. He turned his head away and gagged, but he had to press on. It was only going to get messier from here.

As far up the neck as he could, he sliced across the throat. He grabbed the end of the severed windpipe and pulled, yanking the entrails from the torso. The bladder, still attached to the pelvis, separated as he pulled, spilling feces into the hide and onto the tarp.

"Godammit!" he cursed through gritted teeth, realizing instantly he had forgotten to separate the colon before he pulled. "Fucking amateur."

He picked up a crutch and hobbled to the water tank to fill a bottle, shaking his head in disgust as he went, and came back and turned the deer on its side. "Fucking stupid," he said as he cleaned the soiled meat.

Continuing, he cleaned out the excess membrane and tissue with the knife, then he found a sturdy branch to hang the carcass from, allowing it to cool.

While the deer hung from the tree, he skinned it with cuts along the insides of the legs, gradually working the knife around the body until he could pull the hide away. It came free in long sheets and he tossed them aside.

Despite the rain jacket, he was soaking wet. His injured legs ached. When he had been stuck inside the bunker, all he wanted was to get out. Now he was miserable and desperate to get back in. The irony wasn't lost on him. "A bit more than you bargained for today," he said to himself, shaking his head as he cut slices of meat from the carcass. First the backstraps, then the shoulders, ribs, and finally the hindquarters. He filleted as much meat off the bone as he could and laid it out on the hide.

From the supply shed, he retrieved a cooler and a large bucket of salt. He bundled the meat in the hide and stuffed it inside the cooler, then he picked up the crutches, slung the rifle over his shoulder, and one at a time dragged the cooler and the salt to the hatch, his legs on fire as he trudged across the yard.

When he was finally inside, out of the wet, miserable yard, he breathed a heavy sigh of relief and granted himself a moment's rest. But only a moment. There was still work to do.

He set up the folding table and dragged over the cooler and bucket of salt. He emptied the cooler and cleaned it out, then lined the bottom with a layer of salt. "No refrigerators in the apocalypse," he said to himself. "Gotta improvise."

He cut the meat into thin strips and laid them over the salt, then covered them in another layer of salt. Alternating layers of meat and salt filled the cooler until only a slimy mess was left on the table.

Ready to collapse, he closed the cooler's lid and pushed it to the wall. "What a day," he said, exhausted.

He poured a cup of water from the dispenser and washed down a small handful of ibuprofen pills. The mess on the table caught his eye and he growled. One last thing he had to do before he could crash. Impatiently, he wiped the table down with soap and water, folded it, and returned it to its place against the wall.

Finally, he could rest. He stripped off his wet clothes, dried off with a towel, and shuffled to his bed in the corner like a zombie. Exhausted, he collapsed face-first onto the mattress and clicked off the lantern.

He drifted out of consciousness. The doe's piercing black eyes haunted his dreams.

A faint buzzing noise rose in the air, somewhere far off. It grew louder in sharp bursts until it pierced through the wind and echoed around the neighborhood. It didn't sound to Christopher like a car or a truck, but it was motorized, whatever it was.

He hurried across the yard on his improvised crutches, rifle slung over his shoulder. Leaving the crutches propped against the hickory's trunk, he climbed the ladder to the platform. At the top, he got into firing position, steadying the rifle against the railing.

The sound of the approaching motor intensified. He lifted his head, listening. The roar of the engine seemed to multiply as it ricocheted off the houses. "There's more than one of them," he said under his breath, then, between the sound of the engines, a shrill scream pierced the air.

A figure came into view on the street. A woman. She was running from the east down the middle of the road. He had an unobstructed view from the platform. He put his eye to the rifle's scope. She was no older than twenty, blonde hair whipping back and forth as she ran. Mud and grass stained her torn clothes. Sweat, mucus, and tears streamed down her face.

"What the fuck is going on?" he whispered.

The sound of the approaching motors reached a crescendo and the girl came to a stop. She looked exhausted, staggering like a drunk as she turned and looked back down the street.

Several ATVs came into view and circled the girl. He counted four vehicles through the scope. Six men. Surrounded and outnumbered, the young girl crumpled helplessly to the asphalt, sobbing.

The men were outfitted in camo and wore helmets with dark visors covering their faces. Each had a gun holstered at their side. The ATVs circled the girl in the street several times, engines roaring, before they came to a stop, boxing her in. One of the men hopped off the back of an ATV and drew his weapon. Christopher placed the scope's crosshairs on his head.

The distance to the target was approximately seventy-five yards. Child's play for the Remington. He put his finger on the trigger.

The man pointed his gun at the girl and shouted something through his helmet. He couldn't make out the words but kept his rifle trained on the man's head. Two others dismounted their ATVs and approached the girl. They tried to grab her as she fought and screamed. "I'm not going back."

Christopher grimaced.

"There's too many of them," he whispered. "I'll give myself away."

Another man hopped off his ATV to help the others restrain the girl. She kicked wildly at her attackers until the three men wrestled her to the pavement. Two men grabbed her by the arms and yanked her to her feet, then a third reared back and punched her square in the face. The girl's head fell limp and blood leaked from her nose and mouth.

Christopher winced. There was nothing he could do. He could take one or two of the men, but the rest would get away. Then he'd be a sitting duck for the inevitable counterattack. And even if he could take them all out, what about the girl? He wasn't running a battered women's shelter, and he sure as shit hadn't spent years stockpiling supplies just to give them away.

"Sorry, honey," he said as he took his finger off the trigger.

One of the men picked up the unconscious girl and slung her over his shoulder. Her blood splattered on the pavement as she was carried to an ATV. The man plopped her limp body onto the seat, then the camo-clad gang revved their engines and roared away with their prisoner.

The woman in the red truck was one thing—she was alone and appeared unthreatening—but these guys were serious. They were organized. Possibly trained. Dangerous.

Christopher mindlessly stirred a pot of soup as it simmered on the propane stove. He stared vacantly through the wall of the bunker, lost in thought.

ATVs are short-range. They'd use cars or trucks if they were coming from a distance. They're close.

The soup bubbled and steamed.

It's been a while, and they're still alive. And there's a bunch of them. At least those six, and probably more wherever they're camped.

The soup came to a full boil. He continued stirring, absently.

Question is, are they a caravan, just passing through? Or do I have some real unfriendly neighbors?

The soup fizzed over the brim, splashing the stovetop and the card table with boiling chicken noodle soup. "Shit!" he yelped, and he snapped off the burner. The soup settled in the pot. He sat back in the chair and shook his scalded hand.

Surely this group hadn't prepared the way he had, whoever they were. They must be scrounging and scavenging. They had gotten this far, but how long could they keep it up?

He poured his dinner into a bowl, then stared vacantly at the wall as it cooled.

They did have muscle, at least enough to hold women hostage. That was worrying. For the time being, he would be on red alert.

He turned the soup, slowly swirling the noodles and picking up spoonfuls of broth only to dribble them back into the bowl.

An early May rain drizzled gloomily. Christopher took his eye away from the periscope.

Rain again. Third damn day in a row.

Scowling, he crossed another day off the calendar, then dropped to the floor for his daily sets of push-ups and sit-ups, steam about to shoot from his ears like an old cartoon. When he was finished, he dressed in rain gear while chewing aggressively on a granola bar, stuffed into his mouth all at once, then he climbed the ladder with the Remington slung over his shoulder and a crutch tucked under his arm.

He slogged through the soaked grass along the perimeter, leaning on the single crutch. The pain was gone from his ankle but his knee was still fragile, even with the thin brace. Pushing the worry that it could be something worse than a torn meniscus to the back of his mind, he focused on the patrol, circling the property until he determined it was all clear.

He propped the crutch against the hickory's trunk and climbed the ladder to the platform, steadying himself on the rail when he reached the top.

The neighborhood below was gray and soggy. The leaves on the nearby trees hung heavy and cheerless. Dismal clouds covered the sky, backlit by an invisible sun. There was no sign of movement on the ground and no sound aside from the annoying pelt of the rain against his jacket. The goddamn rain.

He puffed his cheeks and blew the air from his mouth, then turned and worked his way down the rain-soaked ladder. On the second rung from the bottom, his left boot slipped, and he dropped the last foot to the ground. Pain shot through his already injured knee as he caught himself on the ladder. He doubled over.

"Fuck."

Groaning through gritted teeth, he picked the crutch off the ground, then limped back to the bunker. At least it would be dry.

His wet boots squeaked when he touched down on the metal floor. He shook his head and flexed his knee.

"Fucking idiot."

He stripped out of his wet clothes and boots, leaving them in a heap on the floor by the ladder, then clicked on a lantern and carried it with him as he limped across the container. Once changed into dry, comfortable clothes, he limped back across the length of the steel box to the mattress in the corner.

He sank into the bed.

His knee throbbed. He needed to take his mind off the pain. With a sigh, he rolled over and plucked *The Road to Serfdom* from the end table. He read by the flat, fluorescent light of the lantern.

Time crept by with interminable slowness. He needed to be outside in the fresh, open air, tending to the crops, maintaining the grounds, keeping a watchful eye over his territory. Instead, it was apparently fucking monsoon season in Georgia and he was stuck inside, a gimp nursing a bum knee.

Someone could be out there. Someone could be plotting a break-in, just waiting for a moment of weakness.

Disgusted with himself, he put his nose back in *Serfdom* and tried to pass the time. The book rested on his knees. He turned page after page until a strange sensation passed through him. A slight twinge. A feeling in the air. Was it a sound? An odd movement out of the corner of his eye?

He lowered the book and squinted into the dark, past the harsh glow of the lantern. His supplies sat on their shelves, neatly organized. His clothes were packed in their crates against the wall. The gun safe was shut and locked.

Rain tapped softly against the hatch.

Once again, he picked up the book and tried to read, but he couldn't shake the feeling that something was *off*. He tossed the book aside with a huff.

He picked up the lantern and held it at arm's length, swinging the light to the east end of the bunker. The shelves, the cooler stuffed with venison and salt, the crates full of clothes, the bookcase, the toilet. He threw the light back to the west end. The gun safe, the water dispenser, the end table, the bed. Everything was in its place.

"Don't crack up down here, man. Keep your shit together."

He set the lantern back on the end table then turned to collapse back onto the bed when something on the floor caught his eye. He rubbed his eyes and squinted.

"What is that?"

He yanked the lantern back off the table and bent down. A line of black ants glistened in the light.

"Are you fucking serious?"

He followed the trail back to the southwest corner, behind the water dispenser.

"No, no, no!"

The ants marched in formation from the corner clear across to the opposite end of the container. He lifted the light and cursed as he followed the line of insects across the bunker.

"Where are you little fuckers going?"

Their trail crossed in front of the bookcase, past the clothes bins, and ended at the cooler of venison, left slightly cracked open. One neat line went up the side through the opening, and another was headed out in the opposite direction, carrying small bits of dried meat. His stomach dropped. "No!" he shouted as he ripped open the lid to find a swarm of small black ants inside. "Fuck!" He kicked the heavy cooler with his bare foot and it tipped over, spilling salt and preserved meat onto the floor. The ants scattered as he tumbled backward, landing on his backside in the middle of the steel floor. The metal rang like a gong.

Pain pulsed through his toe and his lungs burned with rage. He could have breathed fire.

The meat was ruined. All his work, wasted.

Stewing on the floor, he closed his eyes and tried to calm himself.

How could this have happened? How could I have left the lid open on the fucking cooler?

The doe stared at him through the mist, its eyes cold and black.

He hung his head between his knees.

It didn't matter how it happened. It was done. He forced the image of the doe from his mind. He raised his head. The overturned cooler was there waiting for him when he opened his eyes.

He picked himself off the floor and stared hatefully at the neat row of ants making their way back across the bunker, scurrying along their scent trail. Maybe it was the rain that drove them inside. That had happened to him and Amy once. In the middle of a rainstorm, he got home from work to find Amy furiously vacuuming the top of the wall with the hose extension. "What is going on?" he asked, over the whir of the machine. "Ants!" she yelled back, and she pointed to a line streaming in, somehow, through a tiny space in the frame above the sliding glass door. They had marched across the top of the wall, into the kitchen, and down to the sink's dirty dishes. The scene was almost comical, like something out of an old slapstick film. Amy and Christopher worked up a sweat over the next hour, exterminating as many of the invaders as possible and washing away their scent trails. Then, disheveled and tired, they looked at each other and laughed.

He centered himself, calming the dragon fire in his lungs, then pulled a can of Raid from the shelf and shook it. He wondered if this was the same colony he and Amy had repelled years ago.

"Remember me, fuckers?"

Leaving a fuming trail of death in his wake, he sprayed the entire line of black specks while humming *Ride of the Valkyries*. The poison's scent filled the air and he swelled with satisfaction.

"Smells like victory," he said with a nod.

With a whisk broom and dustpan, he scooped as much of the spilled salt and preserved meat back into the cooler as he could, then he dragged the heavy box to the ladder. He changed back into his wet clothes and slipped the Raid into a jacket pocket, then he struggled to haul the cooler up the ladder and through the hatch.

He stood in the wet grass under the dark mid-afternoon sky. The rain soaked his hair as he caught his breath. The cooler rested on the ground at his feet, raindrops splashing against its lid. He opened the box and kicked it over, spilling the salt and preserved meat into the grass, then he picked it up and turned it upside down. He tossed the empty cooler aside, then pulled the Raid from his jacket pocket and shook the can. That was *his* venison. He had worked his ass off for it. If he couldn't eat it, no other living thing could either. He doused the pile of salt and meat in poison then left it to be washed away by the endless rain.

He returned to the bunker and swept up the thousands of tiny carcasses with a damp cloth. Their crushed bodies released a foul scent, made even worse as it blended with the smell of the Raid. He tucked his nose under his shirt as he cleaned the floor.

Upon investigation of the crime scene, he found a small crack in the corner behind the water dispenser. Tomorrow he would solder it shut with a blowtorch. He sprayed it spitefully with the Raid in the meantime.

With no energy left to cook a hot meal, he unwrapped a survival bar and chewed it slowly as he stood in the center of his steel cage. The spot where the cooler had been was now conspicuously vacant. He retraced the path the ants had taken, from the empty spot on the floor to the small crack in the corner. He pictured the tiny insects. Thousands of indistinguishable workers marching robotically in lines.

A shiver went up his spine.

The sheets on the bed were jumbled, just as he had left them. *The Road to Serfdom* lay beside them.

Beyond Christopher's evergreen curtain, shoots of grass crept across the neighborhood's driveways and English ivy wrapped around fence posts. He let the yard around his house grow wild like all the others.

Behind the protection of his evergreens, though, he kept the grounds civilized. Shade from the tall hickory kept the grass sparse in the center of the yard but it grew thick on the perimeter. Once per week, he would cut it down to size with his motorless lawnmower and pick the weeds around the greenhouse and the sheds.

It was a bright, clear afternoon under a hot June sun. The yard was freshly groomed. Reading on the platform, in the shade of the hickory's branches, seemed like heaven. He took off his work gloves and put the mower away in the shed, where it would wait for him until next week.

Wiping the sweat from his brow, he stepped gingerly across the yard without the aid of crutches. His ankle was nearly back to full strength but his knee was still weak and unstable. All he could do was wear the thin brace and be mindful of his step.

He descended the bunker's ladder to retrieve a new book from the bookcase and the binoculars from their place on the supply shelves, then he returned to the surface and picked a ripe squash from the greenhouse.

Carefully, he climbed the ladder on the hickory, binoculars around his neck, book and food in hand.

At the top, he sat on the platform, resting against the tree's thick trunk. The fresh green leaves rustled in the breeze. He took a deep breath and cracked open *No Country for Old Men*, a book he had been excited to read. The movie was badass—a rare Academy Award winner he could actually respect.

He read through the afternoon, pausing every so often to glass the neighborhood. Shadows stretched across the yard as the sun sank in the sky. The air glowed magic hour blue.

Finally, a perfect day.

Twilight fell over his domain. He climbed down from the tree and scrounged up dinner, a cup of rice from the shed and red pepper from the greenhouse.

Three months. His stores were holding up well. He was proud of himself for planning so carefully and rationing so effectively. There would come a time when food would be harder to come by, and he would have to venture out into the world to hunt wild game and supplement his stockpile with scavenged nonperishables. But it would be years before then. He was sure of it.

Christopher went back to the bunker and cooked a rice and pepper stir fry. He ate by the light of the lantern and read a little more of *No Country* before drifting into a tranquil sleep, wrapped in the afterglow of the day.

Christopher crossed another day off the calendar. He exercised. He ate a bowl of oatmeal and took a bite from the squash leftover from the day before. He dressed for the day in a pair of gray cargo shorts and a green Army t-shirt. He slipped on the knee brace, armed himself with the Glock and Remington, and checked the periscope.

"What the hell?"

He pressed his eye closer to the lens.

"What the fuck? That can't be."

The doors of both sheds were hanging open.

He jerked the scope to the east. The greenhouse's door was closed. He scanned slowly across the yard. No visible intruders.

A sickening rage boiled in his gut as he stepped back from the periscope and stomped toward the ladder. "I know I locked those doors," he said in a rough growl, and he climbed to the surface without any regard for his ailing knee. "If anything is gone, I swear to God..."

He opened the hatch without a sound and peeked over the lip, quickly scanning the yard, then stepped slowly onto the grass. He drew the handgun from its holster.

He moved forward tactically, weapon forward, eyes sweeping side to side as he stormed toward the sheds. The combination locks were cut and lying on the ground. A sinking feeling took hold in his gut. Pushing past the door, he stomped into the food shed.

"Fuck," he screamed, not caring if anyone was within earshot. "*Fuck*."

Whoever had been inside was long gone, and they had left with nearly everything. All the rice was missing, as was the entire crate of survival bars. A few lonely cans of soup, beans, and vegetables were scattered about, but the shelves where hundreds had been stacked were nearly bare. Several boxes of dried fruit, granola bars, and crackers had also been stolen. Packets of heirloom seeds were strewn across the floor, clearly picked over. Even his bin of water purification tablets was gone.

Snarling, he stormed out of the food shed, huffing through flared nostrils, and threw open the door of the supply shed. He stepped inside. Several canisters of propane were missing, along with some flashlights and lanterns. The batteries had also been rummaged through, but most of his tools and supplies remained in place.

Maybe they didn't want to make much noise. Maybe they got spooked and took off before they could complete the job. Maybe they just wanted to get in and out as quickly as possible. Or maybe, after packing up the majority of his food reserves, they didn't have room for much else. Whatever the reason, the rational side of his mind knew it could have been worse. The emotional side couldn't see the silver lining. All it could see was bright, furious red.

His jaw clenched tight enough to crack a marble. He squeezed his eyes shut and clenched his fists, trying to breathe.

All those years of planning, undone in a single night. And right under his nose. It was a violation.

"Fuck *you*!"

He thrashed violently, knocking a bin of small parts from its perch. Screws and washers jangled across the floor.

His skin was on fire with rage. He stood over the mess, chest heaving. Then his stomach lurched. He turned on his heel.

"The greenhouse."

Forgetting about his knee, he crashed through the door and ran across the yard to the greenhouse. Its silver lock poked out of the grass a few feet from the opaque door. He knew what he would find on the other side, and rage transitioned to dejection. He took a deep breath as he opened the door and stepped inside, then exhaled slowly, like letting the air out of an old balloon.

A pepper plant lay on the floor, its pot cracked, dirt spilled everywhere. A young eggplant sat alone in the corner. A few carrots remained tucked into their soil. That was all that was left. The rest of his plants had been cleaned out, leaving the glass room shockingly bare.

He rubbed his eyes in disbelief and slumped to the floor, defeated. The empty shelves and tables loomed overhead.

How? *How* did this happen? *Who* could have done this, and gotten away with so *much*, without making a single goddamn sound?

Furious, he turned it over in his mind, molten lava in his lungs. He slammed his fist on the ground.

"Fucking piece of shit! Fuck you!"

His face turned red and his eyes flared with rage.

"You hear me? That's right. I want you to hear me! Come try this shit again! I dare you! I fucking dare you!"

He closed his eyes and hung his head between his knees, breathing, breathing, breathing, until a thought took hold in his mind. He rose to his feet, a sense of purpose in his eyes. His body tightened. He was a rock. A sledgehammer. A missile.

This act would not go unpunished. The people responsible would be found.

He tore through the greenhouse door, back into the yard, and pressed through the evergreens on the ridge. In the yard below, two distinct lines were pressed into the grass.

"They backed right in like they fucking owned the place."

He stared at the tracks and spat, then raised his eyes to the street. Saliva dripped from his chin. He nodded to himself.

"Fuck it."

He turned back through the evergreens and hurried through the hatch. He traded the Remington for the M4 and grabbed the keys to the SUV from inside the gun locker, then climbed back up the ladder. Whoever was responsible—the ATV riders, the woman in the red truck, or anyone else—had a bullet with their name on it.

His pulse quickened as he raced down the hill and went through the house to the garage. This was happening. He was doing this. He opened the SUV's door and tucked the M4 against the seat on the passenger's side, then yanked open the garage door. The street was clear. He sat down in the driver's seat, slammed the door shut, and turned the ignition. The engine sputtered for a moment, struggling to turn over, then roared to life.

He backed down the driveway and pulled out into the street. The tracks left in the overgrown grass turned to the east. It was a start, at least.

He yanked the wheel and pressed the gas gently, keeping the engine quiet. His pulse thumped in his hands as he gripped the wheel. Even riding in an MRAP through an active war zone was never this eerie. There, he was with a team of the toughest men on the planet. When their massive, armored truck rumbled down the road, everyone got out of the way. But these streets were ghostly. The stillness. The silence. Abandoned, burned-out cars. All the empty houses, some with broken windows. The overgrown grass and weeds made the once-familiar neighborhood feel foreign, haunted, like he was being watched.

He crisscrossed the neighborhood but found no sign of his thieves. He sighed. If he was going to find anything, he would need to cast a wider net. He whipped the SUV around.

He pulled to a stop at the neighborhood's main entrance and reached for the blinker, then pulled his hand back and shook his head. With long looks up and down the road, he made sure the coast was clear, then he hit the gas and turned north.

The two-lane road was lined with green-leaved river birch and tall junipers. Other neighborhoods, similar to his own, branched off from the road. The thieves could be hiding in any one of them.

"Where are you, fuckers?"

He had driven this road countless times before, never giving a second thought to the houses he passed along the way. They had always been a generic blur of stucco, brick, and glass. Now he searched every property as he passed, scanning for any sign of life, any clue that might lead him to the thieves and his stolen property. There was only desolation and the beginnings of decay.

A small development of five large houses, situated along a semi-circle drive, sat behind a tall, black gate on the right side of the road. The gate was bashed in, metal bars warped and twisted.

A row of modest, single-story homes sat on the other side of the road. Green algae had spread over their cheap siding and weeds were growing through their brick stoops.

Two cars sat off the roadside, smashed together and shoved up over the curb onto the sidewalk. Hoods popped open and fenders mangled, the vehicles had disintegrated into each other, their engines melted and charred black.

He drove somewhat aimlessly down the long residential road, having left before developing a strategy. He should have been doing a systematic grid search, starting from his house and gradually working outward, street by street, but he found himself caught up in the sights along the road. It was a surprisingly welcome change of pace to have something to *do* and oddly exhilarating to be *out*. But it would have to be a short-lived excursion. An intersection with a four-lane road was a quarter mile ahead.

That'll be far enough for today.

The intersection was two miles from home. A long way back if he ran into any trouble. The farther out he got, the more vulnerable and untethered he began to feel, like swimming out into the ocean without enough energy in reserve for the swim back to shore.

He had been impulsive, exposing himself to too much risk without a plan. He would regroup and try again—there was no way those fuckers would get away with this—but he needed to get home safely first.

There was an old apartment complex just ahead on the left, before the intersection. A good place to turn around. The tops of the complex's buildings came into view. He approached slowly and swung the SUV into the entryway at a wide angle, then slammed hard on the brakes.

"What the hell?"

He sat in the driver's seat, frozen, unable to process what he was seeing. It couldn't be real. He sucked down a gulp of air and gripped the wheel with tight fists.

People. Everywhere. Milling about in the open. Strolling casually along the sidewalk. A pack of children ran across a patch of grass. A man threw a tennis ball for a dog to fetch.

A young girl spotted the SUV and pointed, then everyone in sight turned their heads. A jolt of panic shot through him. He had been seen.

He hit the gas. Tires squealed and the SUV lurched over the curb as he took the turn back onto the road, throwing him into the steering wheel. The vehicle thudded onto the asphalt, tossing him back in his seat, and he stomped the pedal to the floor. His heart raced as he roared down the deserted two-lane road.

Wild-eyed, he reached up and grabbed the rearview mirror and angled it to see back down the road.

"What was *that*? What the *fuck* was that?"

The SUV's speedometer approached triple digits as the vehicle tore past a SPEED LIMIT 45 sign and nearly flew off the road rounding a bend. He sucked in a panicked breath and gripped the wheel tightly as he eased his foot off the gas. He'd be back home in a few minutes. He had to get a hold of himself.

He slowed the car to a crawl as he approached his neighborhood, then brought it to a complete stop at the turn. The SUV sat in the middle of the road. The engine idled. Christopher sat in the driver's seat, chest heaving as though he had run a sprint. He gripped the rearview again. The road was empty.

"Who the fuck were those people?" he said, catching his breath.

The area was quiet and still. Releasing the tension from his chest, he gently pressed the gas and turned into his neighborhood.

Christopher walked up the hill and through the evergreen shrubs, then he stood and stared at the open sheds. He closed his eyes and inhaled deeply, then let the breath out slowly as he shook his head.

"Not again. Not tonight."

He closed the doors to the mostly empty food shed, then stomped across the yard to the bunker with determined strides. He went down the hatch, and when he reemerged in the yard a few moments later he was carrying blankets and a pillow.

He stepped inside the supply shed and shut the door behind him.

Christopher sat on the corner of the bed on a cold, wet day, huddled under a heavy blanket, knees tucked to his chest. The solar-powered lantern rested on the end table, casting him in a cocoon of fluorescent light. Long shadows stretched across the corrugated steel walls, disappearing into the darkness at the far end.

He scratched the scraggly beard he had been growing for the winter and squinted at the calendar on the wall. November. Five months since the heist with no sign of the thieves, or anyone else, for that matter. No contact with the ATV riders. No sightings of the red pickup. No further contact with the apartments down the road.

A functioning colony. That's what it looked like, anyway. He still couldn't wrap his mind around it. It defied logic. It defied rational explanation. He chewed his lip and shook his head whenever he thought about it—a splinter in his mind he couldn't shake loose.

He rubbed his tired eyes. How long had it been since he had a decent night's sleep? Days? Weeks? Months, even? Time had lost its meaning. The days blurred together.

After the robbery, he slept in the shed for several nights. If anyone came back for a second reach into the cookie jar, he'd be waiting inside with his Glock in hand. After a week of uneventful nights in the shed, he went back to the bunker.

He had built the bunker to avoid exposure to the outside world, to be able to hide in plain sight. But after the theft, being stuck underground night after night, unable to detect creeping intruders, drove him mad. He would lie awake in the dark, straining his ears for hours and jumping at every tiny sound. Once, in the middle of the night, he woke from a half-sleep to a strange scratching sound, faint and repeating. He climbed out of the bunker with a flashlight only to find a family of raccoons clawing at the hatch, their eyes glowing in the light until he shooed them off.

For a while, he took to sleeping on the platform in the hickory until a late-night rain forced him to slog back to the bunker, soaking wet.

He thought about spending nights in the house. He could sleep on a real bed with the windows open so he could hear outside. It was a tempting idea, but it would have been a defeat, a surrender of sorts. The bunker was his fort, his castle, and he wasn't ready to give up yet. He would man his post.

His defenses needed reinforcement, however. He had assumed houses would be the juicy target for scavengers, that he was safe behind his evergreens. The theft had proven he wasn't as invisible as he thought. Whoever had stolen from him had rendered the alarm on his front door irrelevant, bypassing the house entirely and heading straight into the backyard. Who had done it? How did they know? He drove himself half-crazy thinking about it. But, even though he might never get satisfying answers, he had to do *something* to give himself peace of mind.

One day, he waited until dusk, then set out into the neighborhood, scavenging chain-link fencing from nearby yards and bringing it back in sections. The next day, he reassembled the fence on the ridge behind his row of evergreens, leaving a small opening hidden in the corner on the west side. He could slip easily in and out, but anyone stumbling onto his property would find an added barrier—just enough of a deterrent to prevent another theft.

The extra security helped to ease his mind, but as disconcerting as the robbery had been, it was the colony down the road that gnawed at him the most.

All those people. A whole community, just two miles away. Who were they? How was such a place possible?

He had seen people strolling around in the open, children running happily about, a dog playing fetch. It was as if the world had ended everywhere but there, its people spared from the greatest cataclysm in human history, allowed to carry on with their lives as if nothing had happened. *How*?

It was an existential threat, an affront to human nature itself. In the weeks after its discovery, he would find himself standing in the yard, staring blankly in the general direction of the apartment complex, through the trees, toward the horizon.

He had been on top of the world, powerful and superior, reigning over his kingdom of one. Now he was trapped on a deserted island, small and weak, just off the shore of a great continent.

He sat in the bubble of white light and took a bite of a puny, sour apple, one of the measly few the apple tree had ever produced. He shook his head.

"That tree ain't worth a damn," he said to himself as he chewed. "I've half a mind to chop it down and use it for firewood. 'Least then it'd be fucking useful."

He swallowed the bite down his dry, scratchy throat and grimaced. The water dispenser was empty. He would have to trek into the house to retrieve a new jug, up the creaky ladder to the attic. But not today. His knee still hurt. If anything, it had gotten worse. His chest ached, too.

Am I dying?

There was work to be done, but, at that moment, dying on his bed was the more appealing option. The bunker would be his coffin. Alone and in the dark, but at least he'd go out on his own terms, in his own bed. He made his peace with it.

He tossed the half-eaten apple into the shadows. It landed with a soft thud somewhere on the cold steel floor. He pulled the blanket over his head and collapsed onto the pillow.

His limbs were numb. He flexed his hands and scrunched his toes, trying to regain feeling. His mind was sluggish and cold, like a bowl of Jell-O sloshing around in his skull.

Under the blanket, his slow, squishy thoughts drifted to his childhood bedroom where he and his older brother Joshua would push their beds together and build forts with sheets and pillows. Mom would yell from downstairs, telling them to settle down, and they'd pretend to sleep for a few minutes before going back to playing, then Mom would yell again.

He tried to push the vignette from his mind. Though the thought of the late-night pillow forts distracted him from the dank chill of the bunker, recalling even warm and cozy memories of his brother eventually led his mind to the accident.

Joshua had been driving home after working a shift at the mall, not long after getting his license. The highway was dark.

According to the police report, he changed lanes, sideswiping a car that had moved into his blind spot. Startled by the impact, he overcorrected and slammed into the median at full speed. He was dead before the paramedics arrived at the scene. Mom was inconsolable. Dad was a military man who pushed the pain deep down and told Christopher to be a man and do the same.

Dad was killed two years later in a helicopter crash on the base—a training accident. At the funeral, an officer he didn't recognize gave him a pat on the back and told him he had to be the man of the house now.

Five years later, not long after he had started college, Mom died, too. The official cause of death was heart disease. In reality, it was a slow suicide. She ate to fill the hole in her broken heart and clogged her arteries in the process. He dropped out of school and enlisted to fight in Iraq.

Under the blanket, a tear rolled down Christopher's cheek. Embarrassed, he wiped it away with a sniff. Then he remembered he was alone.

Christopher groaned as he came down the ladder from the attic, another jug of water over his shoulder. He placed it by the others, along the wall in the bedroom. Fourteen down, one to go. His knee was weak and pulsed with pain on every trip, but the work had to be done.

The water had been safe in the attic, but it was a pain in the ass having to come into the house for it, up a flight of stairs and a rickety ladder, and schlepp it back on a bum knee. Better to get the pain and hassle out of the way all at once.

He headed back for another jug. The wooden rungs of the ladder creaked as he climbed up to the dark and dingy attic. The air was warm and musty compared to the chill in the rest of the house. Loose insulation was spread over the floor, packed between wooden support beams. The jugs of water sat along the wall in the southwest corner of the attic. He limped across the plywood boards laid out over the beams. His knee threatened to buckle under the abuse, and he knew it would burn like hell later, but bringing fifteen jugs of water down to the sheds would buy him at least two months before he would have to climb up to the attic again. Maybe he could even stretch it to three if he rationed strictly.

He picked up the fifteenth jug and threw it over his shoulder with a grunt. At least five dozen jugs remained. "Until next time, ladies," he said, then he walked across the attic and backed down the creaky ladder one rung at a time, using his free hand to stabilize himself on the railing.

Amazing such a flimsy thing can hold my weight.

Just as that thought crossed his mind, the second rung from the bottom snapped under his foot and he tumbled backward into the closet, crashing against the drywall. Water sprayed his face as the jug smashed against the wall and then the floor, leaving him in a wet heap at the bottom of the ladder.

Groaning, he lifted his head off the wall and rubbed the back of his skull, then he held his hand in front of his face. Blood dripped from his blurry fingers. Pain radiated from his elbow and shoulder. Between his sprawled legs, the jug quietly drained into the carpet.

It was a bitterly cold New Year's Day, by Georgia standards. The snow falling from the sky was also uncommon. Christopher climbed out of the bunker and gauged the powder's depth with the butt of his Remington—three inches on the ground already—then turned his face to the sky. Fat flakes drifted silently toward the earth with no sign of stopping.

He left footprints around the perimeter as he did his usual security check, the wet snow sloshing under his boots. It would soon be a solid sheet of ice if the temperature kept falling. He zipped his field jacket tight.

After checking the fences and surveying the area, he climbed the ladder to the platform, brushing the snow from each rung as he ascended. When he reached the top he was struck by the serene landscape below. There were no footprints beyond his evergreens, no tire tracks on the street, only a pristine blanket of pure white snow as far as he could see, covering the houses and their yards and the road.

He glassed the neighborhood's doors, windows, and yards through the binoculars, as he always did, and found no sign of life from man nor animal. Nothing had been disturbed and there was a sense of complete stillness. Silence. Peace. All the trees were frozen stiff and there was no wind to rattle their hardened branches. He took the rifle from his shoulder and leaned it against the railing. Snowflakes drifted gently from the charcoal sky to the porcelain earth.

A sensation of absolute solitude washed over him. No squirrels or chipmunks were scurrying across his yard, no summer sounds of insects or birds. He was the only living thing in sight, standing over the frozen ruin of what was once a living neighborhood.

He propped his elbows on the railing and rested his chin on his hands. He was staring somewhat absently at the house across the street when Alice Russo wandered into his mind. Alice was one of the popular girls, and she was perfect—not a single blonde hair was ever out of place on her perfect head—and he had worshiped her in the way only a high school boy could. Intensely. Desperately. Painfully. And she had to know he felt that way. She *had* to. They sat next to each other in English. They passed notes. They talked on the phone for hours after school, reading poetry and song lyrics to each other. They even vowed that if one of them died the other would give the eulogy at their funeral. How could she *not* feel the same way he did?

Eric Williams, who lived on the next street over in the house directly behind Christopher's childhood home, was throwing a party on a Friday night. Alice was going to be there. *Everyone* was going to be there. Except for him. He wasn't invited.

On the night of the party, he went upstairs to the bathroom and turned off the light. He watched from the window, across their adjoining backyards, as guests filled Eric's kitchen and living room, waiting for Alice to appear. He stood in the dark for an hour, staring across the infinite expanse of those few hundred feet like Gatsby staring across the waters at Daisy's green light, until Alice's perfect blonde hair finally glided past a window in Eric's crowded house.

His insides fluttered. There was still time. He could run over there and knock on the door. It would probably be fine. Eric wouldn't mind, he was sure of it. They weren't *close* friends, but they were classmates and neighbors—they had grown up together. Not getting an invite was probably just an oversight. He stood in the dark, debating with himself. One minute, he was going, for sure, and he was going through his dresser for cool clothes to put on. Then, the next, he was talking himself out of it, too proud to show up where he wasn't invited. He went back to the bathroom window and stared late into the night.

On Monday, talk of the party was all over school. He was standing at his locker between classes when he heard the rumor. Alice Russo made out with Joey Donovan at the party. He slammed his locker shut.

"Fuck you, Eric," he said, his breath's vapor blending with the falling snow.

He climbed down the ladder.

Before he could get back to the relative warmth of the bunker, he needed to water the plants in the greenhouse. He stomped through the snow toward the rain collector, thinking about how nice the air in the greenhouse was going to feel. He reached for a bucket and bent down to open the tap. An icicle hung from the spigot. He knocked it off with a swift chop then placed the bucket under the spigot. The cold metal screeched as he twisted the knob to the left, but no water flowed.

"What the hell?"

He slapped the barrel. It was heavy, definitely not empty. He pulled off the lid. Plenty of water all right, but it was a solid block of ice.

"Shit."

He would have to get the water for the plants from the jug in the bunker. As he turned toward the hatch something on the side of the barrel caught his eye and he turned back. "No." He stepped closer and bent down. A hairline seam ran down the side of the plastic. He rubbed it with his thumb and shook his head. A definite crack. "No fucking way," he said, just as it made a popping sound and the fracture grew up the side.

"This is Georgia," he said, rearing his leg back. "It's not supposed to get this fucking cold." He kicked the barrel and it partially dislodged from the drain spout. "God-damn am-at-teur mis-take," he yelled, landing a kick on each syllable until the barrel detached and toppled into the snow. He stepped toward it, raised his leg, and brought the heel of his boot down hard onto the barrel, and he slipped and fell backward into the snow.

Flat on his back, chest heaving, he suppressed the urge to scream as his breath evaporated into the falling flakes. Anger burned in his chest. Atlanta winters are mild, with average lows above freezing throughout the season. Despite his rationalization, deep down, he knew it was his fault. He should have drained the barrel when the weather turned cold. Not that it mattered. The rain collector was K.I.A., and all he could do was swallow his anger, catch his breath, and eventually pick himself up off the snowy ground.

He brushed the snow from his pants and jacket and stood up straight. The sheds at the end of the yard caught his eye. His stomach dropped. If the rain collector had frozen...

"The jugs."

He limped to the shed and dialed the combination into the lock. The door swung open with a creak. He clicked on a lantern. Thirteen water jugs sat along the back wall. The water inside was cloudy through the blue plastic. He got down on his knees and tilted back the nearest jug. A large chunk of ice shifted in the water.

"Shit."

Would there be enough space inside for the expanding ice? The water was too valuable to risk, especially with the collection tank gone. He hung his head. Each forty-two-pound jug had to be moved.

He squatted down and gripped the first jug's handle with one hand and wrapped his other arm around the barrel.

"This is going to fucking suck."

He stood, lifting the heavy, half-frozen container, trying not to wrench his back or put too much weight on his injured knee. With the container hugged tightly against his chest, he stepped out into the yard, snow coming down harder than ever. The freezing air numbed his cheeks as he stomped through the snow.

When he reached the bunker, he set down the jug so he could pull open the hatch, then he heaved it over his shoulder and carefully descended the ladder. Below ground, he set down the jug with a groan and shoved it up against the wall. Cold air poured through the open hatch.

"Twelve more. Jesus Christ."

With each trip to the shed and back, the air was colder, the snow deeper, his bones wearier. By the fifth jug, his knee was throbbing and he couldn't feel his fingers. Mucus ran down his flushed face and froze in his scraggly winter beard. By the sixth trip, his lungs were burning. By the seventh, a strange fatigue was setting in, like his brain was turning to mush, sloshing around in his skull with each step. He kicked the nearly frozen jug up against the others and staggered back to the ladder for number eight.

He emerged from the ground and stepped into the yard. A cold wind rose as he trudged toward the shed. Tree branches clacked like castanets over the melody of the winter breeze. He breathed an exhausted sigh as he entered the shed and picked up the eighth jug. A sharp pain pierced his knee. He winced but the muscles in his frozen face barely moved.

He carried the jug into the yard, his eyes dry, his mouth dry, his heart beating rapidly. Too rapidly, like a runner finishing a marathon, sprinting to the finish line so he can collapse on the other side. The wind howled above him. With the jug on his shoulder, he looked up into the falling snow and gasped for breath. The sky swirled and turned black.

Christopher came to, face down in the snow. He rolled over and wiped his face, unsure if he had been down for a few seconds or an hour. The jug of water lay beside him, half-buried in snow. He slowly got to his knees, then his feet, and picked up the jug. Bleary-eyed, he suffered down each rung of the ladder into the bunker.

He shuffled to the wall and set the jug by the others. It was frozen solid, the plastic slightly contorted.

"That's it," he said. "No more."

He closed the hatch and stripped off his wet, stiff clothes. His skin was numb and raw. A shiver rattled his bones as he crawled into bed and wrapped himself in blankets.

The shed's door creaked as it swayed in the wind, five jugs of water left to freeze.

Christopher sat on the bed in the bunker with a worn paperback copy of *Fight Club*. He rubbed his eyes and cast the unopened book aside, then tossed his head back against the wall and groaned. He was tired. Bored. His mind crawled, heavy and sluggish, like a waterlogged octopus slithering over dry land.

It was early February. A year since civilization fell. Though it was a moment he had spent so much time preparing for—a moment that, in his heart of hearts, he had *hoped* would occur—he didn't feel like celebrating its anniversary. He didn't feel like doing anything. Even the thought that spring was on the way left him numb and cheerless, as much as he wanted this miserable fucking winter to end.

He was anxious. He couldn't sleep. He had begun having strange chest pains, like a string tightening around his heart. A lingering cough burned his throat and lungs. He would bolt awake in the night, gasping for breath. One of these nights, he might go to sleep and never wake up. It was a living hell—desperately needing rest and rejuvenation but dreading sleep—fearing to let his consciousness drift away, out of his control. He existed in a state of strung-out insomnia. Everything a copy of a copy...

He got dressed and went outside, bringing *Fight Club* with him. Maybe reading in the brisk late-winter air would wake him up. At the very least, it would force him to feel *something*.

He sat in a lawn chair under the hickory in the center of the yard. A dull gray cloud cover blanketed the sky. The air was chilly. He tried to read but couldn't focus on the words.

A brown thrasher sang from a nearby branch.

A woodpecker rapped on a house across the street.

The drab atmosphere was pregnant with an eerie tension. A quiet foreboding. An unspoken dread.

He peeked over the top of the book, feeling exposed. Vulnerable, out in the open. A sitting duck.

Was he being watched?

Could they sense his weakness?

Had they come for him at last?

A cold breeze blew straight through him and he shivered.

He raised his head. Everything was in its place.

He drew short, shallow breaths. His heart rate quickened. His eyes darted from one side of the yard to the other.

He stood and dropped the book, then paced across the yard and pushed through the evergreens. Ducking low behind the fence, he checked every sightline. When he was satisfied the area was clear, he paced to the opposite side of the yard and did the same.

He climbed the ladder to the platform and leaned over the railing. His territory was empty and still. He dropped his head and exhaled slowly.

A whole year. Don't start cracking up out here, Chris.

The breeze blew his long, disheveled hair into his face, and he let it. He whispered into the air, "I need something to *do*. I need... a mission."

The woodpecker continued peppering the house across the street. He lifted his head and shot a glare in the direction of the sound.

"Will you ever shut up? I can't hear myself think," he said, then he cocked his head and stood up a little taller, an idea forming.

"The houses."

He climbed down from the platform, his heart pumping with life, his mind focusing.

It would be dangerous. Any time spent beyond the evergreen curtain meant leaving his retreat unguarded, and every time he stepped off his land he risked exposing his position. But after a long, hard winter, after the break-in, after losing his rain collector and several jugs of water in the freeze, he was tired of being on the ropes, taking punches. It was time to go on offense. He would do a sweep of the nearby houses and bring back any valuable supplies he could find.

He prepared as night fell, the rush of adrenaline even more intense than it had been on Day One. The excitement—the thrill of anticipation—reminded him of the war.

Just like huntin' insurgents in the Sandbox, he thought, except there would be no one to watch his six.

He dressed in ranger green fatigues and pulled a camo neck gaiter over his head. He loaded extra mags for his M4 and Glock and packed them into his chest rig, strapped on over his fatigues, and put fresh batteries in the night-vision goggles before securing them on his head. He pulled a mini-sledge from the shelf and slid it through a hammer holster, which he attached to his belt, and slung an empty duffle bag over his back.

He climbed the ladder, emerging in the yard under the veiled glow of the moon. He sucked in the cool air, getting his heart rate under control. Professional soldiers are trained to focus on the task at hand, and tonight he was a professional soldier again.

He flipped down his night-vision goggles, crossed through the gap in the fence, and went down the hill. Though slowed by his injured knee, he still moved over the long grass with stealth and swiftness, his M4 at the ready as he slipped into the front yard of the house directly to the east of his own.

His head swiveled, checking his background as he approached the front door. He turned the knob. It was unlocked and opened with a creak. Eye over the barrel of his M4, he stepped inside, leaving the door open behind him as he crossed through the foyer. He was certain no one was inside—he would have noticed people living next door—but he cleared the house by the book, systematically moving from room to room to confirm it was empty.

He headed to the kitchen and opened the pantry. Long-expired cereal. An old box of teabags. A mostly empty box of cheese and peanut butter crackers, the kind that comes wrapped in individual servings. He grabbed the few that were left and stuffed them into the duffle. The fridge was bare except for some old bottles of ketchup and mustard on the door.

"Cleared the place out before they left."

He closed the fridge and turned to the sliding glass door at the back of the kitchen. He stepped toward it, adjusting the focus ring on his night-vision. The backyard came into view and his eyes drifted to its back corner. He pictured the doe standing there, quietly chewing on overgrowth along the fence, shrouded in mist.

She looks up and their eyes meet.

He took a breath and stepped back from the door. He shook his head, clearing the image from his mind, then turned and headed back to the front door at a half-jog. He passed through the threshold, back into the muted silver glow of the night sky.

He continued down the block to the east and turned the next house's doorknob. Locked. He looked through the window beside the door. The kitchen table, straight back through the foyer, was neatly set with silverware and fancy china. To the left, chairs sat neatly upright in the sitting room. The floors were clean. If he hadn't known better, he might have thought this house was about to host a dinner party.

He pulled the mini-sledge from its holster then bashed the doorknob with a swift downward stroke. The knob clattered on the stoop. He pushed the other end through the door with the barrel of his M4, the thud audible through the door as the knob landed on the hardwood inside. He holstered the sledge, pressed the door open with his boot, then stepped inside.

An odd smell hung in the air. Ignoring the odor, he moved swiftly through the house, first to the left, sweeping through the sitting room, then the laundry room at the southeast corner. He swung around, his M4 tucked against his shoulder, and strode through the kitchen toward the living room. The putrid stench intensified.

He stopped in his tracks. Two shadowy figures sat on the couch.

"Stay where you are! Hands up!"

The backs of their heads remained still. He crossed the threshold into the living room, keeping his weapon trained on the dark figures as he stepped in front of them.

"I said hands up!"

The corpses were blackened, nearly mummified skin wrapped tightly around bony limbs. Their clothes hung loosely over their decayed bodies and a dark black stain had soaked into the cushions beneath them. A fly buzzed past his face, then another. He swatted them away and lowered his weapon.

He pulled the gaiter over his nose and mouth and stepped closer. A dark fluid had oozed from their mouths, staining their clothes, and something had eaten away the flesh from their faces. He stepped to the opposite end of the couch. The larger figure held a small revolver. "Suicide," he whispered, shaking his head.

He turned in place. Small, dark clumps of something were scattered across the carpet. He bent down. "Cat shit." He looked up at the rotting corpses. "That explains the eaten flesh." He stood and took a step toward the kitchen but stopped. There was a dark shape beneath an end table in the corner. Kneeling, he found the remains of a small animal, its bony body curled up in a ball. "Rough way to go, kitty, trapped in here with them," he said, nodding toward the bodies on the couch. "They took the easy way out."

He left the three carcasses alone to rot in the living room and went back to the kitchen. In the fridge were four unopened bottles of water. The pantry was a bust except for a box of oatmeal. He added the paltry findings to the duffle bag.

He looked up to the ceiling and grimaced. There would be plenty more houses, hopefully without the stench of rotting corpses. He would skip going upstairs.

He exited through the knobless front door and stepped onto the walk. He froze. Less than one hundred feet from where he stood, a pickup truck was parked in the middle of the street, facing east.

Through the night-vision, a silhouette in the truck's cabin was visible; a small-framed person with shoulder-length hair. The figure leaned to their right and looked through the passenger-side window. They raised their arm. Christopher lifted his M4, then a powerful beam of light blasted through the truck's window, blinding him. "Gahh!" He flipped up his night-vision lenses and squinted into the light, then raised his weapon to his shoulder and shifted his weight to a firing position. The bright light shut off and the truck's tires squealed.

A sharp pain shot through his knee and it buckled beneath him. He cried out and crumpled to the ground.

The pickup lurched down the road.

He rolled and picked himself up off the cement walk and limped forward into the yard. The truck's engine roared as it raced down the block into the darkness. He aimed and fired. One shot, then another, and a third, until the truck's tail lights disappeared around the corner.

Christopher lowered his weapon. The roar of the engine faded into the distance.

Christopher worked in the yard on a pleasant mid-March afternoon. The long, gray winter had come to a merciful end.

Beyond relief from the lifeless cold, he had little to celebrate. His knee was weak and caused pain during every chore, his stock of supplies was dangerously low, and since the second appearance of the woman in the red truck his chest ached nearly all the time. He could never quite catch his breath.

She was still alive and somewhere close. And she had seen him, this time for sure. He replayed the confrontation in his mind, hoping the bullet holes in the back of her truck had sent a clear message: Stay the fuck out of my territory.

He positioned three empty water jugs along the supply shed's wall and jerry-rigged a funnel system from the gutter to the jugs using a garden hose. Around the base of each jug, he nailed a short stack of two-by-fours in a square, securing them in place.

He stepped back, breathing heavily, and looked at his work. "It'll have to do," he said with a grimace, and he rubbed his chest.

He was suddenly hot. Hotter than he should be, like an egg could fry on his forehead. He wiped the sweat from his brow with the back of his wrist. His heart began to thump loudly in his chest. Too loudly. His pulse drummed in his ears. Something was... *wrong*. He needed air. His chest heaved and he gasped for breath, and then he was cold. Colder than he should be. Shivering, he dropped to his knees. A sharp pain flashed through his chest, as though an invisible hand had reached inside, grabbed his heart, and squeezed.

Am I having a heart attack? Am I dying?

He collapsed to the ground. His hands tingling, body quaking, he curled into a ball and breathed rapid, shallow breaths.

This is it. I'm going to die out here. Alone. In the dirt.

Every breath stabbed his heart. He tried to press through the pain, taking in slightly more air with each gulp, until he could fully expand his lungs. He flexed his tingling hands, squeezing them into tight fists repeatedly until the feeling returned to his fingers. His breathing slowed to normal.

He rolled onto his back, then closed his eyes and put a hand on his chest. In and out. In and out.

The sun beat down on his face until the sense of doom had passed. Exhausted, depleted, the world above dissolved. He slipped into a dreamless sleep on the dirt by the shed.

A long gust of wind rustled the freshly sprouted leaves, easing Christopher into consciousness. He lifted his head and rubbed his eyes, unsure why he was lying in the yard. He sat up and saw the improvised rain collectors, remembering the attack he had suffered.

How long have I been out?

A cool breeze blew through the yard. A muted sun hung low over the western horizon.

All afternoon. Shit.

He rubbed his chest and took a deep breath. He was still alive. Whatever it was, it had come and gone.

The breeze washed over his face, running through his long hair and scraggly beard. He closed his eyes and listened to the sound of the wind as it rushed through the trees. It was almost like an ocean.

His mind drifted away to the beach: the sinking sun casting tangerine rays on his skin, waves breaking on the sand, fizzing on the shoreline like soda poured over ice.

A wave crashed loudly and his eyes shot open.

Thunder rumbled in the distance. The sky darkened and the wind rose. The neighborhood trees swayed and hissed.

"Storm's coming," he said aloud as if talking to someone else.

He warily picked himself off the ground, and once he was on his feet he rubbed his chest and took a breath, then he gingerly gathered up his tools and supplies from the yard and locked them away in the shed.

The sound of the windblown leaves grew louder. Thunder crashed, closer than before. He crossed to the northwest corner of the yard then squeezed through the small opening in the fence. He pushed through the evergreens and stood on the ridge. A sheet of menacing clouds was bearing down from the west, covering the setting sun in a blanket of dark seaweed green.

"Goddamn. Gonna be a bad one."

He returned to the yard and scanned for loose objects. It was clear except for the lawn chair under the hickory. He limped across the yard as lightning strobed the atmosphere. The wind roared and marble-sized hail pelted the ground as he picked up the chair and locked it in the shed. Sharp raindrops whipped through the air. Against the wind, he trudged back across the yard toward the bunker, his hand shielding his face until he reached the hatch. He opened it then stepped onto the ladder. Hail crackled on the lid as he held it half-closed over his head, something telling him to stop.

He took one last look at the yard as the trees danced wildly overhead. The greenhouse. The apple tree. The outhouse. The hickory and the platform in its branches. The supply shed. The food shed. The new rain-collecting jugs. The evergreens ringing the perimeter.

Lightning flickered and thunder crashed, rattling the handle in his hand. He secured the lid then hopped down to the floor, landing with a metallic thud.

He fumbled in the dark until he found the solar lantern and turned it on. The wind howled above as he pulled his handgun from its holster, giving it a quick wipe down before securing it in the weapons locker.

He looked up at the ceiling and inhaled deeply, then let the air out with a long, steady blow, easing the tension in his chest. He kept breathing as he changed out of his wet, grimy clothes. With each breath, he told himself he was safe.

If he didn't know better, he might have thought he'd had a panic attack. But that couldn't be. Sure, things hadn't gone quite as planned and maybe he was a little stressed, but it was just a spell of bad luck. From here on out he'd be fine, goddammit. He wasn't some little bitch. How many people could survive for over a year on their own in the apocalypse? He was the fucking man. A panic attack? No fucking way.

He nodded in reassurance and got settled on the bed, propping up a pillow between him and the corrugated wall. *The Time it Never Rained* sat at the end of the bed. The rain and hail tapped on the hatch. He smirked at the irony. "It's rainin' now." There was a pang in his heart and the smirk evaporated from his face.

He hated thunderstorms. The powerlessness of it. The lack of control as he sat underground, hoping his property wouldn't take any damage. Ride it out and pray, that's all he could do.

A deep breath. In and out.

He reached for the book and opened it to where he had left off.

Thunder boomed, reverberating through the pillow. The percussion on the hatch intensified. Wind thrashed in bursts and waves. This was no ordinary rainstorm. He rolled his eyes toward the ceiling and tossed the book aside.

Another crash of thunder rattled the bunker.

There was always something rattling, roaring, or booming in Iraq: IEDs, grenades, drone strikes, artillery fire, the heavy rumble of MRAPs. The volume of military life was always cranked up to eleven. It kept him on high alert until mid-way through his second tour. The cacophony eventually became such a normal part of life that it dissolved into white noise. By the time his MRAP unit was ambushed in a small village, he had achieved a sense of harmony with the chaos, finding serenity in the bedlam. He was untouchable. Bulletproof. He would swim through the ocean of the war without getting wet.

Their orders were to patrol the streets of a village after intel indicated possible insurgent activity in the area. They got this type of assignment all the time—the locals were always trying to use the Americans to settle petty scores—and they were almost always a waste of time.

It was a dusty town in the middle of nowhere and they weren't expecting much cooperation. Either the intel was bullshit, and the locals would have nothing to say, or it was correct, and they'd be too afraid to be seen talking to the Americans. But orders were orders. They would knock on doors, talk to the locals, and see if they could dig anything up.

Johnson parked the MRAP in the middle of the dusty road. Christopher and the rest of the men piled out the rear door. Rubble was strewn across the road, lined with crumbling stone structures, and it was deathly silent. There was no one in sight.

The first round zipped past the men and struck the side of the truck with a loud metallic ping. The second cracked through the air from another direction. They were caught in a crossfire.

"Take cover!" yelled Henderson, just before taking a shot to the chest. He crumpled to the road. Johnson climbed down from the driver's seat while the rest of the men scrambled for cover. Henderson lay on the dusty road, coughing up blood.

Two insurgents fired from behind a stone wall to the north. Johnson knelt beside the MRAP's massive front tire and returned fire. A sniper took aim at the ambushed men from the roof of a two-story structure at the end of the street. Henderson fell silent.

Christopher hurried to the passenger side of the truck with Ruiz and Williams. He crouched behind the rear tire while the others darted south toward a bombed-out building. "I'm exposed here," Johnson yelled, then he bolted across the street toward an alley. Gunfire kicked up dirt and gravel on the road as he ran. He took a shot to the thigh and hobbled off the road, then turned around and raised his weapon. A cloud of pink mist sprayed from the back of his head then his body hit the ground.

"Shit. Johnson's down!" Christopher shouted over the gunfire.

Ruiz found cover behind a pile of rubble. Williams hid behind the remnants of a phone pole. Christopher shielded himself behind the MRAP.

With the three remaining men pinned in place, the firing stopped. A hush fell over the village.

"What do we do, James?" Williams shout-whispered.

"Do you have a shot at the sniper?"

Henderson sputtered and coughed but lay motionless on his back. Christopher peered around the tire. "Henderson's still alive."

"We can't leave him," Ruiz said. "Cover me."

Ruiz dashed into the road toward the fallen man. Christopher sprang up and laid down a burst of suppressing fire toward the wall, using the MRAP for cover. Williams fired at the sniper's rooftop from his position behind the pole. A single shot rang out from the rooftop. Williams slammed against the stone wall then fell to the ground. Christopher turned back to continue his suppressing fire so Ruiz could retrieve Henderson. Another shot from the rooftop clanked against the back of the MRAP, a foot away from Christopher's head, and he pulled back behind the tire.

Ruiz grabbed Henderson by the collar then dragged him toward the MRAP. Bullets peppered the street. Christopher rose to return fire. On his periphery, a window on the southern side of the road opened. "Ruiz, get back here!" he yelled, just as a blast of smoke came from the window. The rocket-propelled grenade detonated, rocking Christopher off his feet.

His ears rang as he staggered to his feet. A flaming pile of debris burned on the road where Ruiz and Henderson had been.

They were all dead. He was alone.

A shot zipped past his head.

Outnumbered, all he could do was flee. Panting, he jogged around the front-end of the MRAP and climbed up to the door. Three shots clanked off the armored truck as he jumped into the seat and slammed the door. He hit the gas and the vehicle lurched forward, bullets pinging off the metal as he escaped into the desert.

Another clap of thunder rumbled the bunker. Debris continued to pelt the hatch. *The Time it Never Rained* mocked him. "I won't give up," he said to the book. "Not now."

A low rumble came up through the floor, vibrating through the mattress and the pillow behind his back. "What is that?" He trained his ears on the sound. It was almost like a roll of thunder—a deep, elemental bass—but steady and sustained rather than sharp and explosive. It grew louder and more intense, like someone vacuuming on the next floor up. He put his hand on the wall. There was no doubt about the vibration. His eyes darted around the room. "What the fuck?"

Terror crept over his face as the vacuum buzz became a screeching roar, like a freight train hurtling through the night. Wide-eyed, he stood as the sound filled the room. Loose supplies on the shelves rattled. Cans of soup toppled over, clanging against the steel floor. The gun safe and the water dispenser shook. He held out his arms for balance.

The freight train roared overhead.

He pressed himself into the corner and braced against the walls. He jammed his eyes shut and sank into a crouch. His body clenched tight, he screamed until the storm fell silent.

The sky was a piercing shade of baby blue and the morning sun bathed the earth in a crisp, golden light. Christopher opened the hatch and limped into the yard, his long, sweat-soaked hair stuck in his unkempt beard. His eyes were bloodshot and swollen, like bowling balls jammed into his skull. Drained of color, his face sagged lifelessly, hollow and resigned. The still-wet grass glistened as he sulked like a ghost over the yard, silently canvassing the ruin.

The great hickory tree in the center of the yard had fallen, its massive trunk splintered at the base, taking the platform nestled in its branches down with it. It lay across the yard, the greenhouse crushed under its mass, leaving a twisted mess of wood, aluminum, and fiberglass smashed into white spidery webs.

Most of the evergreens from the west side of the property lay scattered across the yard, their skinny trunks snapped like toothpicks. The storage sheds had been wiped off the face of the earth—an evergreen rested on the plot where they had stood only hours before. Plastic storage bins lay empty and broken around the yard. Tools and spare metal parts poked out of the wet grass, gleaming in the sun. The few water jugs within sight had been punctured and spilled.

He turned to the west, lethargic and droopy-eyed. All that remained of the house next door was a pile of brick and wood.

He lazily tilted his head to the north. His house was still standing, barely. The siding on the west side was peeled away, exposing torn rolls of insulation. The attic was visible through a large hole in the roof.

"The water," he said to himself in a cracked, raspy voice, barely above a whisper. "It's all gone."

Christopher turned around and ducked under the hickory's fallen trunk. The outhouse was nothing but a few broken panels of wood lying in the corner of the yard.

The perennially barren apple tree had been blown away. Only a stump remained.

He walked his devastated property, unable to muster the energy required for anger. The physical damage was catastrophic but the psychological was even worse. The storm had snatched his soul straight from his body. He surveyed the wreckage through blank, hollow eyes.

He passed through the opening in the fence, descended the hill, then kicked through the long, wet grass. He came to a stop in the side yard and turned to the northwest. The storm had left a clear mark on the world, churning up the street's asphalt and leaving a trail of devastated houses in its wake—neat piles of rubble that probably stretched back for miles. To the left and right of the trail, the houses were oddly untouched. It was uncanny. The storm's distinct path led directly to his property like a runway.

"Just my luck," he said, flatly.

He came around to the front of the house and stood in the driveway, shoulders hunched, arms hanging lifelessly at his sides. He looked out across the neighborhood at the trail of rubble, then turned to face his house. The front door was gone, blown off its hinges, and all the shutters had been stripped clean from the facade, except one left dangling from a single nail. The windows were shattered.

A long two-by-four had impaled the garage door. It jutted out into the driveway at a sharp angle. He reached up, grabbed the end, and pulled. The wood wouldn't budge. He tried again, with both hands this time, but it remained firmly jammed in place. It was almost like it was stuck in something inside...

He closed his eyes and exhaled. He knew what he would find if he walked through the house, past the front door tucked under the couch in the living room, and down the hall to the garage, but he went nonetheless.

He opened the garage door. The stench of gasoline hung in the air. He grabbed a flashlight from a bin and clicked it on. It was even worse than he thought. The long piece of wood was lodged in the back end of the SUV. It had entered the vehicle through the tail light and sliced through the gas tank. Gasoline was still dripping down the rear tire and pooling on the smooth concrete floor.

For a moment, there was a pang of rage in his gut, but it quickly gave way to the same hollowed-out acceptance he had been feeling all morning.

The car was destroyed, right along with everything else. Of course it was. One more kick to the nuts.

He clicked off the flashlight and dropped his head.

This was the end. Though he had lived for over a year while so many others had died, he had failed. So much had gone wrong, even before this final humiliating blow. And it wasn't just bad luck. He had made mistakes. Too many mistakes. He could see that now.

He nodded his head, admitting his failure to himself. He would salvage what he could and hang on for a while longer, but he was weak and getting weaker, and he had lost the fighting spirit. Days were all he had left now. Weeks at most. He would exhaust his dwindling stash of food, then go out with dignity, on his own terms, standing up like a man.

He turned to leave, then froze.

The low rumble of motors vibrated the garage. The sharp squeal of brakes. Muffled voices.

He quickly shuffled through the door, back into the house, and through the foyer. He hid behind the wall and peeked through the open threshold where the front door had been.

A convoy of three vehicles was parked on the street directly in front of his house. A black SUV, a red Prius, and the last vehicle was the red pickup he had seen twice before. This time, the driver wasn't alone. Three people sat in the bed, pointing at the damaged houses. The doors of the SUV and the Prius opened then several people stepped onto the pavement. The people in the truck's bed hopped out and joined the others.

He stayed out of sight behind the door frame, watching and listening as the group stood on the street and talked. He counted six people on foot but couldn't make out what they were saying. Most appeared to be unarmed but one man had a rifle slung over his back and a woman had a handgun holstered on her hip. The three drivers stayed in the vehicles.

The group turned toward his house and began walking up the driveway.

Christopher reached for his Glock. He patted his hip. It wasn't there. He wasn't even wearing his holster.

"Shit," he whispered.

Quietly, he backed away from the door frame then tip-toed through the living room to the kitchen. He silently opened the sliding glass door then slipped into the backyard. Making sure he wasn't seen, he hobbled up the hill, passed the few remaining evergreens, went through the fence, then disappeared down the hatch.

The wrapper of a survival bar crinkled as he pulled at the seam and exposed the depressing brown brick inside. He took a bite and stared blankly at the bunker's corrugated wall as he chewed.

"God, this must be what a horse's ass tastes like."

He raised his arm with a robotic indifference and broke off another bite with his teeth, then dropped his hand to the table with a thud. His fingers were bony. He rotated his wrist. How thin and frail he had become. His shirt draped loosely over his frame. He picked at the fabric, making a tent over his chest, then let it fall.

Spring had given way to summer, and the bunker was sweltering. The sticky heat would have been more tolerable above ground, in the open air, but there was nothing left to do outside. He had salvaged what he could from the wreckage. Everything was underground.

He choked down the last of the survival bar and picked up the lantern as he stood. The harsh light illuminated the only two water jugs salvaged from the attic. The rest may have been hurled all the way to Alabama, for all he knew.

Carrying the light, he shuffled across the room toward the bed, kicking through the wrappers and empty cans littering the floor. The fluorescent light reflected in the mirror and he caught a glimpse of himself as he passed. He took a step back then turned to face himself. The man on the other side of the glass was someone he no longer recognized. His imposing, muscle-bound body had withered. His light brown hair had grown long and wild, down to his shoulders. His thick beard was dirty and unkempt, its length extending to the middle of his chest. Pale skin clung to his thinning face, dark bags under his bloodshot eyes.

A dull pain radiated through his chest. He stared at the stranger, pressing his fingers against his sternum, trying to breathe.

His eyes fell on the calendar beside the mirror.

"Shit." He grabbed the pen and held it over the page. "How many days has it been?" He hadn't seen anyone since the convoy after the storm, but time had lost its meaning underground. "Fuck it. What difference does it make?" He dropped the pen to the floor, tossed the lantern onto the end table, and collapsed onto the bed.

One eye stared vacantly over a clump of bedsheets. A cock-roach scurried across the floor into a mostly empty can of soup. He sneered, then buried his face in the sheets.

A hard object was tucked uncomfortably beneath his hip. He struggled awkwardly with the sheets and pulled his copy of *On Liberty* from under his body. He rolled onto his back and held the book up to the fading light of the lantern. "Goddammit. I just charged you," he said, dropping the book and picking up the lantern. He gave it an exasperated smack as the light quietly extinguished, leaving him alone in the dark.

He felt around on the end table for his Glock. His blind reach sent a dirty bowl off the edge of the table. It clattered to the steel floor along with the dirty spoon inside it. He winced at the noise, then continued the search with his fingers. Finally, he found the gun and tucked it into his waistband, then he tiptoed over the mess with the solar lantern in hand.

He climbed the ladder, turned the latch, and pushed open the hatch, muttering to himself as he emerged from below.

He looked up at the sky. The twinkling stars looked back.

"Fuck," he said, "I give up." He shook his head and climbed out of the bunker.

With a sarcastic, exasperated laugh, he tossed the lantern into the overgrown grass then sat down beside it. He reclined, resting his head on the long, dew-covered blades. Crickets chirped peacefully. The air was warm and moved with a gentle, calming breeze.

The pain in his chest flared again. He took a deep breath of the soothing air, glad to be free of the bunker's stale atmosphere.

The heavens shimmered, within sight but impossibly out of reach, and it occurred to him just how small he was, and how alone—utterly, hopelessly alone—against the vast expanse of the universe. A single tear ran down the side of his face. He wiped it away with a bony finger.

"I pushed them away. All of them," he said to the night sky. "Everyone. They're all gone."

His lips pursed and quivered. He jammed his eyes shut.

"I could have saved them. I could have saved *her*. I pushed her away."

He opened his eyes to the stars and pictured Amy. She is sitting on the couch in the house, reading while he cooks dinner in the kitchen. "Anything I can do to help, babe?" she asks over the sound of green pepper sizzling on the stovetop. "Just keep lookin' pretty," he shouts back. "I'm takin' care of everything." He turns and sees her smile without looking up from her book.

"I'm taking care of everything," he whispered into the night air. "I'm taking care of everything."

Another tear leaked from his eye and fell into the grass.

His heart was stabbed by another sharp pain. He whimpered as he rubbed his chest. Air flowed into his lungs with each labored breath, but it was futile. All the oxygen in the world wouldn't be enough.

His weak, sickly breaths became a sputtering, wheezing cough. He spat a wad of phlegm into the grass then laid his head back down.

The sounds of the night surrounded him in the darkness. A chorus of katydids filled the air. An owl hooted softly in the distance. The sound of his own heart, too, pounded in his ears. Beating. Thumping. Drumming. Louder than a heartbeat should sound. He wiped his eyes and tried to breathe.

"I'm dying," he whispered. "I'm dying out here."

He shut his eyes and reached for his holstered gun. Clutching the weapon to his chest, he took a deep breath and opened his eyes to the expanse above. A final tear rolled into the grass.

A gust of wind rose in the air, rustling the leaves, then receded.

Across the yard, the house creaked. He jolted upright and strained to listen. Was someone there, or had the damaged structure shifted in the wind? He sat completely still, waiting. The house creaked again.

Forgetting the pain in his chest, he got to his feet and stepped quietly across the yard. It's probably nothing, he thought as he crossed through the fence and scanned the back of the house from the ridge, but I'm not taking any chances.

The house stood quiet and still in the darkness, its jagged, damaged shape foreboding.

Something wasn't right.

He descended the hill, wishing he had his night-vision goggles. There was no time for that now. He was on his way to meet whatever fate awaited him. No turning back.

He limped toward the house, kicking through the long grass until he reached the window near the back corner. Glock at the ready, he squinted through the window's dirt-caked screen and grimy glass to the dark interior of the living room. Only the vague silhouettes of the furniture were visible. He slipped across the back of the house to the sliding glass door.

He caught his breath as he stood at the door and gripped the handle.

If it's my time, I'm going out standing up.

There was a swish as the door peeled away from the frame and a low rumble as he inched it open. When there was enough room, he stepped silently into the kitchen, where he stood still for several moments, listening and staring into the darkness. The only light was the pale ambiance of the stars filtered through grimy glass. The song of the night insects was the only sound. Eyes wide, he waited, listening. Nothing moved. There were only black shapes set against black walls.

He lifted his foot, took a step forward, and placed it down silently on the kitchen tile. Staring into the dark, he waited several seconds before taking another deliberate step. He breathed slow, measured breaths, and gripped the gun firmly. The weapon was heavy in his thin hands, but he summoned the last ounce of energy from the bottom of his soul and focused. He was a patient predator, in control of his mind and body, ready to strike. Tomorrow, he could die, withered and spent. Tonight, this was still his castle.

The house remained still, and so did he. In this infinite stretch of time, it occurred to him that this—the exact circumstance unfolding at this very moment—was what he had dreamt of when he began prepping. Here he was, living his deepest desire, playing out his darkest fantasy. The lone wolf defending his territory. He allowed himself an instant to savor the moment.

Had it always been there, buried somewhere deep inside, or was this primal desire conditioned, shaped by circumstance? Had he chosen this, purposely, consciously?

It didn't matter now, he was here. Whether by nature or nurture, by fate or choice, every moment of his life had led him to this dark hallway. And though he had become a pathetic shell of a man, he would see his path through to its end.

He crossed from the kitchen tile to the hardwood in the hall leading into the family room. The floor creaked under his weight. He froze and listened.

The crickets and katydids chanted in dueling rhythms.

Something moved, in the living room, straight ahead. Someone was there. He could feel it. He could sense their quickening breath. They were scared and alone. He had them.

He charged into the room with three authoritative steps and aimed the Glock toward the sound. "Freeze!" he shouted.

There was no response.

The floor creaked again.

"This is my house," he yelled. "Who's th—"

There was a guttural shriek and bright flash of light, then a deafening bang filled the room. He recoiled but quickly rebounded, shifting his weight to the right, and fired two shots in the direction of the flash before ducking behind the end of the couch.

The intruder yelped. It was a man.

Christopher gathered himself behind the couch, about to rise for another volley when he noticed the searing pain in his shoulder. "Son of a bitch," he said, gritting his teeth.

The man whimpered and groaned then took off toward the open door frame at the front of the house, his steps thumping down the foyer. Christopher peeked over the couch just as the man fired two random shots behind his back as he ran through the doorway, out into the night.

He stood and pressed the wound on his left shoulder. "Go ahead and run. I know you ain't going far." He wiped a handful of blood on the arm of the couch as he followed the man.

Though losing blood, he approached the open threshold tactically, flashing a glance through the door to confirm the way was clear. Satisfied, he followed the trail of blood out the door, the splatter glistening in the starlight. It ran down the front stoop, onto the walk, and into the overgrown grass. From there, he followed the fresh impressions left in the yard until he picked up the blood trail on the sidewalk and followed it across the street. He walked up the driveway of the house directly across from his, then tracked the intruder's footsteps through the grass. They led to the far side of the house. He readied his weapon and followed the tracks around the corner until he found the man sitting on the ground, slumped against the side of the house.

"Don't move," he commanded as he came around the corner, weapon trained on his mark's head. He stood ready to fire.

The man remained motionless.

He stepped closer, circling in front of the target, and found him staring blankly at the moon, the life drained from his eyes.

He was clutching a black backpack to his chest and a gun lay on the ground at his side. Christopher kicked the weapon away and crouched to meet his adversary's empty gaze.

The stranger was young. About the same age as himself, or maybe a little older. The poor bastard was in rough shape, too. Skin and bones, a scraggly beard was patched across his face and neck. Ratty, worn-out clothes hung loosely over his frame.

The adrenaline had begun to wear off and Christopher remembered the wound below his collarbone. He pressed it with his fingers and blood oozed through his shirt.

"Damn you," he said through his teeth. "You could have picked any of these houses to hole up in, but it had to be mine. Look what you fucking did. Look what you made me do."

He stared into the man's eyes, seeing himself in the vacant orbs. He grimaced and turned away, then sat down beside the corpse and leaned back against the wall.

"Mind if I sit here awhile?"

He glanced at the man seated beside him.

"It could be me sittin' there, instead of you," he said, almost like they were old friends. "You winged me pretty good back there. I guess it was just my lucky night."

He exhaled, releasing the tension from his chest, and raised his eyes to the starlit sky.

"I've killed before, you know. Not in the war though. First time I killed a man was right over there, in front of my neighbors' house, just as the shit was hittin' the fan. I didn't really think much of it at the time. Just some punks who had it coming. Besides, they were coming for my house next, so it's not like I had much of a choice, you know?"

The dead man sat still, his arms wrapped around the backpack.

"This feels different though. Feels like, maybe it didn't have to go down this way. You aren't some punk, far as I can tell, anyway. After all, you lasted this long. You were probably just looking for some food and a place to crash for the night. Not hurtin' anything. Just minding your own business. Until I came along and cornered you."

The crickets and katydids continued their song. The warm night air was still.

"Until I came along..."

He closed his eyes.

"I really thought I could make it," he said. "I know you probably don't give a shit, considering, but I was prepared for this. I spent years gathering supplies. I thought of everything. It was all set up."

He ran his hand through the long grass beside him and tore a handful of blades from the ground.

"But it all went to shit. It was all for nothing. Won't be long now till I'm just as dead as you."

He chuckled to himself and shook his head, a smirk on the corner of his lip.

"I'm losing it out here. I'm really losing it, aren't I?"

The vast expanse of stars caught his eye. Under its pale glow, he rested his head on the house and leaned back for a better view.

"If only this world weren't so fucked up. If only people were... better. You know? Maybe we could have avoided all this."

The stranger stared blankly ahead while Christopher explored the cosmos.

"You ever think of how alone we are out here? I know that's a cliché thing to say when you're looking at the stars, but you're the first person I've talked to in four hundred days, so cut me some slack."

He came back down to earth, where his new friend sat beside him, unmoved.

"We're just out here, floating around on this little rock. Just a tiny, insignificant speck of dust, all alone. It's all so pointless, isn't it?"

The man had no response.

"I'm sorry," he said, turning to face his defeated foe. "I know. Too little, too late. I don't expect you to believe me, and I don't expect you to forgive me, but I mean it. I'm sorry. Maybe we could have even been friends, in a better world."

The black backpack clutched to the stranger's chest caught his eye. He reached out and pulled it from the man's grasp. The corpse's lifeless arms dropped to the ground.

The pack was heavy and its contents jangled as Christopher set it on his lap. He unzipped the bag and reached inside.

"Let's see what you've got here."

Christopher kicked through the clutter on the bunker's floor and managed to find a battery-powered flashlight in the darkness. He clicked on the light and groaned as he peeled off his blood-soaked shirt, then he stood before the mirror and evaluated the gunshot wound. The round had entered below the clavicle and exited cleanly on the other side. He measured the wound's distance from his heart with his thumb and index finger. Two inches from instant death.

He pulled the first-aid kit from the shelf and cleaned the wound as well as he could, wincing as he dabbed rubbing alcohol over the torn flesh, then wrapped his shoulder in gauze and tape. Slightly dizzy, he blinked his eyes and sucked down a gulp of air. He had already lost a lot of blood. Time was running out.

He swallowed a handful of pills for the pain and put on a new shirt. With the flashlight, he found the bug-out bag buried in the corner, untouched since his first night in the bunker. He set the bag by the ladder, then stuffed a duffle with clothes and several boxes of ammo, then placed it under the hatch by the bag. From the water dispenser, he filled a bottle to the brim and slid it into the side pocket of the BOB, then loaded the Glock with a fresh mag and slid it into the holster on his hip.

He turned slowly with the flashlight, scanning the underground hideaway. The bunker's air was dank, stinking of stale sweat and the rotten remnants of canned food. Its atmosphere was claustrophobic, as though the corrugated steel walls were clenched like a fist around the dark, cluttered room.

He dragged the light over his books, left spilled on the floor from their shelves, then continued around the room, past the urine-caked composting toilet in the corner and the dwindling store of food on the shelves, until he landed on the sad, rumpled bed in the corner.

"This place is a tomb," he said.

He raised the beam to the calendar on the wall.

"June. Sixteen months. Only sixteen months."

He paid a final visit to the man in the mirror. His thin face was even paler than before. He flattened out his long beard with a stroke of his hand, then dropped his head and nodded, collecting himself. He raised his head and looked himself in the eye.

"It's time," he whispered in the dark.

His vision blurred and he steadied himself on the shelf, then forced his eyes open with a deep breath.

"Move out, soldier."

His eyes solemn and weary, he picked up the black backpack that had belonged to the stranger. He added it to the pile under the ladder, then he reached up and opened the hatch. The early morning sun poured through the opening, splashing the interior with an amber glow as he carried the bags above ground.

Once topside with his gear, he lingered in the damp grass, the ruin of his once secluded retreat sprawled before him. The greenhouse still lay in a crumpled heap under the felled hickory. Uprooted evergreens still littered the yard.

Sun rays slipped over the tree line to the east, warming his pale cheeks. It was going to be a miserably hot Georgia day, he could already tell.

"No time to get sentimental," he said, reaching for the first of the three bags.

He put his arms through the straps of the heavy duffle and wore it on his back, wincing as they dug in against his shoulder wound. The BOB went on over his chest like a baby carrier. Weighed down by the two bags, he slowly knelt and picked up the stranger's black backpack by its loop.

His injured knee twinged under the pressure and he took a moment to adjust to the weight. This was going to be painful, there were no two ways about it, but his mind was made up.

After acknowledging the yard with a final nod there was nothing left to do but go. He turned and exited through the opening in the fence and headed toward the street. When he reached the sidewalk, he headed east.

He was abandoning his post. It was a retreat. A surrender. A defeat. He was a coward, unable to face his demise with dignity and self-respect like he had planned, and it made him sick.

He swallowed his pride and walked on, putting one foot in front of the other, refusing to give his house a final glance over the shoulder. If he looked he might turn back.

Continuing along the street, he passed the empty houses of his neighborhood until he came to the main road. He crossed to the sidewalk on the other side and headed north.

The sun continued to rise in the sky. The air was getting hotter and stickier by the minute. He tried to stay in the shade as he trudged along. Sweat beaded on his forehead and dripped down his face. His thin frame strained under the weight of the bags. Each step forward was excruciating.

He thought of the ruck marches back in basic. Twelve miles in under three hours while carrying a rifle and a load of seventy pounds. He had the best time in his platoon. But that was when he had been in the best shape of his life. Now, he was out of shape, malnourished, and losing blood. He struggled down the road like he was wading through molasses.

The straps cut into his flesh like razors. Blood leaked from the wrap around his shoulder and soaked through his shirt. He plodded forward, delirious. How much time had passed or how much distance he had covered, he had no idea.

His heart raced. His vision blurred. His mouth was dry and his lungs wheezed. Red and yellow spots flashed in his eyes. He staggered forward as the road began to spin.

He had to stop.

He set down the black backpack as gently as he could, then lifted his head and groaned as he threw off the other two bags. He collapsed to the ground in a heap and gasped for air, his shirt soaked with sweat and blood. His ears rang. A speed limit sign dipped and spun, and the trees danced and swirled overhead, then everything was erased by a bright white light.

Something lapped against Christopher's face. The sensation was far off, distant like a dream. Then it came again, this time closer and more real. It was soft and wet, like a mop soaked in warm, soapy water. The slimy brush lapped against his cheek a third time.

He opened his eyes.

As he came to, his vision slowly focused on his outstretched feet, sprawled out in front of him like a pair of skis. He was lying on the dirt, just off the sidewalk. His uninjured arm was draped over the duffle bag. His head was propped awkwardly against a wood fence.

A strange sound came directly from his left—a high-pitched whine or whimper of some kind—and he drowsily rolled his head toward it. Two big, brown eyes stared back at him.

He jerked his head back and scrambled dizzily to his feet. The dog sat on its hind legs and looked up at him, tilting its head to the side. It had a golden coat, a graying black snout, and a streak of white down its front.

With a glance, he checked to make sure all three bags were still there, then turned back to the dog. "Go on!" he said, shooing the animal away with the back of his hand. "You heard me, get!" The dog's eyes opened wide and it barked, then it went on sitting there, staring at him and panting happily. "Shhh." He looked nervously up and down the road. "You're gonna get me killed, you dumb mutt."

The BOB had landed a few feet away and he reached out and pulled the water bottle from the side pouch. Keeping his eye on the dog, he unscrewed the top and took a sip. The dog shifted its weight back and forth on its paws, then pointed its nose hopefully toward the bottle. "This isn't for you," he said and again waved the animal away. "Go on, get out of here." The dog whimpered, then got down on its belly and looked up at him with sad eyes. He slid the bottle back into the pouch. The dog stood up and barked. "Okay, okay. Jesus Christ, if it'll shut you up." He took the bottle out and unscrewed the lid. "Sit," he commanded, and the dog sat obediently. He stepped hesitantly forward. The dog wagged its tail and panted expectantly as he held out the bottle to its mouth and poured. The animal lapped the water out of the air. "Okay, that's enough," he said, pulling the bottle back. The dog barked and playfully jumped up onto Christopher with its front paws. He petted its head and read the shiny tag on its collar. "Coco."

The road was still empty, the sun directly overhead.

"Okay, girl, I've got to keep moving."

He picked up the bags and loaded the weight back onto his shoulders. Blood seeped from the bandage. "Keep moving," he said as he continued northward on the road. Coco followed at his feet.

As he trudged on, he kept his gaze below the horizon. It was too far away, his progress too slow. The trees and road signs in the distance never got any closer. He focused on his steps and the ground directly in front of him.

One foot in front of the other. Keep going. Don't look up. Just keep pushing.

The sun was an anvil. Sweat poured down his face. He wiped his brow with his free hand and sucked down air as deliberately and rhythmically as he could. In through the mouth, out through the nose. He cursed the sun and its sweltering Southern heat, knowing he had no choice but to make the journey during the day due to the gunshot wound. It was a race against time. He would have died waiting for nightfall.

The straps burned his shoulders. The strength in his hand began to fail. He clenched his teeth as he struggled to hold on to the black backpack.

His will was fading, like drifting off to sleep. It would have been so easy to let go, to slip into the dark abyss. He had burned all the energy he had to make it this far, and he couldn't make it any farther.

At least he tried, he told himself. He had done his best to plan and prepare, and he had lasted longer than most. But this spot on the sidewalk, along a deserted, apocalyptic road, would be where his journey came to an end. He accepted that and took his final step.

Coco trotted out ahead then took off running around the bend in the road. "Where ya going, girl?" he muttered, dazed and weary, and he took a few more steps to see where the dog had gone. He staggered around the bend. His destination came into view, just ahead.

He stood there for a moment and looked at the entrance of the apartment complex, his face pale, his eyes drooping, his long hair disheveled, his clothes soaked in sweat and blood, too exhausted to feel relief or terror.

He looked to the sky and closed his tired eyes, then took a deep breath, gifting his blood enough oxygen to make it these last few feet. He let the air escape slowly from his nose, then he opened his eyes and stepped forward. One foot, then the next, until he teetered through the open gate.

Children were playing with Coco on a patch of grass when one of them turned toward him and yelled out, "Someone's here! Someone's here!" and another shouted, "He found Coco!"

Others turned and looked as he staggered forward, then a small crowd quickly gathered but kept its distance. He must have looked like he had trekked through the desert. "Get back, kids!" someone said as he made his way onto the property.

Delirious, his vision blurred. The voices of the growing crowd whirled around him, distorted and echoing like he had tin cans over his ears.

"Who are you?"

"Where did you come from?"

"What's your name?"

He set the black backpack by his feet, then took the bags from his shoulders and dropped them to the pavement.

"Christopher," he said, his voice thin and cracking. "My name is Christopher James."

Then the world went black.

NEW CONCORD

Children laughing. The pitter-patter of little feet. The sounds were soft and indistinct, coming from some distant place, but rose until the playful squeal of a child jolted Christopher awake. His eyes shot open and he bolted upright, finding himself on a bed in a small room. His heart thumped loudly in his chest.

It was dark except for a sliver of amber light slipping beneath a shade pulled over a window on the wall behind him. The room was free of clutter and appeared to be very clean. An antiseptic scent hung in the air, similar to his dentist's office.

From the bed, he looked around the room. There was a door on the adjacent wall. To his right, an end table sat beside the bed. His bags were arranged neatly on a wooden dresser in the back corner of the room.

To his left, a bag of fluid, glowing amber in the window's light, hung from an IV stand. It dripped silently into a tube, which he followed with his eyes until he discovered a needle inserted in his hand. He threw off the blanket and found himself in a hospital gown.

I'm not dead, he thought, remembering the trek from his house to the apartment complex down the road.

He reached for his shoulder and pulled the gown's fabric aside. The gunshot wound was wrapped tightly in gauze and medical tape. He slowly rotated his arm. Stiff and numb, but not much pain.

The shock of waking up in an unfamiliar place subsiding, he realized he was groggy and sluggish, a slight haze clouding his mind. He put his hands to his head and found a bandage above his left eye.

A warm breeze drifted in from the window. The shade gently moved with the air and tapped against the wooden frame. The sound of children running and playing outside filled the room. It hadn't been a dream.

He pulled the tape from his hand and slid the IV needle out of his vein, then he threw off the sheets and swung his legs over the side of the bed. The room wobbled as he put weight on his feet and stood. He steadied himself on the bed and took a breath, then took short, cautious steps toward the window until he could reach out and put his hand on the wall.

He pulled the window shade open. Daylight flooded the room, stinging his eyes. He turned away with a groan and shielded his face. Once adjusted to the light, he saw the room's walls were plain white and were undecorated except for a generic painting of flowers in a vase. A small device sat on the end table by the bed. It was attached to a wire that ran into the wall.

He turned back to the window.

He was at ground level. The room faced an open area in the center of the apartment complex, and people were milling about, right out in the open, walking casually from place to place. A pair of young men tossed a frisbee back and forth. A woman was tending to the flowers in a garden. A group of children playing tag ran past the window, laughing as they chased each other, ducking and dodging. A small congregation stood around a stone circle in the grass—a well? No one appeared to be armed.

"It's like they didn't get the memo," he whispered. "These people are fucking crazy."

He shook his head as he scanned the grounds. The place was insanely vulnerable. After all, he had walked right in, so the perimeter was obviously not secure. It didn't look like they had bothered to install any defenses or security measures whatsoever. It was totally exposed—an open-air community filled with seemingly ordinary people.

The people. How many were there? He could see at least a dozen from his vantage point at the window. Surely there were many more.

"This place is a death trap," he said. "I made a mistake."

He shook his head. They had patched up his arm, and he was grateful for that, but how could he stay in such a place? As serene as the environment through the window appeared, it wasn't safe. He would thank them then get the hell out of this place.

He pulled the blinds most of the way down but left an opening at the bottom so some light could come through.

The sound of footsteps approached through the door behind him and he spun around. The latch turned then the door swung open. A man in a white coat entered the room.

Christopher shifted his weight defensively.

"Easy, easy," the man said as he raised his arms, holding a clipboard in one hand. "I'm the doctor. Dr. Rajavi. I see you're out of bed."

The doctor was tall and looked to be middle-aged. He dropped his hands back to his sides. "Mr. James, I believe. Christopher. Is that correct?"

The doctor took a step closer and extended his hand. Christopher kept his eyes locked on the doctor and remained tense and rigid, rebuffing the doctor's handshake. "Rajavi?" he asked coldly, "What is that?"

"It's my name. My family's name."

"What kind of name is that?"

"It's Iranian," the doctor said.

Christopher narrowed his eyes and kept his arms at his sides. The doctor went on, unfazed.

"You were pretty banged up, Mr. James. I've had you sedated for a couple of days now," he said, then he looked down at the chart on the clipboard. "Brought in unconscious due to dehydration and blood loss, not to mention the head trauma sustained from hitting the pavement out front. You're lucky you didn't fracture your orbital," he said, glancing back up to meet Christopher's eye. "We operated on the gunshot wound to your shoulder, and we were able to stop the bleeding and get it closed up. Unfortunately, major trauma isn't my area of expertise, and our resources are limited here. You're going to live, but you may have some permanent muscle and nerve damage. Hopefully, with time and physical therapy, you'll be able to regain most of the shoulder's mobility. I also closed up the gash on your head with a few stitches. You'll probably have a scar. And finally, once we had the immediate concerns taken care of, we tested you for the virus. Negative."

Christopher didn't acknowledge the doctor's summary. He burned holes through the man's head with his eyes.

"I noticed the brace on your knee," the doctor said, ignoring Christopher's hostile demeanor. "Can you tell me about that?"

Christopher slowly inhaled, then slowly exhaled.

"Mr. James, I can't help you unless you talk to me, and I assure you that all I want is to help. Can you tell me when the injury occurred?"

He looked down at the ground and sighed. "Last year."

"And it's never improved?"

"No."

"Sounds like a ligament tear. Probably the ACL. The meniscus will often heal on its own, but an ACL tear requires surgery."

"Can you do that?"

"Unfortunately, no. I'm not an orthopedic surgeon, and this isn't a full-scale hospital. It's just me and my intern. And we have a dentist on staff, too. I'm afraid the best we can do is to find you a better brace to stabilize the knee. Once you're ready to be discharged, I'll take a look in storage to see what we've got."

"Once I'm ready?" he asked in a low, gruff voice.

"I want to monitor your recovery for a few more days. You've been getting antibiotics to prevent post-op infection, and I want you to continue that for now. And I want to make sure you're clear of concussion symptoms before we let you go. Plus, you need to get your strength back up. You need hydration and regular meals."

Dr. Rajavi walked to the window. Christopher rotated, keeping the doctor in front of him. The doctor pulled down the shade, darkening the room.

"Go easy on your eyes for now, Mr. James. I'm sure you're eager to get up and about, but it's best you stay in bed and rest while you recover."

The doctor walked to the door, then turned to face his patient.

"Listen, Christopher, I know it was difficult out there. If I had to guess, I'd say you were trying to make it on your own. You survived for over a year, and that is a great accomplishment, but frankly, given your injury and your state of malnourishment, you weren't going to last much longer. You got here in the nick of time. And I want you to know, things will be better for you now. You're lucky you found us. You're in good hands here, I assure you."

He looked back at Dr. Rajavi. Was he being duped somehow? Lured into a false sense of security? He was a stranger to them. Why were they so trusting and accommodating?

The doctor pointed to the door with his thumb. "There's a bathroom with a composting toilet just through this door," he said, "and I'll have some food and water brought in for you shortly. After that, we'll run some tests to see how your recovery is coming along. Hang in there. Brighter days are ahead."

Dr. Rajavi turned and left the room.

His head spinning, Christopher got back into bed and turned over his new circumstances in his mind.

There was a swift knock on the door. Christopher shot his eyes across the room from the bed but didn't answer. After a polite pause, the latch turned, then the silhouette of a woman carrying a tray pushed through the door.

"Oh hey, glad to see you're awake!" the woman said in an excessively cheerful tone. "How are you feeling?"

He didn't respond, keeping his eyes on the woman as she approached in the dark. She had a slender build and judging by the pitch of her voice she was young, probably only in her twenties. She stepped toward the bed without hesitation.

"It's okay," she said, "you don't have to say anything right now. I'm sure you're starving."

She set the tray down on the bed beside him then partially opened the shade to let a bit of light into the room. As he had presumed, she was young, no more than twenty-five, and she had light-brown hair, pulled back and held up by a claw. She wore a white coat just like the doctor's.

"I've brought you some food. You were malnourished when you came in, so we need to get you back on a well-balanced diet. Then you'll start to feel like a real person again, good as new."

Her bubbly demeanor was annoying, but at least she didn't seem threatening.

He looked down at the food on the tray. He couldn't believe it: a plate of grilled chicken strips over a bed of rice, with steamed broccoli and diced carrots on the side, and a glass of water. It was the sort of meal he used to cook with Amy on warm summer evenings before watching the sunset from the patio. His mouth watered, and he swallowed noticeably despite trying to hide his eagerness.

"Well, I'll leave you to it," she said with a friendly zing in her voice, then she turned to walk out of the room. "I'm Natalie, by the way," she said, turning back. "Natalie Webber. I was in med school when... well, you know... when it happened. So you can't *quite* call me doctor." She smiled the sort of cheeky, toothless smile that hides a painful thought, then she pointed to the device on the end table beside the bed. "Anyway, if you need anything just press the buzzer. Dr. Rajavi's office is just across the breezeway."

He nodded, and Natalie turned and left the room. When the door closed behind her, he picked up the tray and devoured the food.

Christopher woke the next morning with a clearer head, the sedatives worn off overnight. Natalie brought in breakfast. Scrambled eggs, diced tomatoes, and pan-fried potatoes.

Where was this food coming from? He had planned and prepared for years, meticulously collecting a stockpile of essentials for survival, but his meals never tasted so good, and he certainly didn't have chickens or potatoes. These people couldn't have prepared the way he had. No fucking way. How were they doing this?

With a few meals in his system, his strength began to return. Dr. Rajavi's morning check-up showed he was clear of concussion symptoms. Natalie applied a fresh wrap to his surgically repaired shoulder. "Remember, that's going to need physical therapy," Dr. Rajavi said.

The next morning, Christopher got out of bed and opened the window shade. It was another bright day, and the sun warmed his pale, malnourished skin. He pulled the window open and let fresh air into the room. Birds chirped pleasantly in the trees. Maybe it was just his imagination, but the air seemed clearer than it had ever been, smelling clean and crisp. He took a deep breath, feeling more alive than he had in months.

There was a hard banging on the door, an urgent pounding of a fist. He waited and instinctively readied himself in a defensive posture. The door remained shut. It rattled from another pounding. He approached with caution then slowly turned the latch. He kept his weight behind the door and cracked it open only a few inches. On the other side of the threshold stood a woman. She looked him dead in the eyes. He recognized her face immediately.

"Let's talk," said the woman from the red truck.

"We haven't been formally introduced," she said through the cracked-open door. "Let me in, we'll get to know each other."

Christopher scanned her face. Her lips were clenched shut, her eyes narrow. She was trying to appear tough—that was obvious—but was she putting on a front, or did she mean him harm? "I promise not to bite if you won't," she said as if reading his mind.

The door creaked as he pulled it open slowly and stepped backward into the room without a word. He kept his eyes locked on the woman as she pushed past the door.

She was shorter than he imagined but athletic. Her toned muscles were exposed by a tight green tank, which she wore tucked into her jeans. Though small in stature, she looked like she could run through a wall if she tried. Her skin was fair but freckled, and her dirty-blonde hair was pulled back behind her head in a tight ponytail. Her dark hazel eyes were piercing even in the dim light slipping into the room past the shade.

"We've met before, of course. Well, in a manner of speaking." She nodded over her shoulder. "The doc here had to dig the glass from my truck's window out of my shoulder after our last encounter. Scarred for life."

She paced deliberately around the room.

He clenched his jaw and turned as she moved.

"So? Anything to say for yourself?"

He breathed long, silent breaths.

"The real talkative type, I see."

She stopped and turned to face him.

"They tell me you said your name was Christopher before you hit the deck out there. Christopher James, is that right?"

He nodded once.

"I'm Jordan Byrnes."

She cocked her head, then sighed when he didn't respond.

"Nice to meet you, too," she said, rolling her eyes.

She staked out a position in the room with a firm stance and shook her head, then looked Christopher directly in the eye.

"Look, I'll just get down to it. So far, since you've been here, there hasn't been any trouble. You've been here recovering, and it seems like that's going fine. But being as you were out there for so long, alone, fending for yourself, heavily armed, dangerous... I just want to make sure we're not gonna have a problem. Especially given our little confrontation a while back. Kinda got the impression you might have trouble playing nice with others."

He inhaled sharply and glared. Jordan stared back at him.

"We have a good thing going here," she continued. "Nobody wanted this shit to happen, but we've worked hard to make the best of it. I'll tell you right now, I may have been overruled about letting you stay here, but there's no way in hell I'm gonna let some tacticool psycho disrupt what we've built here. You got that?"

He clenched his fists and took a breath, a rage boiling in his chest, then dropped his head and slowly let the steam escape his lungs. He raised his head and again met Jordan's eye.

"We've got an open gate policy and we're sticking to it, even for you. You're welcome here, just like anyone else who shows up half-dead with a bullet wound." Her eyes unwavering, she pointed a finger at his chest. "We're giving you a fair shot. Do not make us regret that."

He inhaled sharply. What gives this bitch the right to talk to me like this?

"Listen, I know you tried to make it out there on your own. You're one of those survivalist-prepper guys, right? The real self-reliant type? You're used to doing things your own way, on your own terms. That may have worked for you for a while, but you're not alone anymore. This is a community. There are a lot of good people here. If you want to be here, you need to understand that. My advice, see this as an opportunity for a fresh start. As long as you make an effort to buy into what we're doing here, you'll be allowed to stay. Is that clear?"

He didn't like her aggressive stance or her tone of voice, but what choice did he have? He was standing there in a hospital gown, completely at the mercy of these people until he could regain his strength.

"Is that clear?" she repeated.

He nodded to appease her.

Jordan held his eye and pursed her lips inquisitively.

"This place isn't a prison, you know. You can leave whenever you want, and we won't stop you."

He tilted his head.

"But remember," she said, raising a finger, "you came to us. Maybe you lasted on your own longer than most people could, but whatever happened to you out there, it brought you here. Think about that before you do something idiotic, like running off in the middle of the night."

She had a point. He had shown up at their doorstep, broken, bleeding, and close to death. There was no denying his failure. He exhaled slowly.

She crossed her arms over her chest and tapped her foot on the floor.

"So, we have a deal? Don't *be* a problem, you won't *have* a problem. Sound good?"

He nodded.

"Can I get a verbal confirmation here?"

"Agreed," he whispered after a pause.

Jordan's face relaxed, her eyes flashed. "Good," she said with a perky smile. "Glad that's out of the way."

He relaxed his defensive stance as well. With the tension broken, he became suddenly aware of his hospital gown's thin fabric. Sheepish and vulnerable, he looked down at himself. Jordan followed his gaze.

"I'll... get out of your hair," she said, walking past him to the door, then she turned to face him again. "Look. Sorry for ambushing you like this. But it had to be done. If you were in our position I'm sure you'd have done the same. Our next chat will be friendlier, I promise."

Christopher shifted awkwardly and cleared his throat with a dry cough.

"Dr. Rajavi says you'll be ready to get out of here in a couple days. Once he discharges you, I'll show you around. And then I'll introduce you to Simone."

"Simone?"

Jordan smiled. "She's the heart of this place."

Sitting upright in bed, arms folded over his chest, Christopher anxiously shook his leg. He turned around and peered out the window, then shifted his gaze to the door across the room. A whole week stuck inside. He wanted out, despite serious mixed feelings on the matter.

He wondered if this was how it would feel to be a POW, wanting to escape but having nowhere to go, trapped behind enemy lines. Though, he was free to leave at any time...

Why hadn't he left? He was well enough. There weren't any guards at the door. He could get dressed, grab his bags, and walk right through the front gate. No one would try to stop him. Yet there he was, in his hospital room, waiting obediently to be discharged.

He turned again to the window, to the green world on the other side. Someone was pulling water from the well. A young boy ran playfully down the sidewalk. He turned and fell back into the pillow with a sigh.

There was a knock on the door, so gentle he almost didn't hear it. The latch turned then the door cracked open.

"Mr. James?"

He shifted on the bed as a tall, thin woman entered the room. Black-framed glasses ringed her brown eyes, and curly brown hair fell over her shoulders. She wore a long, beaded necklace over a steel blue tank top that hung loosely over denim capris wrapped tightly around her legs.

"My name is Sharon Sullivan," she said, disregarding his failure to confirm his identity. "I'm the counselor here. Would it be alright if we talked for a little while?"

She stood and waited for a reply. He gave her a cold stare, his face hard and tight, his eyes peeking out from under his brow, then he turned his gaze back to the ceiling.

Sharon went to the side of the room and walked back with a chair. She placed it beside the bed and sat down, crossing one leg over the other, then flipped open a notepad and clicked a pen.

He flashed his eyes at the sound.

The counselor sat still, the pen hovering over the paper.

He looked away and chuckled dismissively. "So, what, you're gonna do the whole shrink routine? Psychoanalyze me?"

She jotted down a note on the pad.

"What a joke this is," he said. "Look at you. Such a fucking stereotype. You look like you just graduated last fall. Are you even qualified?"

She continued to write.

"Don't think I don't know what you're doing. I know how this works. I tell you I don't want to talk, but you just sit there quietly and let me vent because I'm just *oh so glad* to finally have someone to listen to me, and before I know it you've cracked my head open like a peanut and I'm spilling my guts about how everyone abandons me and I'm always left sad and alone. Boohoo. Poor me." He shifted to face Sharon. "I know your game."

She lifted her pen off the paper and raised her head. "Is that true? Everyone abandons you?"

"See, you're doing it right now," he said with a laugh. "Fuck this. I'm not saying another word."

Sharon scribbled more notes on the page.

He lay back on the bed, crossed his arms, and stared stubbornly at the ceiling.

"Actually, Mr. James, I only meant for today's session to be introductory. I know you've been through quite a traumatic experience. If you're not ready to talk about it, that's perfectly fine. I'm not going to force you." She took a breath and leaned back slightly on the chair. "And yes, I had been a licensed psychologist for two years prior to the pandemic and collapse."

He gave Sharon a side-eyed glance, keeping his arms crossed tightly in front of him.

"For today, I just want to know one thing," she said. He turned back to the ceiling and grumbled under his breath. Sharon ignored his petulance and continued. "From what I understand, you spent a long time out there on your own. Isolated."

He kept his eyes on the ceiling.

"Prolonged isolation... it can do strange things to people. We're social creatures, not meant to be alone for extended periods of time."

He uncrossed his arms and turned to the counselor, his lips pressed tightly shut.

"Now, I don't know exactly what happened to you out there, and I don't know the circumstances that brought you to us. Maybe it was purely desperation, because of your injuries, and now that you're healing you're thinking of running away from here, leaving the first chance you get." Sharon leaned in closer and spoke softly. "Or maybe you had a real change of heart. Maybe, somewhere deep down, you realized that you couldn't go on alone."

His eyes flashed with anger. "You don't know a damn thing about me, lady."

"You're right, I don't. But I want you to know, just in case you're having doubts about it, whatever it was that brought you to us, well, you made the right decision."

His chest rose and fell. He closed his eyes and huffed. "You said you only want to know one thing," he grumbled. "What is it?"

Sharon set the notepad on her lap and closed the pen with a click.

"Mr. James—Christopher—it's not going to be easy for you to integrate into a community of people, after what you've been through. You've got a hard road to recovery in front of you, and not just from the physical injuries you've suffered, but the mental ones as well. All I want to know today is whether you're willing to commit to the recovery process. The physical *and* the mental. You seem like the type who would take on a physical challenge without a second thought, but the mind is just as important as the body. I'd like you to agree to see me for regular sessions once Dr. Rajavi discharges you. Will you do that?"

He turned away from the counselor and stared at the ceiling. Sharon sat in silence with him.

The thought of sitting through therapy sessions made him want to puke. But there were no guards at the door. The gate was open. He could leave at any time.

"Fine," Christopher said without turning toward the young counselor. "If it'll get you out of here, I'll do it."

Dr. Rajavi entered the room after a swift courtesy knock.

"All right, Mr. James, how are we feeling today?"

Christopher sat up. "Better."

"Good, good. And the shoulder?"

He rotated his left arm and nodded to the doctor.

"Very good," said Dr. Rajavi. "Well, it's been ten days since you arrived. You're finished with your antibiotic cycle, and I think you're ready to get out of here. What do you say?"

His stomach fluttered with butterflies and he inhaled discreetly to calm them. He nodded. "I'm ready."

"You're still going to need physical therapy for that arm. Come back tomorrow morning and we'll set you up with Jason. He was a trainer at a gym. Fair warning, he doesn't mess around."

"Neither do I," Christopher said, stone-faced.

"Good then," said the doctor with a smile, then he cocked his head and looked Christopher directly in the eyes. "It's going to be a long road back." There was something in his voice that suggested he was talking about more than just the arm. Christopher held the doctor's eye and nodded with a stoic resolve.

Dr. Rajavi turned and started for the door, then stopped and turned back. "Oh, I almost forgot. We found a knee brace for you. Much sturdier than the one you had before. It's never going to be fun walking around on a torn ligament, but until an orthopedic surgeon turns up it will have to do. I'll have Natalie bring it in for you. Then you can rejoin the land of the living."

The doctor shut the door behind him, and Natalie soon arrived with the brace, as promised. It was lightweight but sturdy, with flexible stabilizing hinges on the sides and thick Velcro straps above and below the knee. He tossed his old, thin knee wrap on the bed and slid on the new heavy-duty brace. He fastened its straps then took a few steps around the room to get used to its feel. "That's more like it," he said, and he looked at the worn-out elastic sleeve on the bed and saluted casually. "Thank you for your service."

He shed the hospital gown then rummaged through his duffle for a change of clothes. He slid a pair of jeans over the brace, then threw an Army t-shirt over his bony frame. Back in real clothes, his back straightened, and he stood taller, like a real human being rather than a caged rat.

He put the bug-out bag over his shoulders then picked up the duffle with his good arm. He looked down at the black backpack, then his injured arm, and groaned. Natalie came scampering through the door to help after he pressed the buzzer on the end table. She picked up the black bag then he followed her out of the room. They passed the bathroom and went through the apartment's living room, transformed into a hospital. There were two more beds along the walls with a divider between them. At the other end of the unit, a surgical prep area occupied what used to be the kitchen, its cabinets labeled for various medical supplies. They exited the apartment, and Christopher closed the door behind them. A sign hung on the door: EMERGENCY ROOM. He looked across the breezeway. PRIMARY CARE.

"These rooms are for emergencies and hospitalizations," Natalie said, then she pointed to the door across the hall. "Dr. Rajavi keeps his office in the Primary Care unit, where he sees people for regular check-ups. And just over there is Dentistry. We also have offices for Physical Therapy, Aerobics, and Counseling. This whole building is the Health Wing. When you come back to see Jason for PT, his office is the next breezeway down."

They walked down the steps toward the parking lot in front of the building, and Dr. Rajavi was there waiting. Jordan was also there, leaning impatiently against the railing at the bottom of the steps. She looked at him out of the corner of her eye as he passed.

"Take care of that arm, and let us know if you experience any complications," said Dr. Rajavi. "And don't forget about physical therapy. It's important."

The doctor extended his hand. Christopher hesitated for a moment, then reached out and shook it.

"Good luck, Mr. James."

Christopher nodded.

Natalie set down the black backpack, then rushed forward and embraced Christopher in a hug, pinning his arms to his sides as she wrapped around his torso. "I'm so glad you came to us. You're gonna be just fine here, I know it."

His body stiffened in her grasp. His fists clenched. Until arriving at this place, he hadn't even talked to another person in over a year, let alone had physical contact with one. He wanted her to let go, but he resisted the impulse to lash out and push her away. There was something about her unabashed kindness that disarmed him, an earnestness that melted his hardened shell, and he relaxed.

Jordan smirked as she leaned against the railing. "Alright, alright, can't you see the man is freaked out?" she said, and Natalie detached. "Besides, he's mine today."

"Sorry," Natalie said, looking up at him, "got a little carried away."

Jordan shook her head and rolled her eyes. "You can drop your bags here. Follow me."

He shot her a distrustful look.

"No one's gonna jack your shit. Let's get moving."

He reluctantly piled his bags at the bottom of the stairs, then followed Jordan across the parking lot to the sidewalk.

A warm breeze blew through his long hair and beard. The hot sun on his skin was revitalizing. Others seemed to agree as the grounds were alive with people basking in the balmy weather. Some turned their heads and stared as Christopher walked by with his guide.

"Don't worry about them, they're just curious about you after the way you showed up," Jordan said. "Quite a dramatic entrance. You've been the talk of the town."

He wasn't reassured. The butterflies struck again.

"Plus, it doesn't help that you look like Forrest Gump after he ran across the country. Get a haircut, settle in, and soon enough you'll just be one of us." She paused and glanced up at him. "That is, if you can handle it."

"Handle it?"

"Yes. If you're up to the challenge."

"Like some kind of test?"

Jordan smirked. "Yeah, something like that."

The sound of laughter fluttered through the air. He looked up, following the sound, but couldn't see where it was coming from.

"So, what is this place? Some kind of cult?"

Jordan laughed. "Does this really look like a cult to you? Man, you've really done a number on yourself." She shook her head. "Look around. It is what it is. Just ordinary people living together. It's not that weird."

"What does everyone *do* here?"

"Whatever they want," she said, and Christopher cocked his head. Jordan glanced up at him. "I mean, we have responsibilities. But mostly we just... live. You'll see."

They came to a stop on the sidewalk in a spot where the road forked. From where they stood, they could see the complex's front gate and the road beyond it. Jordan gestured in that direction.

"There's where you came in. You can only see a couple buildings from up there on the road, but there are actually sixteen apartment buildings on the grounds." Jordan pointed at the gate, then turned toward the property, drawing an imaginary line with her finger. "Starting from here, the road makes a big circle through the complex—we just call it the loop—and the apartment buildings are scattered all around it. In the center is an open grassy area we call the green. The building that used to be the leasing office sits on the edge of it, inside the loop."

Jordan resumed walking along the sidewalk. Christopher followed. It occurred to him, as they strolled along the loop like it was an ordinary summer morning, that he had driven by these apartments hundreds of times but never really looked at the buildings until now. Each was two stories tall, their facades made of wood siding painted putty gray, punctuated by sections of red brick and balconies with wooden railings and slats. There was nothing sleek or modern about the structures. They looked sturdy, lived in, and had a rustic sensibility, nestled among the hundreds of hickories, maples, and oaks that had grown tall over the community.

They continued along the loop, passing a small group of people arranged in rows under a large, shady tree on the green. Their legs were stretched far apart in a lunging pose. In unison, they made a slow movement with their arms.

"Yoga," Jordan whispered. "Cathy runs daily classes."

He shook his head. "How are you doing this?"

"Doing what?"

"*This*. All of it," he said. "Living here. *Surviving* here, after all this time. Who *are* you people? How had you prepared? What training do you have?"

Jordan laughed. "Training? Are you serious? There are over *two hundred* of us here. That's a lot of life experience to draw from, man. Everybody has their own set of knowledge and skills, you know? We learn from each other."

Jordan pointed across the green.

"See that well over there?" A woman was raising a bucket to the surface with the pulley. "Digging that thing was one of the first big community projects we took on together. We held a community meeting and figured out who knew something about geology, who had experience in construction, and so on. We put our experts in charge, found the best spot to dig, came up with a plan, gathered the tools, organized volunteers, and got to work. And now we have clean drinking water."

He pictured his backyard. It would have been impossible for him to attempt such an undertaking on his property, on his own. So impossible that the idea hadn't even occurred to him.

"What's that?" he asked, pointing to a small, enclosed structure made of wood beside one of the apartment buildings.

"Oh, that's an outhouse. We built one for each apartment building after the plumbing stopped working."

"Who maintains them?"

"We take turns cleaning them out, usually in pairs. Each building is responsible for its own. There's a schedule. We do have a few composting toilets scattered around, mostly in common areas and in the Health Wing, like the one at Dr. Rajavi's office, but we could only find a few of them on our scavenger runs."

He didn't mention his composting toilet in the bunker.

"What about showers?"

"We built two community showers, one at each end of the green, and people use the one closest to their apartment unit. Overhead rain collection tanks funnel the water to showerheads below."

"Everyone showers together, right out in the open?"

"Well, the showers are enclosed, but they're public and unisex, yeah. Why, you shy or something?" She winked at him, and he began to stammer through a response. She stopped him abruptly. "It's not a big deal," she said. "Just a little skin. Besides, there's a limited amount of water, so people are in and out pretty quick, and most people skip a day."

They kept walking along the pavement and approached an area enclosed by a tall chain-link fence. "And right here," Jordan said as she pointed ahead, "we converted the tennis courts into a chicken coop. After everything settled down, we sent out teams to collect live chickens from local farms. Just like the well project, we figured out who had experience with livestock and put them in charge. And now we breed chickens. We use their eggs and slaughter a few for meat now and then."

Another good idea, just as impractical as the well. There was no way he could have set up a chicken coop in advance without complaints from neighbors. And in a survival scenario, the clucking and crowing could attract attention.

"You aren't worried about people finding you here?"

"Does it look like we're hiding?" she said with a laugh. "We *want* people to find us."

His mouth hung open.

Jordan smiled. "Don't worry, it'll make sense. If you stick around long enough."

They turned a corner, and a bright reflection flashed from a nearby rooftop.

"Solar panels. These buildings get the most sun," Jordan said. "We collected them from the rooftops of abandoned houses and brought them back here. We add more any time we find them out there."

"The buzzer in the doctor's office..." he said mostly to himself. "You have actual electrical power."

"Some, yeah," Jordan said with a grin. "We ration it pretty strictly. The doc runs a small fridge for the medicines we've collected, and there's enough juice to let us run a few community lights for a couple hours in the evenings."

They rounded a curve and approached a building that looked slightly different than the rest. It had the same color scheme and rustic aesthetic as the rest but was smaller—not as wide and only a single story with a vaulted roof. They fell silent as they approached the building. Their boots clicked on the asphalt. A warm summer breeze carried the sound of children playing from somewhere in the distance. Bewilderment washed over his face.

"You look like you've seen a ghost. Your eyes are as wide as fucking saucers."

His jaw clenched.

"You seem really thrown by this place—by what we're doing here. And hey, I get it. You were a prepper, out there on your own. Making plans, stockpiling supplies..."

A bolt of anger flashed through him. His eyes narrowed. "Don't mock me," he said with a growl.

Jordan threw up her hands. "I'm just saying, we took a different approach. You wanna know how we got started here?"

As uncomfortable as this experience was, as insane as these people seemed to be, he was curious. Pooling their knowledge and experience was one thing, but how did they get off the ground? How did hundreds of people willingly, voluntarily decide to stick together through the end of the world? He couldn't wrap his head around something so impossible.

He relaxed his face and took a breath, then turned to his guide.

Jordan nodded.

"It started with a woman named Simone Jackson," she said. "Simone has lived in this apartment complex for many years. Before all this, she used to organize community block parties twice a year. One at the beginning of spring and another in the fall. She would print fliers and get management to put them up, and then she would go door to door to personally invite everyone who lived here. These parties, man, they were amazing, like a holiday just for us. Everyone came. And, you know, it's an apartment complex, so people were always moving in and out. But Simone believed that a community shouldn't be made up of strangers.

So, these block parties—they made sure the long-timers got to know all the new people. And everyone got to know Simone, of course."

She came to a stop in front of the one-story building and turned to face him.

"Here's the thing about Simone. Back in the day, she was an activist. Marched for civil rights, protested Vietnam, volunteered with the Panthers' Free Breakfast program. She was an organizer, you know? The real deal. She was always fighting for people, bringing together the community for a cause."

Jesus, a Black Panther? One of those commie extremists? Dear God, what have I gotten myself into?

"So when shit started hitting the fan, as I believe you preppers like to say, and it was obvious that something really bad was happening, Simone kept us together—most of us, anyway—the same way she did when she was inviting people to the block parties. She knocked on doors and kept people calm. She told us it would be smart to stay put, and that we should stick together as a community if things really fell apart out there."

He scoffed. "Everyone went along with that? Just because she said so?"

"Not everyone. Some people were determined to leave— trying to get to their relatives and things like that. But most of us stayed, yeah." Her face swelled with pride. "While the rest of the world was ripping itself apart, we held tight. And it happened because the community had already been formed. We all *knew* each other, you know? And because we trusted Simone."

It sounded crazy. There was no way he would risk his life to help his neighbors, especially if it was a militant black radical asking. In survival situations, it's every man for himself. People can't be trusted. And yet, here he was, standing in what appeared to be a peaceful, functional community of people who had weathered the apocalypse together.

"Those early days—those first few weeks, really—they were terrifying," Jordan said, "but we made it through because of Simone. There's a good chance most of us would be dead right now if it weren't for her."

He crossed his arms. "So she's, what, your governor? Your president?"

"She doesn't have a formal title. No one here does. And we didn't bother with any sort of official vote either. It would have been unanimous anyway. Simone's our leader because she just *is*. She's the one who stepped up to lead when it mattered most. It's as simple as that."

In the Army, hierarchy maintains order and discipline, and he was trained to salute the rank, not the man. But even so, he had great commanding officers—men who were smart, decisive, and tough as nails. Men he considered to be exceptional leaders. Men whose authority was not to be second-guessed. But this old lady, with no formal authority whatsoever, with no official command structure, had not only assumed leadership of this community but kept it going strong for well over a year. And in the face of the greatest catastrophe ever faced by mankind, no less. It made no sense. There had to be something else—something Jordan wasn't saying.

Simone Jackson. Unanimous leader. Respected by all. Fuck that.

"So," Jordan said with a smile, "you ready to meet her?"

"She's in there," Jordan said, and she pointed toward the building with her thumb like she was hitching a ride. "You go on in. I'll hang out here while you get to know each other." Christopher looked at the door, then back at Jordan, doing his best to hide his apprehension. "Go on," Jordan urged, flicking the back of her hand at the door. "Babysitting you isn't the only thing on my calendar today."

He hardened his face and stepped up to the door, which looked worn but sturdy, painted a shade of deep scarlet. He turned the knob and pulled but the door jammed in the frame. He yanked again and the hinges squealed as the door swung open. The scent of wood and old books wafted past him as he crossed the threshold into the lobby of what used to be a leasing office.

The high-ceilinged room glowed amber in the light shining through its tall, shade-covered windows. Dust in the air caught his eye, illuminated by a thin beam of light stretched across the open room. A pattering approached on the floor and he looked down to see a pair of cats scurrying past his feet, one chasing the other until they neared the wall and their paws slipped on the hardwood floor and they went down in a tangle of fur. One cried at the other before they untangled and tore off after each other through an open door.

"Don't mind them." The woman's voice came from somewhere out of sight. "It might not look it, but they're best friends."

He stepped in the direction of the voice through the dusty rays of light, his footsteps echoing in the emptied-out office space. Planks of wood lay stacked on the floor along much of the wall space. From the office directly ahead, there was a groan followed by a heavy thud. "I'm back here, honey."

He crossed into the office and found a woman struggling to push a cardboard box full of books across a desk, sweat beaded on her brow.

"Perfect timing," she said as she looked up at him, breathing heavily. "Give me a hand with this last box, will you? It's just down here."

He just stood and stared at the woman as she rummaged through the box on the table and pulled out stacks of books with both hands. There was something hypnotic and disarming about the way she worked, methodical yet graceful. She wore a hunter green work shirt with the sleeves rolled up and the collar flared, and khaki hiking pants rolled up just below her knees—a functional outfit that conveyed a sense of style. She wore clear-framed glasses and couldn't have been more than five-foot-three. Her skin was a radiant dark bronze and her silver, wiry hair was cut short and swept back from her face. In the golden glow from the window, it looked like white-hot flames danced on her head as she swayed on her heels with the books stacked in her arms.

"Well, you just gonna stand there or you gonna help an old woman out?"

He snapped out of it and looked down at the box with a grimace, then glanced over his shoulder, back the way he had come.

There was just something strange about the people here. Something *off*. They were too blunt, too direct, yet also, somehow, too friendly. It was as though the complex's gate was a portal of some kind, and crossing through it had transported him to an alternate dimension with a strange, foreign culture. This woman didn't know him, and neither did Jordan or anyone else he had met here, yet everyone in this place spoke to him in a way that was too familiar, too casual, like they were already old friends long past the point of polite restraint.

His instinct was to retreat through the lobby but, instead of heading for the door, he found himself lifting the box and heaving it onto the desk alongside the other, just as the strange, too-familiar woman had asked.

"Thank you," she said with a smile as she brushed the dust from her clothes, "I was really dreading that last one."

He moved to the side of the room and put his back against the wall, then dropped his gaze to the floor. The woman looked over at him.

"Oh, where are my manners? I'm Simone. And you must be Christopher."

He lifted his eyes but didn't respond to the greeting. Simone scanned the distant look on his face, then went right on talking as she unpacked the books from the boxes.

"We decided to turn this old leasing office into a library, so we've all donated our books. Been collecting them from the surrounding area, too. Now they'll be available to everyone.

She set a book down on the pile.

"Sounds like you've been through quite an ordeal, but I take it Dr. Rajavi gotcha all patched up?"

He nodded.

"Good, good," Simone said as she reached in for another handful of books. "Then again, I suppose we've all been through an ordeal, haven't we? It was quite a thing, seeing everything come undone the way it did. Quite a thing."

He cocked his head to the side and cleared his throat. "It was only a matter of time."

With a book in her hands, Simone looked up at him over the rims of her glasses. "You could be right about that," she said after a moment. "I suppose something had to give, eventually." She stood still as if deep in thought, then she nodded and gestured toward him with the book. "You know what I miss most about the old world? Movie theaters. Boy, I loved the movies. The whole thing, even waitin' in line for a ticket—made it feel like an event. I know they came out with all those big TVs, but there was nothing like seeing a movie on the big screen. And you know what really made the difference?"

He shifted his weight from one foot to the other and blinked at the question.

"It was bein' part of the *audience*. Don't you think? The electricity of the crowd. Made the whole experience come to life."

He didn't have an opinion on movie theater audiences and didn't know what the hell the crazy old lady was going on about. He shuffled his feet anxiously, his back still pressed against the wall.

Simone glanced up at him. "What do you miss most, Christopher? If you don't mind me asking, that is."

His friends from school flashed through his mind, and then his Army buddies. He thought of his brother, forever young in his memory. He pictured Amy, pressed up against him on the couch.

"Nothing," he said. His eyes were vacant as he stared down at the floor. "I was glad when it happened."

"Is that right? Nothing at all?" she asked, nodding her head. "Well, that's a shame. Though, I suppose there *was* plenty to dislike about the way things were." She turned back to the books but eyed him from the side. "Let me ask you, what made you want to live all alone, out there in your backyard?"

His eyes focused and his muscles clenched. He raised his head.

"Jordan spotted you right off, of course. Didn't really seem like you wanted any company though, so we let you be."

They knew I was there the *whole* time? Could that be possible?

His stomach churned at the thought.

"My sheds. My supplies. *You* stole my stuff."

"No, no. We didn't steal from you. That's not how we do things."

"Then... who?"

"Lord knows. In those early days, people were runnin' 'round all over the place, scavenging anything they could. Coming across your stash must've been like hittin' the jackpot."

"*This place* is the jackpot," he said. "It's highly visible and has no defenses in place, which puts a pretty big target on your back." Simone nodded along as he spoke. "Jordan said you *want* people to find this place. You're not afraid of outsiders coming and taking what you have?"

She continued to sort through the box of books, stacking them into piles, and Christopher was oddly mesmerized. "Well, you might not agree with it," she said, "but I'm sure you know the saying. There's safety in numbers. We might not be trained soldiers such as yourself, but there are a lot of us." She stopped sorting and looked up at the frail man who leaned against the wall. "Ask yourself, would you come storming in here on your own? Or even with some backup? Or might you think twice about that shit?"

He met her eye and exhaled slowly. She was right.

"That's what I thought," she said. "Besides, you might be surprised by the fight we'd put up if it really came down to it."

He knew they had at least *some* weapons, but even if they had a few former cops or soldiers in the community, most of these people were ordinary civilians who would surely shit their pants in a firefight.

"We don't expect it to, though," Simone continued. "Come down to a fight, that is. I'm sure Jordan already told you, we keep the gate open most of the time, and so far that's worked out just fine. Anyone can come strollin' on in, just like you did, and anyone here is free to leave any time they please. This is a community. It's not a fortress, and it certainly ain't no prison."

He pictured himself standing in his yard, watching the shipping container being lowered into the ground. A little fortress just for him, he remembered thinking, puffed up with superiority over the stupid, unprepared masses. The captain of his own ship, the king of his own castle.

The corner of his lip curled into an almost imperceptible smile.

Then he remembered the bunker's cold steel walls, closing in on him at night. The suffocating darkness.

The line of his lip flattened and a glaze washed over his eyes.

"You never answered my question," Simone said, bringing him back from his thoughts.

"What question?"

"Trying to live alone like you did. You obviously went to great pains to hide, to separate yourself from other people. You didn't even respond when we came to see if you needed help after the storm. Why?"

He shook his head. "I..."

Simone set down the book she had in her hand and turned to face him.

He looked up, his mouth open, not sure how to put into words something he had always just *known* on such a subconscious level, something held so deeply in his bones. It was simply common sense, he wanted to say. People suck. They're selfish, greedy, and cruel. It's human nature. Everyone knows that. And even the people you care about most eventually disappear from your life, leaving you to fend for yourself. That's just the way it is. In this life, when push comes to shove, you're on your own. No sense in pretending otherwise.

Venom boiled in his gut as he rehearsed the rant, and it spread upward through his chest until it reached the tip of his tongue, which he pressed against his clenched teeth, ready to spit. He met Simone's eye and geared up with a sharp breath. She looked at him over the rims of her glasses, waiting for him to speak, then the air went out of his lungs.

"I don't know," he finally answered, deflating. "I really don't know anymore. At the time... I thought it made sense. It was the *only* thing that seemed to make sense. But now, trying to explain it, it's... exhausting."

Simone pushed her glasses back up her nose, a look of deep empathy swelling in her eyes.

"I didn't think I needed anyone," he continued, his face beginning to redden. "I thought other people would drag me down and hold me back. They'd debate every decision and divide my resources, and I couldn't have that. No, once all the rules go out the window, it's the strong and the prepared who survive because they take what they need and do what needs to be done, without hesitation, without accountability to anyone but themselves. Others just become liabilities."

Simone inhaled and pressed her lips together, her eyes never breaking away. She nodded, telling him to continue.

"I was prepared!" he said, and his raised voice echoed through the empty rooms and high ceilings of the office. He recoiled from the volume of his own reverberating words. His eyes welled up. "I thought of everything," he said in a hushed voice, barely above a whisper. "I thought of everything. I was prepared. I was *prepared*."

Simone took off her glasses and cleaned them on her shirt. "Listen, honey, I can't change anything about your past—who you were and what you've done—and neither can you. What's done is done. All you can control is who you're gonna be from here on out. And maybe you don't yet realize it, but I think you've already made a pretty big step in changing the direction of your life."

"How so?"

"Seriously?" she said with a sarcastic bob of the head. "You don't remember draggin' your broken, bleedin' ass two miles down the road, right to our doorstep? You decided not to lay down and die alone in your backyard. You made a *choice*,

Christopher, a real choice, and now you're here with us. A chance to start again."

He wrinkled his nose and shut his eyes, trying to conceal how close he had come to tears.

Simone crossed her arms.

"Jordan was giving you a tour of the place today, right? And what did you see out there? Did it look like some crazy dog-eat-dog hellscape to you? Did any of those kids running around out there look like they were up to any Lord of the Flies shit?"

He rubbed his eyes, a hint of a smile forming on his cheek. He shook his head.

"Let me tell you about those kids. A lot of 'em don't even have their biological parents here. You know that daycare center just down the road? Well, two days after everything went to hell out there, we sent out some cars to scout around, see if anyone in the area needed help. The way everything crumbled so fast, turns out some people never made it to pick up their kids. Two days they had been there, stranded, just waiting for mommy and daddy to show up and take 'em home. So, we put a sign up on the door saying where we'd taken 'em, and then we brought all those kids here. Been raising them ever since."

"Who has? You?"

"The community, Christopher. It takes a village. You know that old African proverb, right? We put the concept into action. Some people volunteered to be primary caregivers, but everyone here helps to raise those kids in one way or another."

"That's crazy."

"Is it? Listen, I know those kids miss their parents. The older ones, especially. But, considering the circumstances, it's been working out just fine."

His face contorted, puzzled.

"Look, don't get me wrong, it's a tragedy what happened to those kids' folks. I wish it hadn't happened, and I wish we could have saved more people, I truly do. But despite everything that happened, there's a silver lining for everyone who made it here. This is a chance for us to start over. And I don't just mean us as individuals, I mean *us*. Our whole society."

Simone put her glasses back on and took a soft but commanding step toward him. She looked directly into his eyes. Though he towered over her, it was her presence that dominated the room. He wilted as she came closer.

"Everyone gets a second chance here, Christopher," she said as she reached up and touched him on the shoulder. "This is *your* chance to start over. The old world? Gone. Nothing more than ash scattered in the wind. And in its place, we are building a new world. Here, everyone's basic human dignity is recognized. We lift each other up. We work as a community. We survive, *together*."

His pulse quickened. His teeth clenched.

"I know this is not going to be easy for you," Simone continued. "But if you give us a chance—if you give *yourself* a chance by taking down those walls you've put up, if you allow your mind to be unchained—you will thrive here in ways you never knew were possible. I promise you that. So, what do you say?"

A strange sensation passed through him in a single slow pulse. It was like standing on the edge of a cliff, but without the fear of death, only the warm breeze kissing his skin, inviting him to take the final step over the edge. *You will be okay, I promise*, the wind whispers as it gently blows through his long hair. *I will catch you*, it says, and all that is left is to let go—to surrender. He closes his eyes and steps forward, over the edge, and a cleansing sense of relief washes over him as he free falls—a liberation he never knew he needed.

"Do you think you can do that, Christopher?"

Simone's soft but powerful voice broke his fall and carried him back into the room.

He dropped his head and a tear rolled down his face into his scraggly beard, then he rose to his full height, baptized, feeling stronger than he had in months.

"Yes," he said. "I'm going to try."

"I'm glad. We will add your distinctiveness to our own," she said with a deadpan expression. "Resistance is futile."

He looked confused as he wiped the tear from his face.

"Sorry, honey," she said with a laugh, "just a little Trekker humor to lighten the mood a bit. And don't worry, now that you're out of the hospital and one of us, we've got a real room for you. You'll be in apartment 1404. I hope you don't mind, but I took the liberty of having your bags brought up to the room. I had a feeling you'd want to stay. Jordan'll show you the way. And if you need to go back to your house to pick up anything you left behind, just ask. We'll arrange a car to take you."

"Thank you," he said, spent, powerless to do anything but acquiesce. His lungs opened as if he had just completed a marathon, pathways for blood and oxygen suddenly clear—a release of tension he didn't know he was holding onto so tightly. He was suddenly airy, lighter on his feet.

"Oh, I almost forgot," Simone said, walking to a pile of books along the wall. "Came across this earlier today and I think you might find it worthwhile." She picked a book off the top of a pile and handed it to him. "Consider it the library's first loan."

He held the worn paperback in his hands. On its cover was a blue-tinted image of an old man imposed over a black background. He was wearing glasses and resting his chin in his hand. The name Viktor E. Frankl was spelled out in large, lavender print at the top, and the title, *Man's Search for Meaning*, was in smaller, white text below.

Simone put her hand on his back and guided him out of the room, back toward the front door. The cats were curled up together, sleeping on a stack of planks in the corner. "See, I told you they're best friends."

They reached the door and Simone turned the knob and pushed it open, then he followed her outside. Jordan was beside the door, leaning against the side of the building.

He turned to Simone, a suspicious look on his face.

"How did you know I was a soldier? I never mentioned that to the doctor."

Simone smiled.

"Let's just say you struck me as the type. Plus, that Army shirt you got on kinda blows your cover, dontcha think?"

Christopher looked down at the worn green t-shirt, embarrassed.

"So, what do you call this place?" he asked.

A wide grin spread across Simone's lips. She turned to stand beside him and put her hand on his back. Shining in the bright summer sun, her face beamed with pride as she looked out into the community. She held out her other arm and swept it dramatically across the apartment buildings, the loop road, and the green field at the center of the grounds.

"Christopher James, welcome to New Concord."

"This is you," Jordan said.

She and Christopher stood in a breezeway in front of the door marked 1404. It was a plain door, painted an inviting shade of teal blue, no different than any of the other teal blue doors in the hall.

Jordan nodded reassuringly.

He took a calming breath, then pursed his lips and exhaled slowly through his nose.

This was it. Soon this door would be opened and he would cross the threshold to a new life on the other side. It was like the opposite of Caesar crossing the Rubicon. A moment of weakness and failure rather than one of strength and will. Some unquantifiable part of himself would be lost, and there would be no way to recover it. He wondered if wild stallions miss running free once they've been tamed. Or do they blissfully forget the liberty of the open range, the prairie wind blowing through their manes?

He, a trained soldier, an expert survivalist, was accepting charity from a radical black hippie running some sort of post-apocalyptic commune. It was a cruel twist of fate, a cosmic joke of some kind. But he wasn't laughing. The people here didn't have his knowledge, his training, his skills. Who the fuck were *they*? And yet, they had somehow thrived while he had failed. There was no getting around that. He dropped his head in shame.

"Let's get this over with," he said. "You gonna give me the key?"

"All the units are unlocked," she said. "Simone has all the keys in the leasing office, but we all agreed there was no need for them anymore."

He shook his head in disbelief. "No need for them? You don't want to keep people from taking your things?"

"No one here is going to take your stuff. Besides, in case you hadn't noticed, the world has changed. In a way, there is no more *your* things and *my* things. Here in New Concord, at least. Take a look around. We're all in this together, man. If you need something, just ask."

"How 'bout my gun?"

"You'll get it back. But not today."

"When?"

"When you're ready."

His chest tightened and his fists clenched. "When I'm ready? What exactly does that mean?"

"Look, don't worry about it, okay? You're safe here. So get settled in and we'll see how it goes."

He unclenched his body and took a breath.

Jordan smiled. "I'm in 1016. Don't be a stranger."

He nodded.

"Oh yeah, I forgot," Jordan said, pointing at the door with her head, "your roommate's name is Sean."

A surge of anger flashed through him. "My *roommate*? You waited until now to tell me? No. I can't—"

Jordan raised her hand. "Relax. Sean's a good guy. You're very different, but I think maybe you'll be good for each other."

"What do you mean by that?"

"Just give it a chance, okay?"

He took another breath. A roommate. Not what he thought he was signing up for. But what choice did he have about any of this? He had no leverage. He was still thin and weak, not ready to take off on his own. Like it or not, giving it a chance was his only option.

He turned to Jordan, awkwardly chewing his lip. He thought he should thank her for the tour of the grounds, and maybe apologize for the wounds on her shoulder—that's what a normal person would do—but no words came to him. Instead, he met eyes and nodded, hoping she would receive the message.

He turned toward the door.

Christopher stepped into the apartment and closed the door behind him, relieved to be out of public view. He leaned back against the door and closed his eyes. He was tired. Drained. Dr. Rajavi, Natalie, Jordan, Simone. All that *talking*. All those total strangers, gawking as he passed. It was exhausting. He craved a soft bed, sleep.

Then he remembered.

"The roommate."

He opened his eyes. To his left was a closed door. The guy was probably in there. He raised his hand to knock but thought better of it. He stepped past the door.

A narrow entryway opened into a small living room in the center of the unit. He crossed into the room and found his bags piled in front of an open door just off the main living space. He nodded to himself and turned in place.

The living room was cluttered but not messy. Books sat on a dark brown coffee table in the center of the room, stacked haphazardly, jar candles and incense burners beside them. On the mantle were more books, propped up with bookends shaped like cats. There were ashes in the fireplace, likely leftover from winter. A shirt and a pair of jeans hung over the back of the armchair in the corner.

Separating the living room from the kitchen was a bar, cluttered with a stack of plates and an assortment of shot glasses, one left half-filled with a golden brown liquid. He picked up the glass and pressed his nose into it. "Bourbon?" He looked around, then put the glass to his lips and knocked it back. "Oh my God," he whispered as he closed his eyes, savoring the flavor.

He leaned back against the bar. A covered patio was just off the living room through a sliding glass door. Potted plants hung from hooks in the overhang, soaking in the summer sun.

There was a sharp squeak as the door in the entryway swung open. He set down the glass and turned to see a skinny man with long, shaggy hair bounding into the room, his tanned skin fully exposed from head to toe.

"It's all good, I got it!" he called out before nearly crashing headlong into Christopher. "Oh shit, man. Shit, man, sorry. Didn't hear you come in." The naked man stepped back and yelled over his shoulder. "Wendy, what time is it?"

"Sometime after noon, I think," a woman's voice called out from the bedroom, followed by a yawn.

"Damn, man, sorry, I think we kinda lost track of time." He stepped toward Christopher with his hand outstretched. "I'm Sean. Good to meet you, dude."

Christopher pressed his eyes shut and recoiled, not about to shake hands with the nude man.

"Not the warm and fuzzy type, I guess." Sean put his hands on his hips. "It's cool, man, it's cool. No offense taken."

There was an awkward silence as the two men looked at each other for a moment. Christopher stood in a rigid, defensive posture. Sean had a stupid grin on his face and bobbed his head like a chicken.

"So what's your name, man?"

"Christopher."

"Christopher. Nice. Well, hey man, I'm glad we're gonna be living together. Been waiting to get hooked up with a room-mate ever since I moved into this unit."

Christopher grimaced and cleared his throat.

Sean looked down at himself.

"Oh, shit, sorry man, I should probably put on some clothes, huh?"

"Yeah. I think you should."

Sean flashed a goofy grin and pinged back to the bedroom.

Jordan wasn't kidding. He and this guy were about as dif-ferent as two people could possibly be. He shook his head. "What the fuck have I gotten myself into?"

He turned back to the living room. It had a somewhat bo-hemian aesthetic, the way books and candles and glasses were strewn about—the kind of place he imagined an artist or writer might live. The vibe was relaxed, peaceful. Sean might be an air-head, but the place itself was actually pretty nice if he was being honest. He took a deep breath. Maybe this wouldn't be so bad.

There was a picture frame made of cheap plastic on the wall. It was the type that held several photos, arranged in a pattern resembling the petals of a rose. Sean wasn't in any of the pictures. In the center was a portrait of a family standing together on a beach: a man, a woman, and three young children. Along the outside were candid shots of the same children, but they were a few years older. He looked at their faces, seeing how they'd aged. Who are these people? Where had they gone?

"Those are the Johnsons."

He turned to see a young woman standing behind him, wrapped in a bedsheet, a butterfly tattoo visible on her bare shoulder. She had striking red hair, piercing green eyes, and freckles splashed across her nose.

"That's what Simone said, anyway."

"I take it you're Wendy?"

"That I am. And you're the mysterious Christopher James."

He turned back to the photos on the wall. "What happened to them?"

"No one knows. When it happened, they packed up and left. They haven't been back."

"Did you know them?"

"No. I came here after. Like you."

"And Sean?"

"He was here. In another apartment though. They all agreed to use the space as efficiently as they could, so everyone rearranged. Sean volunteered to take in the next straggler."

"He seems like quite a character."

"He's a sweetie."

"So, you're here with him?"

"For today," she said coyly. "I'm in 814, just down the way."

"And tomorrow?"

"I really haven't thought that far ahead, to be honest."

She smiled at him, touched him on the shoulder as she welcomed him to the community, then turned and went back to Sean's bedroom as soundlessly as she had come. As if gliding over the floor, she moved with ethereal grace, the sheet trailing her like the skirt of a long gown. He watched her over his shoulder until she disappeared through the bedroom door.

He turned back to the Johnsons. Two brothers in baseball uniforms, embracing. A young girl in front of a Christmas tree. A mother touching her forehead to a baby's, both with their eyes closed. A man holding a fishing rod, standing by a blue pond dotted with green water lilies. Happy, smiling faces in every shot.

"Simone couldn't save them all," he whispered. "The choices we make."

Remembering how tired he was, he looked down at his bags on the floor. He dragged them into the bedroom and closed the door behind him. A dresser made of walnut-stained wood sat by the door, but all Christopher cared about was the freshly made bed in the center of the room. He collapsed face-first onto the mattress and fell into a deep sleep atop the sheets, still in his clothes and boots.

The gang of pursuers was closing in and Christopher needed to get away, fast, but his legs wouldn't respond to the urging of his brain, like he was wearing cinder blocks for shoes. Dozens of the bastards were behind him, each of them featureless, dressed in black, charging ahead. They were relentless. They were gaining on him. "Move, legs, move!" He was frozen by some unknown force, suspended in time and space, until the ground gave way beneath him. He was falling. He reached out and grabbed the cliff's edge with the tips of his fingers and hung on for dear life, dangling over the chasm below until the faceless, black-clad mob approached from above and he couldn't hold on any longer. As he fell into the dark, he opened his mouth to scream but his lungs lacked the air to make a sound. Something grasped his shoulder and his muscles snapped instinctively to ward off the invisible assailant.

"Hey man, easy, easy. It's just me."

He opened his wild eyes to find Sean standing over him. "What the fuck? Get off me!"

"It's cool, dude, it's cool. You've been out like a light all afternoon. Didn't want you to miss dinner, that's all, man."

He sat up and flailed at his roommate. "Get the fuck out of here. Don't come in here like that again—you or anyone else."

Sean put his hands up and backed toward the door. "Sorry, man, won't happen again. Personal space and all. I get it, I get it. But hey, listen, man, they hit the gong at chow time. I'm going down for some grub if you wanna head."

"Head?"

"If you wanna head down together, man. You gotta be starving."

He put his feet on the floor and his face in his hands. "Just get out of here, okay? You go ahead. I'll find it."

"Cool, cool. Okay, well, see you soon, bro. And hey, sorry again for spooking you like that. Won't happen again, man, Scout's honor."

Sean held up the three-fingered Boy Scout salute as he backed out of the room and closed the door behind him.

His heart was still racing after being jerked so suddenly from the nightmare. "Jesus Christ," he said as he rolled his eyes and huffed, exasperated.

He stood and looked around the room. It was small as far as bedrooms go, but palatial compared to the dank confines of the bunker. Its windows and white walls made it feel larger than it was.

He looked at himself in the mirror above the dresser. He was going to have to go out there and face everyone. His hands were shaking. He squeezed them into fists and took a breath.

He thought about the photos of the Johnsons, then looked down at the intruder's black backpack on the floor. He exhaled slowly.

Not today.

He nodded to himself, then left the apartment.

Voices drifted through the air. A woman's laugh. A child's playful yell. He followed the sounds across the paved loop road and onto the green in the center of the community until he could hear the murmur of conversation—a sound remembered from another lifetime.

As he approached, he wiped the sweat from his palms on his pants and tugged at his shirt. Then he saw them—everyone—gathered under a large canopy erected beside the community clubhouse. Food was spread across a bar in large pots and pans. People holding plates stood in line. Those who had already gotten their food were seated at picnic tables arranged in long rows, eating and chatting casually under the canopy.

He stopped and took in the scene from a distance, unsure how to proceed and bewildered by the sheer audacity of what he was witnessing. It was unthinkable. Once again, he found himself wondering: Had no one told these people this was the apocalypse?

He scanned the crowd. No one had seen him yet. He could turn and leave, and it would be like he was never there. His stomach panged with hunger. Maybe he could get in and out before anyone noticed. He circled the periphery of the gathering until he found a route to the back of the line that would draw the least attention. He stepped up casually, keeping his eyes down as he got into line, and inched toward the buffet.

Once he reached the bar, he picked up a plate and quickly served himself. He would have been dumbstruck by the array of options—strawberry salad, deviled eggs, rice, sauteed mushrooms, an assortment of steamed vegetables, and even apple pie—if he hadn't been in such a rush to pile food on his plate and sit down unnoticed. Without paying any attention to what he was doing, he grabbed a serving spoon and shoveled food onto his plate, then, hands shaking, he repeated the process at the next station. Avoiding eye contact, he scurried off to find a seat away from everyone else, settling near the rear of the canopy.

Shoulders hunched, he hovered over his plate. "Goddammit." He had ended up with only rice and mushrooms. Never mind. He would eat quickly then sneak back to his room.

So far, he hadn't drawn any attention to himself and no one had approached him. That was good. And even though his plate wasn't filled with the same array of fruit and vegetables as everyone else's, the rice and mushrooms looked good. His mouth watered as he stared at the food. It was then he realized he had forgotten to grab a fork. "Fuck," he whispered as he lifted his head and craned his neck. A basket of silverware sat at the end of the bar. "Shit." He could feel his heart thumping in his temples. He looked down at the food. "Fuck it," he said, and he leaned over the plate and started shoveling it into his mouth with trembling fingers.

Just finish this plate and get out of here.

Chewing frantically, he stuffed his face until his jaw began to tire. He didn't notice the buzz of conversation under the canopy had faded to near silence until the only sounds were his fingers scraping against the plate and food grinding between his teeth. He looked up nervously.

Simone stood on a crate near the bar and looked out at the residents of New Concord. "Hello, my friends," she said with a beaming smile. "I'd like to introduce you to our newest neighbor, Christopher James."

Simone gestured in Christopher's direction from the other end of the canopy. Everyone turned to face him, and their eyes stabbed like knives. He wanted to melt through the bench and disappear, but there could be no cracks in his facade, no sign of weakness. He gulped down the food in his mouth, stiffened his back, and met their eyes with his.

"Christopher had a rough road getting here," Simone said, still standing on the crate, "but he made it. Let's all make sure he feels welcome."

Simone clapped her hands then everyone joined her in a round of applause. Several people seated near Christopher slid over to greet him. A bearded man patted him on the shoulder, and his muscles tensed at the man's touch. The sea of bodies closed in around him. Eyes darting from face to face, he was drowning, being swallowed whole, until he recognized Jordan's face a few tables away. Her eyes locked onto his. She smiled and gave a single nod, somehow anchoring him among the waves. He took a breath and nodded back.

"Stand and introduce yourself, Mr. James," Simone said over the clapping and cheering of the residents.

He had no choice. He peeled his white-knuckled hands from the tabletop and rose to his feet. A wave of anxiety rippled through his core. His hands trembled, and his knees shook as though they might buckle beneath him. His heart pounded in his ears as he scanned the blur of faces in the crowd—all those eyes in blank faces—not registering as individuals but rather as a white-hot mass, glaring at him, burning holes through him, waiting for him to say something, anything.

He swallowed and was about to open his mouth to speak when one face among the blurry crowd caught his eye. A man he didn't recognize, sitting at the opposite end of the canopy. He wore a baseball hat, pulled low over his eyes, and he leaned over the table, arms folded in front of him, chin resting on his arms. Christopher squinted. Beneath the shadow of the brim, the man's eyes were unwavering, like he was staring straight through him. He looked Hispanic, but he couldn't be sure.

Who is this guy? Why is he staring at me like that? Shit, how long have I been standing up here? Say something, dammit.

His skin was steaming hot. He dropped his head, breaking eye contact with the man in the hat. His facade was cracking. He chewed his lip and shook his head.

This is fucking embarrassing.

His eyes glazed over as he opened his mouth to speak, but no words came out. His cheeks burned. Someone cleared their throat, and he turned to see Simone standing on the other side of the canopy. She looked at him and flashed a reassuring yet knowing smile, indicating she wouldn't be coming to his rescue. He needed to get through this on his own.

What was he supposed to say? He had no jokes to tell, no cute stories, no endearing anecdotes. His brain was foggy, and his scalp prickled, like thousands of tiny needles jabbing repeatedly. Helplessly, he stood before the waiting audience, the awkwardness in the air becoming more palpable with each excruciating second until, finally, instinct kicked in. He threw his shoulders back and put his arms to his sides, standing as tall and straight as he could, then lifted his chin, sucked in his stomach, and stuck out his chest. With a crisp and clear military inflection, he shouted, "James, Christopher, Private First Class, United States Army."

He stood firmly at attention, an odd sort of electricity coursing through his veins, while the crowd sat silent and deathly still. After a moment, he relaxed his posture and clasped his hands tightly behind his back. The warm summer breeze rustled the canopy. Birds chirped pleasantly somewhere nearby. The silence of the crowd stretched on for eternity.

"At ease, soldier!" someone yelled, mercifully breaking the tension, and the community erupted into laughter. He unclasped his hands and exhaled, too relieved to care if he was being mocked.

"Thank you, Christopher, thank you," Simone said, raising her voice over the buzz of the crowd, then she waved to indicate he had fulfilled his obligation and could sit back down.

Weak-kneed, his eyelids drooped shut, then he crumpled to the bench and put his hands over his face, stretching the skin over his eyes and rubbing his temples. Eventually, he drew a deep breath and turned back to finish his food, hopefully without any further fanfare.

"It's good to have you here, Christopher. Welcome. I'm Tom."

He looked up from his plate. A middle-aged man stood over him, hand outstretched.

"My name's Carol. You'll love it here."

"Hey, I'm Shanice, welcome to New Concord!"

One by one, members of the community approached him and introduced themselves. Then came the questions. Where had he come from? How did he get here? How had he survived for so long on his own? Was his wound healing well?

He answered in fragments, barely able to get a word out before being hit with the next question. His head was pounding. He closed his eyes and dropped his head. Voices swirled around him.

He stood abruptly and walked away without a word, leaving the crowd under the canopy as he headed in the direction of his apartment.

"Hey, man," someone shouted after him, "normally we stick around and help clean up."

Christopher kept walking.

Christopher crashed through the apartment door then slammed it closed behind him. Injured knee be damned, he tore through the hall, bounded through the living room, and locked himself in his bedroom.

Chest heaving, he fell back against the bedroom door, then closed his eyes and sank to the floor. His nose began to run as his eyes welled up. A tear rolled down his cheek.

"No."

He sucked the runny snot back up his nose and wiped his eyes dry like he was scrubbing a dirty pan, then he jumped to his feet and lunged toward the bed.

"You're not going to cry like a fucking pussy," he said as he flipped the mattress off the box spring in a rage. It crashed against the window, and the shade sprang upward and wrapped itself around the roll at the top, illuminating the room with the last light of the summer day. He huffed, stormed to the window, and ripped the shade back down, then he turned and kicked the bed frame with his boot. He cried out in pain and disgust but kept kicking, again, and again, and again, alone in the darkened room.

The first knock was only a light tap, distant and muted. He ignored the sound.

The bed frame lay in a twisted heap in the center of the room. The mattress was on the floor, pressed up against the wall. Christopher was sprawled across it, buried beneath the sheets, his head tucked under a pillow.

Sometime later, the knock came again, more insistent than before. He rolled over and peered at the door from beneath the covers, then rolled back and shut his eyes.

A third knock. Louder. Heavier. The door rattled against the frame.

"Go away."

He squeezed his eyes tight and pressed himself further into the mattress.

"Hey, man," said an apprehensive voice through the door. "I know you said not to come in, man. Personal space and all. But, uh, you've kinda been in there a long time."

He didn't answer.

There was a long pause. He waited for the sound of footsteps.

"This is Sean, by the way. Should I be worried, dude?"

Christopher groaned, ignoring the pleas of his roommate.

He fell into a sweaty, restless sleep.

As Christopher drifted back into consciousness, Jordan's upside-down face gradually came into focus.

He was sprawled on his back, head dangling awkwardly off the mattress and resting on the carpet. The sheets and blankets lay on the floor, tossed aside. He jerked himself upright and spun around, putting his back against the wall.

Jordan stood in the middle of the mangled bed frame. "Good morning," she said pointedly.

He eyed the door angrily.

"I remember telling that surfer bro out there, very clearly, not to let anyone in here."

Jordan laughed. "Sean's a great guy, but not much of a security guard." She crossed her arms and looked down at the mattress, then gestured to the bed frame with a nod of her head. "Throwing a little tantrum, were we?"

He blew air through his nose with contempt but said nothing.

"No, I like what you've done with the place," she went on. "Definitely gives it your personal touch."

He thumped the back of his head against the wall and grumbled under his breath.

"So, I know you're just settling in and all, but were you planning on leaving this room ever again, or what?"

"What is with you people?" he barked. "Is it some sort of a crime for a man to spend some time alone?"

Jordan puckered her lips and bobbed her head from side to side. "A crime? No. Just frowned upon." She waved her hand in front of her face. "It *smells* like a crime was committed in here though. Did we have a little accident?"

She stepped over the metal rail of the bed frame and knelt to match his eye level.

"Look, man, you've been in here going on thirty-nine hours now. You're freaking people out. You don't think it's reasonable for someone to come make sure there's not a rotting corpse in here?"

He dropped his head and slowly exhaled, frustration giving way to embarrassment.

"Come on, let's get you cleaned up," Jordan said, and she extended her hand. Christopher raised his head, then after a moment of hesitation, he reached out, clasped her hand, and she stood and leaned back and pulled him to his feet. "Grab some clean clothes and a towel."

Jordan led the disheveled, foul-smelling man out of the apartment, first to the outhouse, then to the community shower house nearest the building. The structure was a simple rectangle, constructed from sturdy wood posts driven into the ground and plywood nailed around the exterior. An opening along one of the long sides served as the entryway and secured on the roof sat a water collection system made from plastic storage bins. The shower house's walls were painted sky blue and decorated with doodles drawn by children. A stick-figure family standing by a house. Kids flying a kite under a bright yellow sun. A brown dog, captioned with the name "Coco."

They passed through the entryway, his long arm draped around her petite frame for support, and inside were three showerheads rigged up to spigots, plywood dividers between them. An aging man stepped out of the shower and the far end and toweled off. Christopher groaned and pressed his eyes shut.

"Hey, what did I tell you before?" Jordan said, wagging a finger toward his face. "Just a little skin. Now get over yourself and let's do this. You stink, man."

He flashed his eyes at the old man then whipped them back at Jordan, revulsion on his face. Ignoring his objection, she reached behind him and turned on the water. It drizzled from the spigot, soaking his long hair and his clothes. He closed his eyes, reveling in the lukewarm water as it ran down his face.

"You didn't have to shower with your Army bros?"

"That was different."

"Well, unfortunately for you, in the apocalypse, efficiency has to outweigh our petty personal hang-ups. You'll get used to it. The shampoo's behind you on the shelf, soldier boy. Take those nasty clothes off and get cleaned up. I'll be waiting outside."

Jordan turned to leave the shower house, and Christopher began to pull off the wet t-shirt, groaning in pain as he tried to raise it over his head.

Jordan turned back.

"Shit, sorry, I forgot about that shoulder," she said. "Here, let me help you." She reached out, but he recoiled.

"I can do it."

"No, you can't. You're obviously in pain."

Christopher grumbled in protest but surrendered. Jordan grabbed the bottom of the shirt and gently lifted it over the shoulder wrappings then over his head.

"We might as well take these bandages off, while we're at it. After you clean the wound we can stop by Dr. Rajavi's for a new wrap job."

She slowly unraveled the tape and gauze from his arm, eyes focused intently on the task as the shower splashed her face. Neither spoke. There was something about the way she worked—the close, personal attention, perhaps—that sent tingles down his spine.

"Hey, don't get any ideas, mister," she said, looking up. Christopher quickly broke eye contact, feigning like he hadn't been staring. "I'm sure there's a nice guy buried in there somewhere, but you're not exactly my type."

He opened his mouth to protest, but the last bandage was removed before he could declare his innocence.

"Okay, that's it. Now finish getting cleaned up, and then we'll grab some food on our way to see the doc and Jason."

"Jason?"

"Physical therapy."

He nodded. "Right."

"I'll be outside. Don't take all day."

Jordan left the shower house, and so did the elderly man, towel wrapped around his waist.

Finally alone, Christopher took off his pants and stood under the trickle. The water rinsed the stink from his body, and slowly he came back to life.

Christopher lay on an exercise mat, a tennis ball tucked between his shoulder blade and spine. He raised his arm over his head in a backstroke motion, making sure to keep his elbow straight, then swam it back to his side. The trainer paced around him, keeping an eye on his form.

"Good, good. Keep it going, keep it going."

Sweat beaded on the trainer's shaved head as he circled his client, a sleeveless shirt exposing his muscular arms. His dark umber skin glistened in the sun's hot rays, pouring into the room through the shut-tight windows.

Christopher craned his neck.

"How about some air? I'm fucking dying in here."

"Don't look at me. Keep that head straight. Get that arm all the way back. Quit your bitchin' and give me five more."

He groaned as he repeated the backstroke motion. "Fuck you, Jason."

"Hey, don't take it out on me, I ain't the one who shot ya. Four more."

As much pride as Christopher had taken in his physical prowess as a soldier, he had never enjoyed training the way many military men do. Not *really*, anyway. He could crush a workout with the best of them, but he preferred more stimulating activities, like an obstacle course or even a game of basketball—something fun and competitive. Sitting in place, doing endless reps in the weight room was mind-numbing torture. Especially while it was so goddamn hot.

He finished the set.

"Just kill me now and get it over with," he said, sitting up.

Jason swatted the air dismissively.

"This is only your second session. You better get used to it 'cause you got a long way to go, my man. That shoulder ain't gonna fix itself."

Panting, he stood up and put his hands on his hips. He dropped his head.

"Come on, man, get that head up," Jason said. "I know I'm being a hardass, but you'll thank me when that arm ain't just hangin' there like a limp noodle."

He looked up at the trainer and nodded.

"Okay now. Last exercise of the day. Let's finish strong. You with me?"

"Yeah."

"What's that?"

"I'm with you."

"My man, that's what I like to hear."

The trainer tossed him a resistance stretch band.

"You know the drill. Step on one end and grab the other end tight in your fist. That's it. Thumb on top, arm straight. Give me ten reps, out to the side, shoulder height."

He pulled on the band, slouching to the left with each painful rep.

"Keep that back straight. Come on, five more. Four, three, two, and good. Okay, now out to the front. Ten reps and then you're done for the day."

He grimaced and groaned as he pulled, breathing hard, in through his mouth, out through the nose. Sweat dripped down his flushed face.

"...nine... and ten."

He dropped the band and exhaled. "Jesus Christ," he said as he put his hands on his knees, catching his breath.

"Nice work today. But remember, it's gonna get more intense as you get stronger. More reps, more resistance. So get ready to have your ass kicked on a regular basis."

He nodded.

"I want you back here in two days."

"I'll be here."

"Better be," Jason said with a smile, and he held out his fist.

Christopher stood up straight, met the trainer's eye, then bumped his fist.

Christopher wiped the sweat from his brow and neck with a towel as he walked the short distance through the breezeway from the trainer's room to the therapist's office. Though dreading the therapy session, he felt good. Oddly good. Maybe the exercise had released some dopamine or endorphins, clearing his brain of stress and anxiety. It almost made it worth it to be yelled at by a Terry Crews look-alike for an hour.

He stood in front of Sharon's office and reached for the knocker on the door. A voice from somewhere nearby echoed through the breezeway. He took his hand away from the knocker and pressed closer to the door. Hunching his shoulders, he turned his back to the end of the hall. He dropped his head.

"This is fucking pointless," he said under his breath while kicking at a dead beetle on the doormat. "I don't need this shit."

He turned to walk away just as the door opened.

"Christopher, glad you could make it. I thought I heard someone out here."

Shit.

He froze, then turned to face the woman in the doorway. Her black-framed glasses were instantly recognizable.

"Hope you weren't trying to make a run for it."

"Just wasn't sure I was in the right place."

"You're in the right place. Come on in."

The shuffling of approaching feet grew louder. Voices. Laughing. He shot a glance down the hall. Two women were coming up the steps to the breezeway. Sharon observed his nervous glance and stuck her head out the door just as he hurriedly brushed past her into the office. She moved aside, then again peeked into the breezeway. "Hey, Tina. Hey, Ashley." She waved from the doorway then turned to find him pacing inside. She shut the door behind her.

"Is everything all right?" she asked, stepping into the room.

"Yeah. Great," he said, his eyes on the floor.

Sharon studied him from across the room, keeping her distance.

A slight limp in his step, he moved manically through the modern, minimalist apartment, its aesthetically arranged decor a blur, not fully registering in his mind. His eyes darted from the trendy knick-knacks on the white floating shelves hung on the pure white walls to the useless, orb-like floor lamp in the corner. He was vaguely aware of the fact that he was acting strangely, possibly frightening the counselor. He probably seemed like a dangerous bull set loose in the elegant china shop of her living room, doubling as an office. He charged past her as if she wasn't there.

"Can I get you anything?" she asked.

He ignored her and continued around the room.

"Whenever you're ready you can take a seat on the couch."

A glass vase filled with polished rocks caught his eye, sitting perfectly in the center of a whitewashed table in the corner. He settled on a spot in front of it.

"Mr. James? Would you like to get started?"

"What is the point of this?"

"To help you get settled in. It's helpful to have someone you can talk to."

"No. This. What is the purpose of crap like this?"

"The rocks? They're just decorations. I think they look nice."

Sharon's framed degrees hung on the wall behind a neatly organized white oak desk.

"Seems like a bunch of useless shit to me," he said, scanning the wall. "Screw this. I'm out of here."

He took a step toward the door, and Sharon put herself in his path.

"Let me through."

"Wait," she said, putting her hand up. "You promised me you'd commit to a recovery process. Physical *and* mental, and I see you've already been to Jason's. I took you at your word,

Christopher, and you seem like the kind of man who believes in upholding an oath. Or am I wrong?"

He narrowed his eyes and huffed, then put his hands on his hips and looked down at his feet, shaking his head.

Sharon walked across the room, clearing his path to the door, and sat down in a chair facing the white couch against the wall. She picked up a notepad and pen from the coffee table. "Why don't you take a seat on the couch and we'll get started."

He lifted his head. The door was right there, all he had to do was go through it. He took a breath, then glanced at the counselor.

"This isn't a jail cell," she said. "You're free to go any time you please. But I think you owe it to me to keep your word. And it might sound lame, but you owe it to yourself, too."

With an exaggerated sigh, he turned around and took a seat on the couch, settling on the cushion farthest from the counselor's chair. He sat wedged against the armrest, stiff and upright.

"You're welcome to make yourself comfortable."

"I'm fine. Let's get this over with."

"How are you today, Christopher?"

He shrugged. "I feel fine."

"And how have you been adjusting to life here? It's been a few days now."

He turned away from his interrogator and stared blankly across the room at a white bookcase decorated with a small assortment of books and candles. Sharon clicked her pen and made a note on the page.

"Simone formally introduced you to the community. How did that feel?"

He pictured himself standing under the canopy, the crowd before him. Everyone's eyes, burning his flesh.

"Christopher? How did that feel?"

"Fine," he said. "It didn't feel like anything." The door beckoned from across the room. He tapped his foot impatiently. The head shrinker's judgmental pen swished over the notepad.

"You left dinner shortly after your introduction if I'm not mistaken. Can I ask where you were going?"

He turned his head back to the counselor with a flick of his neck. His lips clenched together tightly, he stared straight through her head, wishing he could make it explode. "That's none of your business," he said in a gravelly voice filled with contempt.

Sharon set the pen down on the page and dropped the pad to her lap. "I understand that this process may feel intrusive, and it's not my intention to anger you, but it's okay if you feel upset. I want to help you process those feelings. You should know, anything you say here in this room is strictly confidential. It stays between you and me. You're safe here."

"This therapy crap is a bunch of useless nonsense," he grumbled, crossing his arms, then he raised his voice to a sardonic whine. "'Oh, doctor, let me tell you about all my precious little feelings.' That shit's embarrassing. I'm not some sensitive little snowflake who needs a safe space to analyze my emotions."

"Is that why you didn't want anyone to see you come in here today? Because it's embarrassing? You're worried people will think you're weak?"

He exhaled slowly through his nose.

"Why are you so worried about what anyone else thinks of you?" Sharon said, picking up the notepad.

"I don't give a fuck what anyone thinks."

"That's not what it seems like to me. It seems like you care quite a bit about what people think of you."

He pressed himself closer to the armrest. He stared at the counselor and seethed.

"Let's backtrack," Sharon said. "Where were you when... it happened? You know, the end of the world."

He uncrossed his arms.

"I was at home. My house."

"Lots of people stayed in their houses. Not many of them lasted as long as you."

"That's true," he said, pride swelling in his chest.

"Can you elaborate? How did you do it?"

"I had food and supplies. A hidden shelter. I planned ahead."

"And how was it, afterward?"

He leaned back. His legs widened.

"It felt good. It felt good knowing I was right, knowing all my hard work was paying off. Vindicated. I felt vindicated."

"Vindicated?" the counselor asked, writing down the word on her pad and underlining it.

"No one could say I was paranoid anymore. All those fools were dead, or about to be. But I was alive. I had everything I needed. I was safe."

"But that didn't last long, did it?"

His muscles clenched.

"No. It didn't."

"What happened?"

"Bad luck."

"What specifically?"

"I got hurt. Everything was harder after that."

"So you thought of everything—food, supplies, shelter— but didn't consider that you might sustain an injury?"

He locked eyes with the counselor.

"I knew the risks."

"What happened next?"

"What does it matter? A bunch of shit went wrong."

"Things that were difficult to overcome on your own?"

He maintained eye contact with the counselor, barely suppressing an explosion.

Sharon waited a moment for a response but none came. She jotted down a note then set the pen down.

"Listen, Christopher, I know this is hard for you, but you're doing fine. You're talking, you're getting things out. We've started a dialogue. That's good progress for today."

He took a deep breath through his nose and let it out slowly, relief flooding his body. He tried not to show how tightly clenched he had been as he stood up.

"Fair warning, though," Sharon continued, "I'm going to keep pushing you out of your comfort zone. Little by little."

Christopher sat at the end of a row of picnic tables. Jordan sat across from him, and Sean was to his left. A group of women sitting farther down the row chatted casually about how good the strawberries tasted and how nice the weather had been lately even though it would be good to get some rain. He didn't attempt to engage anyone in conversation.

Mercifully, Sean wasn't yapping his head off for once. Jordan smiled from across the table but seemed content to let him eat in peace. A flock of children raced through the canopy, weaving between the tables and laughing without a care. The murmur of voices and clinking of silverware on plates created a blanket of white noise which had become familiar and comfortable.

He tuned it out, the way people did in crowded restaurants, and focused on his meal until the murmur quieted, and he eventually noticed its absence.

A man was standing on a crate at the far end of the canopy, waiting for everyone's attention. Christopher's eyes widened.

"He was staring at me," he said mostly to himself.

"What's that?" Jordan asked across the table in a whisper. Christopher dismissed the question with a shake of his head, keeping his eyes locked on the man.

"Hey, everyone, if I could get your attention for just a minute. Thank you," the man said. "I'm going to be leading a scavenger run tomorrow. Standard run. We'll be looking for any useful supplies. Food, tools, medicines, solar panels. And any survivors still out there, of course. I'm assuming my regulars will come along. Dan? Tyreek? Jordan?"

Jordan raised her hand and nodded in the affirmative, as did two others in the audience, whom he deduced to be Dan and Tyreek.

"We'll have room for one or two more in the second vehicle, so if anyone wants to volunteer to come along, come see me after dinner. And like always, if you have any special requests for things you'd like us to look for out there, make sure to let me know tonight. Okay, that's it. Thanks, everyone."

The man stepped down from the crate and sat at a table in the opposite corner under the canopy. As soon as he was seated, a middle-aged man approached. The man from the crate smiled and nodded, then wrote a note on a pad of paper. Then a young woman stepped forward. The man laughed, nodded, and again jotted down a note.

Christopher turned to Jordan. "Tell me about that guy," he said, nodding in the direction of the man.

"Oh, that's Diego," she answered. "Diego Rivera. Real great guy."

"Diego Rivera? Why does that sound familiar?"

"His parents must have been art fans, I guess."

"What?"

"You know, the painter?"

He shrugged. Jordan rolled her eyes.

"What did he do? Before."

"He was a mechanic. He keeps all our vehicles running, and organizes the big supply runs."

He turned back toward Diego. A thin teenage boy slowly approached him. Diego stood and hugged the boy, then he looked him in the eye, a hand on his shoulder. They exchanged a few words. Diego nodded his head and put his hand over his heart.

He turned back to Jordan.

"He was looking at me."

"What do you mean? When?"

"The other day. When Simone made me stand up. He was staring at me."

"I hate to break it to ya, man, but everyone was staring at you."

"Yeah, but this was—"

"I'm sure it's nothing. Diego is cool. You'll see."

He wasn't reassured. He anxiously tapped his fingers over the table like he was playing the piano.

"I want to go," he blurted out.

"Go where?" Jordan replied. "The run?"

He nodded.

"No. Not a good idea."

"I can do it. I need *something* to do."

"No, you're not ready. Your shoulder, for one thing, and..."

He cocked his head and raised his eyebrows. "And what?"

"You're still new here, Chris. You're still adjusting. I know you were in the Army, but on these runs you've gotta be *all there*, you know? You have to be sharp, and you have to trust the others on the team with your life. And they have to trust you with theirs. Can you honestly say you're ready for that kind of mutual trust? Can you honestly say you're up to full speed physically?"

"But..."

"What would you say if you were running an operation and some reinforcement fresh out of boot camp requested to tag along at the last minute?"

He dropped his head. Under the table, he balled his hand into a fist. "Probably... exactly what you're saying now."

"Look, man," Jordan said, putting her hand on the table, "you're going to be great here. I believe in you. But first thing's first. Get yourself healthy, and then you can come along. I promise."

"Hey, Diego! What's up, man?" Sean said from the next seat over, and Christopher turned to see Diego standing behind him.

"Hey guys, how's it going over here?"

"Great, man! Just having a nice chill night," Sean said. "So, going out for a supply run, huh?"

"Yeah, heading out at sunrise. We're planning to push out farther than we've ever gone before, so I expect we'll be gone most of the day."

"Sweet, dude, but be careful out there, alright?"

"Okay, but only because you asked," Diego said as he smiled and nodded, then he straightened up and looked across the table. "So, Jordan, you gonna introduce me to your new friend?"

Jordan gestured toward Christopher with the back of her hand in a playfully exaggerated way. "Diego Rivera, may I introduce you to Mr. Christopher James, newest resident of our humble village. Mr. James, please meet my dear friend, Mr. Rivera."

Diego extended his hand. "Nice to meet you, Christopher."

Christopher gauged the expression on Diego's face. He was acting friendly enough, a smile on his face, but something gave him pause.

"Earth to Chris, you gonna shake the man's hand?" Jordan said through her hands, mimicking the sound of an old radio.

He hesitated for just another moment, then reached out and shook Diego's hand. He had a firm grip and strong, rough hands. Christopher squeezed harder to match. "Nice to meet you, too," he said coldly.

"So, listen, Christopher," Diego said, "I understand you have military experience. Is that right?"

He nodded.

"Once you get settled in and have some time to heal up, I'd love to have you join our scavenger crew. We could use someone with your skills out there. What do ya say?"

He turned to Jordan and a knowing smirk formed on her cheek, then he turned back to Diego. "I'd like that."

"Great. Well, we organize a big run every month, so we'll see if you're feeling up to it next time."

Christopher inhaled and nodded reluctantly.

"Sounds good," Diego said. "Later, guys."

Diego waved, then turned and walked back toward his end of the canopy. Another resident with a request chased after him.

"See, what did I tell ya?" Jordan said. "Diego is an awesome guy."

"We'll see."

Jordan took the lead in the red pickup. A black SUV driven by Diego followed closely behind. The vehicles rounded the loop, crested the hill, then exited through the front gate, out into the expanse of abandoned gas stations, pharmacies, grocery stores, and houses.

Christopher kicked at a loose pebble on the ground and spat as the cars disappeared from view. The purr of their motors faded, replaced by the sound of chickens clucking in their tennis court pen across the green.

I should be out there, he thought, sneering at the wrap around his damaged shoulder. I'm useless here.

The shoulder was healing nicely, according to Dr. Rajavi, and while the rehab sessions with Jason were difficult and painful, he wasn't going to give up.

He looked toward the gate.

"I'll be on the next run. Bet your ass, I will."

He kicked the pebble away and began to walk along the loop. He had nothing to do and nowhere to be. No security checks to perform, no inventory to catalog, nothing to fix or build. Not even physical therapy or counseling sessions. So he walked through the damp morning air, going nowhere in particular, along the loop road.

It was going to be a hot and sticky day, he could already tell. The rising sun had begun to burn the night's dew from the grass. A warm mist hung in the air over the black asphalt.

New Concord's early risers had begun to go about their morning routines, seemingly without a care in the world. He stopped and turned in place, watching as the community sprang to life like a blooming flower.

A woman stepped out from her building's breezeway, and three young children charged past her, bounding down the steps before chasing each other into the green. "Have fun, kids," she yelled out to them, but they were too busy playing to hear. A man and a woman emerged from the shower house together, each wrapped in a towel, and they laughed about something only the two of them would ever know. A teenage girl turned the crank on the well, then poured the water from the bucket into bottles with a funnel.

Footsteps approached from behind, and he turned to see a man jogging toward him. The man waved then continued along the road. He let him pass without waving back, a stupefied expression on his face.

It was all so *normal*, which is exactly what made it so eerie. It was an ordinary community—people just living their lives. How were they so... unafraid? His stomach churned.

A small group of people was gathering on the green near an oak tree with a fat trunk and wide, thick branches. He took a few steps for a closer look, then took a few more. The group was a near-even mix of men and women and included people of many races and ages. The people were greeting each other and unrolling mats on the ground. "About time to get started," a woman said, gently yet clearly, and the group arranged into rows. "Would you like to join us?" The woman was beckoning him with a wave. "Come. Join us."

Not sure if he had been compelled by the soothing, hypnotic nature of the woman's voice or by the embarrassment of being put on the spot, he found himself walking toward the group under the tree. The woman at the head of the group was middle-aged with pale skin, dark brown hair, and piercing green eyes. "I'm Cathy," she said. "Won't you sit with us on this beautiful morning?" She held out a rolled-up yoga mat, which he accepted without a word, then she made an elegant gesture toward an open patch of grass under the tree, all wrist and fingers. "Good morning," people said, one after the other, nodding to him as he passed. He sheepishly nodded back.

He settled on the open patch near the back of the class. The oak's thick branches swayed gently, and a chorus of cicadas chirped through the warm morning air. He unrolled his mat. Everyone else had assumed a cross-legged position and sat with their backs straight. He mimicked their pose.

"Hello, everyone, and thank you for being with me today," Cathy began, facing the class in the same cross-legged pose. "I'd like you all to set aside any troubles you had before this moment. Set aside any worries weighing on your mind. Let the rest of the world fade away and be here with me now in the present. Close your eyes, and we're going to breathe the air together. In. And out. Listen to the sound of your breath. In. And out."

He kept his eyes open. Everyone else had their eyes closed, breathing in and out. He had never been to a yoga class. He had never tried to meditate. This New Age bullshit was the type of thing hippies did in their communes. His cheeks flushed with embarrassment, and he looked around to see if anyone was watching. The green was alive with activity—people were jogging by, children were laughing and playing, a girl was reading on a nearby bench—but no one was paying attention to the yoga class. He turned back to face Cathy and sighed.

Oh, what the hell? Fuck it.

Again, he straightened his back like the rest of the class. This time he closed his eyes and followed Cathy's commands to breathe and to listen to the sound of his breath. Once he surrendered to it, her soft, clear voice became mesmerizing. It was as if she was speaking only to him. A warm pulse began in his head then traveled pleasantly down his spine. The frustration from being excluded from the supply run melted away, the worry about New Concord's security forgotten. With his eyes closed and the breeze drifting gently through the tree's branches, it was as though he was on an island, far away. There were no walls, no defenses, yet he was at the center of the safest place in the world.

Cathy brought the meditation phase to an end then led the class through a series of yoga poses. He did his best to follow along, careful not to put too much pressure on his recovering shoulder or his injured knee, but even the seemingly simple poses were surprisingly difficult to match.

The tree swayed. The summer insects sang.

The class concluded, and he was left sweating and exhausted. He stood to his full height and took a deep breath of the sweet, humid air, oddly relaxed and centered.

He approached Cathy and held out the mat.

"It's yours now," she said. "Keep it for next time."

Christopher headed back outside after depositing his new yoga mat in his room. Mind clear, he descended the stairs from the breezeway, energized, invigorated, awake.

The morning's steam had evaporated under the bright, shining sun, and the light and the heat compelled him outdoors. Besides, if he was going to stay in New Concord, there were things to explore, not to mention that he needed the exercise if he was going to be on the next supply run.

With a slight limp, he walked along the paved loop road. The sun on his face, sweat beaded on his brow. The heat was almost painful, yet satisfying in a way he couldn't describe—somehow life-affirming. He stopped short of a smile but gladly filled his lungs with the warm summer air and wiped the sweat from his eyes as he walked.

He came upon two apartment buildings he hadn't noticed on his tour with Jordan. He shaded his eyes with a salute and squinted into the glare. A worn, dirt path lay nestled between the buildings. Stepping onto the grass, he approached the path then followed it between the buildings. On the other side, standing in the apartment's shadow, a sun-soaked field of crops stretched out before him, at the bottom of a slight hill on the backside of the community. "Holy shit," he said out loud. The sheer scale of the farming operation was stupefying. There must have been several dozen rows of plants spread across a field at least two hundred feet long.

A chain-link backstop for a baseball diamond sat on the corner of the field. Rows of crops ran from the foul line through the infield and out to the outfield fence. Several people were on the field, tending to the crops with watering cans or picking fruit and vegetables, down on their hands and knees. He walked down the hill, careful to keep most of his weight over his healthy knee as he descended the slope.

Waist-high chain-link fencing fully enclosed the field, and he leaned against it, resting his arms on top. The rows of tomatoes, peppers, and corn were easily identifiable, but the variety was staggering. There were strawberries, blueberries, green beans, carrots, maybe spinach, and either cucumber or zucchini, and potatoes being pulled from the ground by a man toward the back of the field.

"Is that Christopher?" an unfamiliar voice called out. He shielded his eyes from the sun and squinted to see who was asking. A woman was waving to him. "Over here, sweetie," she said. "We could use another hand if you're free." She was wearing corduroy overalls over a gray long-sleeve shirt, white curls peeking out from under a beige sun hat with a wide brim. She had to be in her seventies, at least. "You can come through that gate right there, honey," she said with a pronounced Georgia accent, pointing to the opening in the fence a few feet away from where he stood. Without being sure why he was doing it, he found himself lifting the gate's latch. It squealed as he pushed it open. "Grab a basket," the woman shouted, pointing to a stack by the fence. He picked one from the top of the pile then walked toward the lady.

"I'm Jane," she said once he got closer. "Jane Young. Even though I ain't young no more," she said with a smile. She took off her thick gardening gloves and reached out for a handshake. "It is Christopher, ain't it?"

He reached out and shook her hand. "Yes, ma'am, it is."

"Well, Chris—I hope ya don't mind I call ya Chris—today we're pickin' strawberries if that's alright with you."

"Sure," he said, surprised by his willingness. "Why not?"

When he woke up that morning, spending the afternoon picking strawberries with an old lady was not something he could have imagined—not in a million years—but there he was, about to do just that. There was something about Jane's demeanor that made it impossible to refuse her.

They got down on their hands and knees. Jane instructed him not to squeeze the berries in his fingers when he plucked them from the plants, but to cradle them in his palm and place the berry's stem between his index and middle fingers, then pull until the fruit came loose from the bush. They worked down the row, gently pushing aside the leaves, searching for the berries that were ready for picking. The ripe, red berries piled up in their baskets until each was full to the brim.

"Well, I think you've got the hang of it," Jane said. "You'll be an old pro like me 'fore ya know it." He looked up at her and raised his eyebrows. "Not quite as old as me, a'course. You've got a ways yet 'til then," she said, and Christopher smirked, almost laughing.

When was the last time he had laughed? *Really* laughed? He couldn't remember. The happy moments from his past—goofing off with his Army buddies on the FOB, hanging out with his friends after leaving the service, and even his time with Amy—were patchy and faded in his mind, like memories from a past life. Perhaps they were, in a way. That life was over, and all there was left to do was push forward into this new life and whatever it would bring.

He looked up and surveyed the massive garden.

"It's lucky this field was here," he said. "And the fence around it. Helps keep the wildlife away, I'm sure."

"Oh, absolutely," Jane agreed. "The fence keeps out the deer and the foxes, but we do find some smaller critters in here on occasion. We make a nice rabbit stew when we catch 'em."

He chuckled.

"Yeah, the kids was sore their baseball field was taken away," Jane said, "but it was for the greater good, ya see. When ya got people's lives on the line ya got to get your priorities in order."

He nodded.

"What's next?" he asked.

"Now we take these berries up to the kitchen and let the chefs do what they want with 'em."

He picked himself off the ground and flexed his injured knee a few times before they started walking.

"So what happened to that knee, sweetie? I seen ya hobblin' around a bit."

"You'd laugh if I told you," he said. "It's stupid."

"Well go on, I ain't lettin' ya off the hook that easy. 'Sides, I can always use a good laugh."

He smirked as he opened the gate and they started up the hill. "I tripped over a bucket."

"Ha!" Jane laughed, then she covered her mouth.

"See, I told you you'd laugh."

"I'm sorry, sweetie. How'd you manage such a silly thing?"

"I was being careless, trying to carry too much at once. Had a ladder over my shoulder and a bucket of water in my hand, slipped, lost my balance, rolled over the bucket, and heard the knee pop on my way down."

"The doc have a look at it?"

"Yeah. Nothing he can do. Ligament surgery was one thing I didn't anticipate when I was planning."

"Well there's yer problem, sweetie," she said as they passed the apartment buildings and stepped onto the paved loop road.

"What do you mean?"

"Planning."

He cocked his head to the side and looked at her, a puzzled look on his face.

"Well look at us," she said, waving to the community. "You think any of this was planned? Sure, Simone was wise enough to go around keepin' everyone calm and collected like she did, but all this—the chickens and the farm, the community kitchen and them solar panels up there, and everything else we done—we just made it all up as we went along. Now, sure, anyone can have an accident and get their knee tore up. Ain't nothing can stop a random act of God if it's gonna happen. But here, if you ever find yourself up a creek without a paddle, you can bet someone'll be along in no time to bail ya out."

They approached the community kitchen, located inside what used to be the apartment complex's clubhouse.

"Well, here we are," Jane said, then she turned to Christopher and put a finger on his chest. "Don't go forgettin' what I said, Chris. We're all in this together now, ya hear?"

"Yes, ma'am," he said, though he was unsure if he truly meant it.

"Special delivery for my favorite chefs," Jane said as she and Christopher entered the kitchen, baskets of strawberries in hand.

Food preparation stations were set up on sturdy, wooden tables in the center of the room, and cookware was organized on a countertop along the wall. Splayed out on the granite surface and stacked on the shelves above it were pots and pans, strainers and mixing bowls, large knives and wooden spoons, spatulas and tongs, as well as staples like salt and pepper, olive oil, bags of flour, sugar, and rice, and an assortment of spices.

Three young, black men, all wearing baggy, food-stained t-shirts, stood behind the tables in the center of the room, their arms, hands, and fingers working at a frantic pace, chopping, mixing, and measuring. They didn't break their rhythm as they looked up in unison to see who was coming through the door.

"Hey, Mrs. J!" said the young man on the left, over the sound of his knife clattering against a wooden cutting board. He wore a thick gold chain around his neck and a stud in one nostril. His hair was long and curled in tight coils, a neatly trimmed goatee on his chin. "What you got for us today?"

"Oh, nothin' but the finest strawberries, just for you," Jane replied with a grin.

"They look real good, Mrs. J," said the young man in the center of the room as he expertly cut the meat from a chicken leg with a small blade. His hair was shorter than the first's, styled with a fade cut. His pudgy cheeks were clean-shaven. "But not as good as you're lookin' today." The other two chefs howled and laughed.

"He's right, though," said the young chef on the right, a hair pick stuck in his afro. He smiled, flashing a set of pearly white teeth. "Mrs. J, you don't look a day over thirty."

"Oh, stop, you're makin' me blush," Jane said with a wave of her wrist. When the laughter died down, she turned to Christopher. He was hanging back, just inside the door. Jane urged him forward with a nod of her head. "Gentlemen, I'd like to introduce you to my new friend, Christopher James. Well, I call him Chris and he doesn't seem to mind. We met this morning out on the field and he helped me pick all them lovely strawberries."

She turned toward Christopher then pointed to the man on the left.

"Chris, this young man here is Anthony, and to his left is Isaiah, and down on the end there is Jaylen."

All three chefs stopped chopping, mixing, and slicing, and set down their instruments. Christopher took a hesitant step forward in the suddenly quiet room, still holding his basket of strawberries by the handle. He flashed Jane a side-eyed glance and swallowed. Keeping his eyes on the floor, he cleared his throat. "How's it goin'?" he asked in a slightly affected voice, trying too hard to sound cool.

He peeked up to see Anthony, Isaiah, and Jaylen exchange glances, and he stood in agony, awkwardly waiting for a response. Though his face was turning red with embarrassment, he felt like the whitest man on earth. The painful silence stretched on for an eternity.

He held his breath.

The trio of young chefs simultaneously erupted into a blur of smiles, greetings, and salutes. They excitedly spoke over each other, welcoming him to the kitchen and the community.

He exhaled, relieved.

"Hey man, you know, we could use an extra set of hands if you wanna hang for a minute," Anthony said.

"Yeah, them strawberries you just brought in ain't gonna chop themselves." Jaylen said, pointing with his knife to the basket Christopher held in his hand. "What do ya say?"

"We're makin' a chicken stew," Isaiah said, "but the berries'll make a nice side."

He wanted to turn and bolt out the door. What could be more awkward than standing in this kitchen, for who knows how long, trying to make conversation with these three guys? Kids, really, and from a totally different world.

The three young men looked at him, waiting for a response. He was put on the spot, just like he had been at the field by Jane, just like he had been at the oak tree by Cathy. How could he say no?

"Alright," he said, mustering just enough enthusiasm to pass for politeness. "Just for a while."

The three chefs cheered, and Jaylen cleared off a space at the end of his table for Christopher to work on the strawberries.

Jane set her basket of strawberries down on the table. "Well, looks like y'all are gonna hit it off just fine, so I'll leave y'all to it," she said. "Christopher, it was a pleasure meetin' ya this morning. I hope we can work together again real soon."

He nodded. "Nice meeting you, too."

The three men waved and said goodbye to Mrs. Young, then the old lady turned and left through the door, leaving Christopher alone in the kitchen with the chefs. His stomach dropped and his face flushed. Maybe he could make up an excuse and follow Jane out the door.

His eyes hung on the door until one of the chefs approached from the side. A glint of light reflected off an object in the chef's hand, and Christopher shifted his eyes to see Anthony holding a knife. He flinched instinctively and took a step back.

"Yo, relax, man," Anthony said with a laugh. "Whatchu think, I'mma gut you right here in front of everybody?"

He set the knife down on a cutting board in front of Christopher then dropped a bottle of hand sanitizer on the table. "Get yourself a squirt of that, then you can get to slicin' and dicin'."

Isaiah came by and set a bucket of water on the table. "Gotta wash the fruit 'fo you do though."

Christopher looked helplessly at the door, in too deep to back out.

The three chefs went back to their work, chopping celery, peeling carrots, skinning potatoes, and slicing chicken.

"Those strawberries the self-slicin' kind?" Jaylen asked with a smirk and a nod toward the fruit.

Christopher cleared his throat and feigned a smile, then looked down at the table. He sanitized his hands, picked up the knife, and got to work, rinsing the berries in the bucket, then slicing off their tops and cutting them in twos. He put the cut berries in a large bowl while the others worked on the massive chicken stew.

To his surprise, there were no awkward silences. Whether that was a good thing, however, he wasn't sure. While they worked, his three fellow cooks took turns peppering him with questions about his life.

"Where'd you grow up?"

"Got any brothers or sisters?"

"What was your job before the collapse?"

"How'd you survive?"

"What brings you to New Concord?"

"Who's your favorite rapper?"

Coming from people he had just met, the questions were so intrusive, so personal, and he struggled through the conversation. What right did they have to any of his private thoughts and personal details? But the more he talked to these people—people who had been total strangers only minutes before—the more invigorating it became. It filled him with a euphoria he couldn't explain. They were genuinely interested in what he had to say.

He talked and talked, answering their questions fully and honestly.

"I don't know... Eminem?"

Anthony, Isaiah, and Jaylen looked at each other and laughed.

"At least you didn't say Vanilla Ice," Isaiah said.

"Yo, The Marshall Mathers LP is tight though," Jaylen said.

"True," Anthony said, "it's legit."

During a lull in the banter, Christopher looked up and asked a question of his own.

"Let me ask you something. How did the three of you become chefs, here in the community? Did you have to apply or something?"

"Naw, nothing like that. Just signed up for a shift is all. We had a good time doing it that first time, so we kept at it. Simple as that," Anthony said.

"The three of us were cooks at a restaurant," Jaylen said.

"That shitty place on South Cobb Drive, by the Quiktrip. That's where we met," Isaiah said.

"We became friends workin' in that nasty ass kitchen," Anthony said.

"Yeah, man, that place was nasty as hell, but we needed the money," Jaylen said.

"Eventually, the three of us decided to move in together, to save on rent," Isaiah said.

"So that's how we ended up here at the complex," Anthony said.

"After everything went down, it just seemed right that we'd volunteer to cook for the people here," Jaylen said.

"Sure as hell beats the restaurant," Isaiah said.

"Yeah, here we can get creative, you know? Cook what we wanna cook," Anthony said.

"No fuckin' manager breathin' down our necks," Jaylen said, and the others nodded in agreement.

"And we only do this a couple times a week, too," Isaiah said. "There are other cooks besides us. We got a schedule."

Once everything had been chopped, peeled, and sliced, the four men filled two large pots with the ingredients and carried them outside to the fire pits beside the clubhouse. They set the pots down on the grates, filled them with water, and lit the fires. Soon the chicken stew was simmering over the flames, its savory aromas filling the air.

They stood around and talked while the stew bubbled over the fire and took turns stirring the food in the huge pots. Invariably, the stirrer would say something like, "We gonna be eatin' good tonight!" and Christopher's mouth would water.

Other volunteers arrived to help set up bowls and plates and silverware at the serving station. Once everything was in place, and the food was ready, it was time to call the community to the canopy.

"Go ahead, Chris. Hit it," Anthony said, gesturing to the gong hung beside the clubhouse. "You earned the honor today."

"Me?" he asked apprehensively, pointing to his chest.

"Yeah, bro, give it a good whack," Jaylen said.

"Alright," he said as he stepped up to the gong. It was suspended from a wooden frame with a mallet hanging from a rope on the side. He picked up the mallet and looked back at the three chefs. "You got this!" Isaiah said with a smile, then Christopher swung the mallet and hit the gong right in the bullseye. Its distinctive, tinny sound rang out across the community, and gradually the residents began to trickle in and get in line.

Christopher sat at a table with Anthony, Isaiah, and Jaylen, and he and his three new friends talked and laughed and enjoyed the food they had prepared together. The strawberries were the best he had ever tasted.

The vehicles returned while the community ate under the canopy. The residents clapped and cheered as Jordan's red truck and Diego's black SUV came to a stop on the loop, not far from the canopy.

The supply run. He had completely forgotten about it. Between yoga, working in the field, preparing food in the kitchen, and making new friends each step of the way, his frustration from that morning had vanished.

The team exited the vehicles and began unloading the supplies they had brought back. The thin, teenage boy approached Diego, just as he had the evening before. The team's smiles turned to frowns. They all dropped their heads. Diego said something to the boy and shook his head, and the boy dropped his head, too, and slunk away. Diego took off his hat, then turned and kicked the bumper of the SUV.

It was midmorning on an already sweltering summer day, and Christopher was pushing through yet another physical therapy session with Jason. The windows were open, but he didn't have the slightest clue what good that was doing.

"It's like a goddamn sauna in here," he said as he completed a set with the resistance band. Sweat dripped from his brow and down his back as he changed position and began a new set, stretching the band over his head then back down to his side.

"I'd turn on the A/C if it weren't for this apocalypse we've been having lately," Jason said as he circled Christopher, sweat beaded on his shaved head. "Lucky for you though, this is it. You're done."

"Thank God." He dropped the resistance band and picked up a water bottle, then chugged until it was empty. "So when's my next session?" he asked between gulps of air.

"Didn't you hear me, my man? You're done."

A smile slowly crept across his face. "Like, *done* done? Seriously?"

"Hey, you can always come back just to look at my pretty face if you want, but as far as I'm concerned that shoulder is as close to fully recovered as it's gonna get. How's it feel?"

He rotated his left arm. "Range of motion might not be quite what it used to be. But no pain." He smiled. "Feels good. Strong."

"My man. Another satisfied customer." Jason smiled and nodded. "I like the fresh cut, by the way. Finally get tired of the mountain man look?"

His hair was still much longer than military regulation but neatly trimmed to chin length, swept back over his head and behind his ears. He also kept the beard, short on the sides and slightly longer on the chin—rugged but dignified.

"Thanks. Had it done a few days ago." He shook his head and smiled. "Have to admit, never thought I'd sit in a barber's chair again."

Jason extended his hand. "Been a pleasure."

Christopher looked the trainer in the eye. He nodded, then reached out, clasped the trainer's hand, and shook it.

"I might swing by from time to time. For the exercise. Your face ain't *that* pretty."

"Come on in, Christopher," Sharon said. "Please make yourself comfortable."

Christopher took a seat on the center cushion of the couch. Sharon sat on the chair facing him. She was sweating through a red cotton tank top and fanned herself with her notepad.

"Sorry I don't look more professional today. This heat is diabolical."

"At least you weren't just suffering through one of Jason's PT sessions," he said with a smile.

"Oh, you poor thing, I can only imagine."

"The good news is he says my shoulder is fully recovered."

"That's fantastic news, Christopher. Congratulations."

His smile faded. "Yeah."

Sharon flipped opened her notepad and clicked her pen. Christopher eyed the metallic silver object in her hand and took a deep breath.

"So, you're not pleased with your recovery?" the counselor asked, reverting to her professional tone and demeanor.

"I am..."

Sharon held the pen over the page.

"...It's just..."

"It's okay, Christopher."

He turned away and stared through the wall with haunted eyes. He rubbed his shoulder.

"The man who wounded me... I killed him."

Sharon scribbled a note in her book then looked up at her patient.

"Can you tell me how it happened?"

"Does it really matter? He's dead. And there's nothing I can do about it."

"How do you feel about that? Knowing you can't change the past."

"I'm not sure. But today, I was just thinking..."

He pressed again on his healing shoulder.

"... I get to recover, but that poor bastard never will."

"And you feel guilty about that?"

He exhaled slowly and looked up at the ceiling.

"Maybe. He shot at me first, but I had him boxed in. Didn't give him much choice."

He looked down at the floor and shook his head.

"It was my fault."

"How so?"

"He wasn't hurting anyone. He was just passing through."

The counselor looked at him expectantly, her pen still. Christopher met her eye and took a breath.

"I was so out of it, at the end. I didn't even know if it was day or night. I went outside to charge my solar lantern in the middle of the fucking night, and that's when I heard the guy. A random coincidence."

He shifted in his seat.

"You know, I never killed anyone in the war. Can you believe that? They sent me halfway around the world to fight the fucking Hajjis—I mean, the Iraqis—but... I never actually took anyone's life until I got back home, when all this shit went down."

"Were there others?"

"Others?"

"Besides the man who wounded your shoulder. Did you kill other people?"

"Yes."

"How many?"

"Three, on the first night of the collapse."

"How did that make you feel?"

"I felt fine about it. At the time, anyway. They were just some punks robbing the house next door. They killed my neighbors, and they were coming for my house next. They had it coming."

"You said you felt fine about it *at the time*. You don't anymore?"

"I don't know. Defending my territory was the most important thing in the world. It *was* my world. It was all I could think about, even before the collapse. Hell, I was actually *excited* when it happened. Like living out a fantasy..."

He glanced at the counselor.

"... But now... looking back... it all seems so pointless, you know?"

"Why do you think that is?"

"I guess, after a while, I started to wonder what I was staying alive for, out there in the scorching heat or the bitter cold, my food supply dwindling, all alone in that fucking metal box. The more time went by, the more pointless it became."

"What do you think made it pointless?"

He dropped his head and let out a long, deep breath. "I... I don't think I'm ready to say it out loud."

Sharon scribbled a note. "That's perfectly fine, we can come back to it another time." She slashed the pen across the page. "Is there anything else that's been weighing on your mind about that time?"

He took a breath and nodded.

"The deer."

"The deer?"

"A doe. I spotted her in the next yard over, standing alone in the fog. Just minding her own business, eating some overgrowth by the fence."

"What happened?"

"I shot her. Right between the eyes. My God, those eyes..."

Sharon looked up from her notepad.

"... She was looking right at me—right *through* me—like she could see how hollowed out I was. Of course, at the time, I was just thinking, 'Hot damn, fresh meat.' But those cold, black eyes did something to me, the more I thought about 'em. It's like they've been haunting me ever since. I can't tell you how many times I've replayed that moment in my head, over and over. Her, standing there in the mist, turning her head to look at me, like she knew what was coming, but resolved to go out with grace. Almost like she was making a point of some kind—judging me. Exposing my whole life as one big lie I was telling myself. She was defiant, yet... at peace. She didn't try to run. She just stared me down as I pulled the trigger."

The pen rested on Sharon's notepad. She wiped the sweat from her brow. "So would you take it back, if you could?"

"Which part?"

"Any of it. All of it. The man who wounded you, the people who broke into your neighbor's house, the deer?"

"I don't know. Even if I really wanted to, I couldn't take it back. All I can do now is live with it, and try to move on."

"That's right. And do you think you can?"

Christopher stood and paced slowly across the room. A painting on the wall caught his eye—an abstract image of two human heads facing each other, each a kaleidoscope of shapes and bright colors. He stopped pacing.

"You know, I had planned on running off, first chance I got," he finally answered. "Once I healed up and got my strength back, I was gonna take off and start over. On my own, like before." He shook his head. "This place... the people here... before I saw it, I wouldn't have believed it. I would have said it was impossible."

Sharon watched him from her chair as he stared into the painting.

"I think maybe I've been a bad person. I've done bad things, at least. All that time, I thought I was some kind of badass, like an outlaw who refused to play by the same rules as all the suckers. But maybe I was just a coward, hiding and pushing people away. I've hurt people. Maybe the best way to atone for what I've done is to give this place a chance. A real chance."

He turned away from the painting and faced Sharon.

"I'm going to stay."

Christopher walked home from the Health Wing along the loop, sweating through his t-shirt. Despite the humidity, his steps were lighter than usual, like he might break free of the earth's gravity and begin floating over the asphalt, a great weight lifted from his soul.

The green was buzzing with its usual activity. Children were trying to get a kite in the air, without much luck. People were gathered around the well, taking turns filling up bottles, chatting as they waited. As Christopher walked by, an older child carrying a bag of water bottles ran up to him. "Here you go," the child said enthusiastically, handing him a bottle before scampering off to find someone else in need of refreshment. "Thanks," Christopher said, pleasantly bemused. He unscrewed the cap and poured water over his head and rubbed it into his face, then took a long, satisfying gulp from the bottle before continuing along the paved road.

As he approached the 800 building, he saw Wendy wearing a white sundress, her red hair shining in the bright daylight. She was down on her hands and knees in the alley, scrubbing clothes in a bucket with a built-in washboard. When he got close enough, he could hear her humming a familiar tune as she raked a garment against the board. He stopped and listened until she noticed and looked up.

"That song. I can't quite place it," he said, awkwardly covering for himself after getting caught staring.

"Wish You Were Here," Wendy said, shading her eyes with her hand.

"Ah, Pink Floyd. I was more of a hard rock guy, if I'm being honest," he said, "but I like the way you do it."

"When it comes to humming, I'm a virtuoso. As long as no one's listening."

"Sorry, I didn't mean to sneak up on you like that."

She smiled. "No harm done, Mr. James."

"Need a hand with that?" he asked, pointing to her basket of laundry.

"No," she said. "But I suppose I could use the company."

He came closer, and she tossed him a wet pair of pants. "Throw that on the line for me, if you're sticking around," she said.

"No problem." He hung the pants on the clothesline strung up between buildings 700 and 800, then turned back to Wendy. A pair of wet underwear hit him in the face and stuck there. "Hey, come on," he said through the sheer fabric.

"On the line, Mr. Soldier man."

He peeled the undergarment from his face and hung it on the line, then turned around quickly with his hands up, ready to defend himself.

Wendy laughed. "Can't fool you twice." She scrubbed a shirt against the washboard then tossed it to him.

"So what did you do, in the old world?" he asked as he hung the shirt on the line.

"Oh, you know. A little of this, a little of that. I was a hostess, at the end."

"At a restaurant?"

"Yeah, one of those modern, trendy ones downtown. The kind where the staff wears all black and the customers pay for the atmosphere more than the food."

"Was never my kind of place."

"Well, me neither, really. But a girl's gotta make a living."

The sound of the gong rang out over the grounds.

"Thank goodness," Wendy said, clutching her stomach. "I was about to spontaneously become a vampire, and you were about to become my first victim."

"Saved by the bell," he said, the ease of their banter surprising him. Wendy playfully bared her fangs, and he smirked, his head buzzing pleasantly. Were they flirting? He was out of practice, but the feeling was intoxicating.

Wendy reached out her hand and Christopher pulled her up to her feet. "Will you join me for dinner?" She asked.

He smiled and nodded. "I could eat."

"Well then," she said, taking his hand and leading him away, "there's no time to waste."

His heart raced, and the floating sensation from earlier was heightened. He was walking on air now, and he didn't want to come down. He had almost forgotten what it felt like to be touched by another person—by a woman. Even something as simple and innocent as holding hands was exhilarating. Electricity crackled over his skin, and he became oddly aware of his pulse. He hoped Wendy wouldn't notice how hard his heart was beating as they walked to dinner, hand in hand.

"So, Mr. James, tell me who you are."

"I'm... not sure how to answer that."

"Tell me something about yourself. Tell me a story."

A pang of panic rippled through his stomach, threatening to disrupt his airy mood.

"I've never been much of a storyteller."

She looked up at him and he turned to meet her eye. Her deep red hair fluttered freely in the gentle breeze, the butterfly tattoo on her shoulder exposed. She smiled. "That doesn't matter, as long as the story is from the heart."

"Fair enough," he said, gathering himself. "Let me think."

They walked along the loop toward the canopy on the green while he searched his memory for something to tell her. It was a strange and difficult task, searching for something personal—something intimate—to tell someone he barely knew. And stranger still to *want* to. The walls guarding his oldest memories were tall and thick, and to breach them was like stepping into another lifetime, almost as if the experiences they protected belonged to someone else. Wendy looked up and smiled at him. He took a deep breath, pushing past the anxious pang in his stomach.

"I was kind of a scrawny kid," he began.

"Well, this story is already beyond belief," she said playfully.

"I was," he said soberly, and Wendy demurred. "When I was about ten years old there was this pack of older kids that always picked on me. They went to the middle school. I was still in elementary. The way it worked was that the kids in the high school got let out first, earlier in the afternoon, then the middle schoolers an hour later, and then the elementary kids. I was in fifth grade and I was the only elementary kid to get off at my stop, and the stop was down the street from my house, so I had a good ways to walk after I got off the bus. This pack of middle school kids... they got in the habit of waiting for me, always in a different spot along the route to my house, so I wouldn't know where to expect them. They'd ambush me, jumping out from behind a house or a car parked along the street, and push me around, and I would try to ignore them and keep on walking. My blood would be boiling inside but I had no choice but to take whatever they decided to dish out that day. I was outnumbered and they were bigger than me, so there wasn't much I could do. Most of the time they were harmless enough. It was intimidation, more than anything. They'd cuss at me and make me think they were gonna hurt me. Sometimes they'd shoot folded-up paper hornets at the back of my head with a rubber band or they'd grab my backpack and dump it out on the sidewalk and leave me there to pick up my books. Well, finally, I decided I had enough. Ignoring them wasn't working, so I figured I'd try standing up to them. Might as well, right? One day, I got up my nerve, and when they jumped out and started pushing me around I took off my backpack and put up my fists and started trying to fight them off. There were four of them and they were all about a foot taller than me, and one of them grabbed me from behind and held my arms while the others took turns punching me in the stomach. And just before they were about to run off the biggest kid got right up in my face and said, 'This is so you remember not to fight back,' and he punched me in the face, hard, right under my eye. Well, I got home, and my older brother Joshua saw me come through the door, crying and bleeding. I had never told him about the bullies. I was embarrassed, you know? Well, Joshua made me tell him what happened, and who had done it, and he was furious. He was in eighth grade, a year ahead of the bullies, and he knew exactly who they were. We told our parents I got hit with a baseball so they wouldn't be suspicious and then that night we came up with a plan to get revenge. So, the next day, Joshua got off the bus with the bullies and he watched them sneak off to pick out a spot to ambush me, then he circled back to the bus stop. An hour later, my bus dropped me off, and I started walking home my usual way, acting normal, and Joshua hung back, following from a distance, close enough to keep his eye on me but not close enough to give himself away. Well, sure enough, those boys jumped me, like they always did, and they started pushing me around and mocking me for my black eye. They were so busy circling me and knocking me around that they didn't notice Joshua when he came running. He didn't say anything to announce himself, he just ran up and clocked the biggest kid right in the jaw. Laid him out flat on his back. And then he turned and looked at the other kids and asked who wanted to be next. The big kid picked himself up off the ground and spat blood on the sidewalk, then all four of them ran off, and Joshua yelled out after them that he better not hear about them messing with his brother ever again. And sure enough, they left me alone after that."

"Wow," Wendy said. "You were right."

"About what?"

"You're not much of a storyteller."

He cocked his head, taken aback.

"But," she said with a grin, "it *was* from the heart."

"Every word."

"So where's your brother now?"

"He was killed in a car accident three years later. He was sixteen."

Wendy squeezed his hand tighter. "Oh gosh, I'm so sorry."

"It was a long time ago."

"Yes. But he was your protector."

"Yeah. He was," he said, just as the pair approached the canopy.

The food line had already begun to form, and they joined it at the back. When it was their turn, they made their plates, then they picked an empty table and sat down across from each other. Then it was Wendy's turn to spill her guts.

Christopher learned she had been an only child and that her parents had both died young. She was raised in her teens by her mother's unmarried sister, and the two became almost like sisters themselves until Wendy had gone off to college only to drop out after one semester. "We were never quite the same, the two of us, after that," Wendy said. "She made it clear I was on my own from then on, and we lost touch. We hadn't spoken in years, before the end of it all. I have no idea what happened to her."

He was entranced, for once not looking over his shoulder to see who was watching or desperate to flee. The clattering of silverware faded as they spoke. The buzz of conversation under the canopy melted away. He looked Wendy in the eyes, and she looked back into his haggard, careworn pools, and he was unburdened in her presence. She was a fully formed person—centered, present, at peace with herself. Her quiet confidence was soothing, infectious, and thrilling. No one interrupted their conversation.

"We're two lost souls in our own little fishbowl, aren't we, Mr. James?"

"You don't seem lost at all," he said. "You seem like someone who's always exactly where she wants to be."

Wendy beamed at him across the table, her green eyes glowing in the twilight.

"Come on," she said. "Let's get out of here."

They stood and took their plates and silverware to the washing station, then she grabbed him by the hand and led him away from the canopy.

"Where are we going?" he asked.

"My room," she answered.

They didn't speak on the way to her apartment. She pulled him forward, nearly at a run. His pulse quickened. A tingling flooded his brain and ran from his scalp down through his fingertips. He barely noticed the twinge in his knee as he followed her lead.

They reached the building, went up the stairs to the breezeway, then crashed through the door to her unit. She pulled him past the kitchen, through the living room, and practically flung him into her bedroom.

She shut the door behind her.

Christopher stood in the center of the room. Wendy's back was to the door. Out of breath, their chests heaved as they locked eyes.

She rushed forward and smothered him with a kiss.

"Take off my dress," she whispered.

Christopher stood under the oak tree in the Mountain pose, feet together, arms straight up over his head.

"Don't forget to breathe," Cathy said from the front of the class. "Deep breaths. In. And out. Now, Warrior pose. Right leg forward, left leg all the way back. Keep your arms stretched *high* over your head."

He did his best to replicate the teacher's pose despite the torn ligament in his knee. When his legs were in position, he raised his arms, lifted his head, and closed his eyes. He took a deep breath through his nose. A gentle gust of wind rustled the oak leaves. He was calm. Centered. At peace.

"And back to Mountain."

He pulled out of the Warrior pose, put his feet together, and raised his arms over his head. He felt like he was eight feet tall.

"Let's finish today with some breathing and relaxation exercises. Sit down on your mat. Cross your legs comfortably in front of you. Keep your back *nice* and straight. That's it. Now close your eyes, and breathe. In. And out. Feel the connection between your mind and body, and the connection between yourself and the earth. Clear your mind. Allow the stress and tension locked inside your muscles to be released. In. And out. *Breathe*."

Cathay ended the class, and Christopher opened his eyes, refreshed and relaxed. He stood alone at the back of the group and quietly rolled up his mat as the rest of the class mingled under the tree, their conversation beginning to fill the air. He looked over the group, then turned to walk away.

"Christopher," a woman's voice called out, and he stopped and turned back to see Cathy striding toward him. "I had my eye on you today," she said. "You've made quite a bit of progress."

"Thank you," he said, shifting the rolled mat under his arm.

"I hope you're planning on continuing. You've shown a lot of potential."

He nodded. "I think I will. To be totally honest though, before this, I always thought all this yoga and meditation crap was a bunch of hippie-dippy bullshit."

Cathy smiled.

"No offense," he rushed to say.

"None taken," she said, waving the comment away. "You're not the first person I've heard express that very sentiment." She eyed the mingling class under the tree. "There's more than one convert in the group back there."

"Good to know."

"So listen, Christopher, it's such a lovely day. Would you care for a walk?"

He smiled. "Sounds nice, but there's somewhere I have to be. And believe me, if I could get out of it, I would. Maybe next time though."

"I look forward to it, Mr. James."

"Shit," said Christopher, standing over the pit.

"Literally, dude. It's pretty gnarly down there," said Sean.

"Can't believe I turned down a walk with Cathy for... this."

"It's gotta be done, my man. When your number is up for outhouse duty, there's no way around it, bro."

They each put on a dust mask. Sean handed Christopher a long shovel, then picked another off the ground for himself, and the roommates began to dig out the decomposing waste piled up in the three-foot pit. One shovel full at a time, they deposited the foul-smelling goop into buckets.

"The farmers are gonna love this, man," said Sean through his mask. "Fertilizer!"

"At least it's not a total... *waste*."

Sean cocked his head. "Woah. Hold the phone, bro. Did you just make a *joke*, man?"

He shrugged coyly and smiled under his mask.

"Alert the news media! My man here, my main man, Mr. Christopher James, just made a funny. News at eleven!" Sean yelled to anyone within earshot.

"Yes, yes, Hell has frozen over. Now can we get this done, please?" he said, gesturing toward the pit.

"Alright, man, alright. Just thought I'd mark this monumental occasion."

They dug and scooped until their shovels could no longer reach the pile of waste.

"Looks like one of us is going in the hole," Christopher said.

"I'll put on the boots," Sean said.

Sean set down his shovel and picked up a pair of tall, water-proof boots, set aside for precisely this purpose.

"No," Christopher said. "I'll do it."

"You sure, man?"

"Yeah. I'm sure. Give me the boots."

He replaced his shoes with the boots then hopped into the pit, landing with a squish.

"Gross, dude."

"No *shit*," he said, flashing a wink.

Sean threw his head back and laughed. "Bro, two jokes in one day? I don't think I can handle it, dude. I'm dead. I'm dead, man!"

He chuckled to himself, then began the nasty work of shoveling the remainder of the stinking waste into buckets and handing them up to Sean.

Sean sat on the edge of the pit, dangling his feet over the edge. "This is the life, man, you know?"

"Maybe for you, up there."

"True, true. But still, man. Even down there, shoveling shit. Don't you just... feel *alive*? Like, more than you did before?"

He glanced at Sean, then went back to work without answering.

"What did you do?" Christopher asked. "Before."

"I was an outdoorsman. Went hiking a lot. Rock climbing. I loved camping, man. Great way to blow off steam and vibe with nature."

"No, I mean, what did you *do*?"

"Like for a job?"

"Yeah, for a job."

"Oh, man, I worked for some company downtown, in one of those shiny glass buildings that all look the same. I can't even remember the company's name anymore..."

He leaned on the shovel. "An office worker. Wouldn't have guessed that." He shook his head in disbelief.

"... something Dynamics..."

"So, what did you do there?" he asked, trying to regain Sean's attention.

"Oh, dude, I was an I.T. guy."

"I.T.? I *really* didn't see that coming."

"Yeah, man, I was real good with computers. Messed around with them a lot when I was a kid. Self-taught, man, you know? I hated those corporate help desk jobs though. All those bright fluorescent lights in those dull offices with white walls, and seventeen people screaming at you on the phone all at once, you know, man? I don't miss it at all. Yeah, I'm much happier out here, shoveling shit."

Christopher nodded. "I can't argue with any of that. Wasn't much one for the corporate world, myself." He filled a bucket and handed it up to Sean.

"So, you and Wendy, huh?" Sean asked. "You guys looked pretty into each other at dinner the other night."

Caught off guard, he tried to gauge his roommate's expression, then went back to shoveling.

"You saw us?"

"Yeah, man, it was pretty obvious. Off in your own little world. We all just left you two alone."

He rested his shovel against the side of the pit and gathered himself.

"I was gonna try to avoid the topic, to be honest, but I guess it's best if we talk about it."

"What do you mean, bro?"

"About Wendy. You're not mad?"

"Why would I be mad, man?"

Christopher cleared his throat. "Aren't you two... together?"

Sean laughed. "Naw, man! It's not like that."

"So, you're *not* together? Wasn't she with you the day I moved in?"

"Yeah, dude, she was."

Puzzled, he looked up at Sean, squinting into the sun. "I'm confused."

"It's not that complicated, bro. You're just stuck in the past, man, the way things used to be."

"I'm not sure what you mean. People don't have relationships here?"

"Of course they do! We're human beings, man, it's what we do."

"Then...?"

"Look, bro, it's like this. Back in the Before Times, it was like... you had to get a license from the government to get married, and have lawyers divide up property if you got divorced. People tried to *own* each other, you know? Even when people were just dating, it was like claiming a person to be *yours*, like they belong to you. But here, man, all that toxic ownership crap got thrown right out the window. This was a chance to start over. To be free, man."

He stood in silence for a moment, processing what Sean had said. It sounded like some kind of free love bullshit. Maybe a nice idea in theory, but surely it went against human nature. People's feelings would always get in the way.

He pulled down his mask. "So... you're not mad?"

"Dude, that's what I'm trying to tell you, there's nothing to be mad about. I don't own Wendy, man, or anyone else for that matter. It's not up to me to decide who she can be with and who she can't, it's up to her. She can be with whoever she wants. I mean, look around, bro. The world ended. Nobody has any, like, *official claim* on anybody else anymore."

"Nobody here is exclusive? There aren't couples?"

"You're thinking about it too hard, man. You gotta loosen up. If people wanna be together, like exclusively, they can be together. If they don't, they don't. It's up to them, man. It's their choice. But the main thing is to treat people with respect, bro, like human beings, not property. That's all there really is to it. Respect and dignity, open communication, man, and the rest just kinda works itself out."

Christopher nodded, then pulled the mask back over his face. "Let's get this finished up," he said. "Then we can drop off this load of crap at the farm."

"Oh, man, you're killing me today, bro," Sean said with a laugh.

The sounds of construction filled the interior of the former leasing office. Hammering, sawing, sanding. The noise echoed through the building and the smell of freshly cut wood hung in the air. Light streamed in through the windows high above the foyer, casting bold rays across the room, illuminating the sawdust. New Concord would soon have a library.

Simone stood in the center of the workspace. A blueprint in her hands, she directed traffic as workers carried tools and supplies from place to place. Planks of wood, hammers and saws, nails and screws, tape measures, bottles of glue and sheets of sandpaper—Simone conducted the orchestra. Soon, newly built bookcases would fill the space.

Christopher worked diligently alongside a dozen others and hammered one last nail into a tall bookcase resting on its back.

"Okay, I think this one is done," he said. "Let's lift 'er up."

Several people dropped what they were doing and gathered around to help. Everyone grabbed an end and waited for Christopher to give the command to lift.

"On three," he said. "One, two, three, and lift!"

With their combined strength, the crew easily stood the bookcase on its base. Simone cheered, and the rest of the workers joined her in a round of applause.

"Where to?" Christopher asked, and Simone checked the blueprint and pointed to a bare wall across the room.

"Everyone ready to lift? We're going to the far wall over there." He nodded toward their destination, then he turned and shouted over his shoulder, "Heads up, everyone. Make a hole, we're coming through."

He made eye contact with each of his coworkers to make sure they were ready. Once they were in position, he called out another countdown, and together the team lifted the heavy bookcase a few inches off the ground and walked it carefully across the foyer. At Christopher's direction, they rotated the unit and gently eased it into place against the wall.

"Well done, everyone!" Simone shouted from the center of the room, pumping her fist in the air. Christopher dusted himself off and walked toward her. "You're a natural, Mr. James."

"Thanks. I have a bit of experience with carpentry. Not a ton, but a little."

"Oh, that's not what I meant."

He tilted his head and narrowed his eyes, curious.

Simone flicked her glasses down to the end of her nose and peered over them. A sage smile spread across her face.

"You're a leader, Christopher. A natural leader."

The gong rang, then rang again, and again, and again—long, slow chimes that filled the air like church bells, a twinge of melancholy laced through the tinny sound.

Christopher set down *Man's Search for Meaning*, which he had been reading on the couch in the apartment.

"What's all that about? Not time for dinner yet, is it?"

"That's the signal for a community gathering," Sean said. "Hope everything's okay."

The roommates headed toward the green, along with everyone else in New Concord, a murmur growing as the crowd converged.

Christopher leaned in close to Sean. "This is odd, right?" he said, barely above a whisper.

"Yeah, totally. Haven't had an emergency meeting since the early days, if that's what this is."

The residents funneled onto the green, congregating on the grass in the very center of the community. The sun shone brightly as cottony white clouds drifted overhead. People sat on the warm grass. Sean and Christopher followed suit then waited for the rest of the community to gather.

Once everyone had settled in, Simone stepped forward. The murmur of the crowd quieted as everyone sat up to listen.

"Thank you all very much for coming," Simone began, her voice booming over the green. "You're probably wondering why you've been called here today. I wish I could bring you all together under happier circumstances, but I'm sorry to say I have some bad news I need to share with you."

Christopher turned and scanned the crowd. The concern on his neighbors' faces was evident.

"As I'm sure most of you knew, our friend and neighbor Thomas Walker has been fighting type one diabetes, a disease he's had since he was a small child, and I regret to say that Thomas, our little Tommy, lost his battle this morning."

A collective groan rose from the crowd. "No," someone cried, and people all around Christopher shook their heads, pressed their hands to their foreheads, and wiped tears from their eyes. "Oh, man," Sean said quietly, and he hung his head between his knees.

"This was something we knew would happen eventually," Simone continued, "but that doesn't make it any easier. We will all miss his bright smile, his warm laugh, his tender hugs, and the joy he brought to all of us during his all-too-short life."

Christopher leaned over to Sean and whispered, "Who was Thomas?"

"He was that tall, skinny kid. I'm sure you saw him around."

"The one talking to Diego at dinner the other day?"

"Yeah, that was him, man."

Simone gestured to a woman seated near the front.

"Now I'd like to ask Tommy's mother to say a few words, if she's feeling up to it. Diane?"

A blonde woman stood, and Simone embraced her. She sobbed into the leader's shoulder, then gathered the strength to turn and face the community. Her face was red and streaked with tears.

"Thank you all for being here with me. I know my little Tommy would appreciate everyone coming out today. He loved you all very much. He was such a sweet boy and he brought me nothing but joy. I just can't believe he's gone," she said, dropping her head.

"We're all here for you, Diane," said a voice from the crowd.

"Thank you. I know you are." She raised her head and wiped the tears from her eyes. "And thank you to Dr. Rajavi, for always taking such good care of Tommy. He really loved you, and I know this is a really hard day for you, too. I also want to thank Diego and Jordan and their team. It was because of you, always putting yourselves at risk, out there looking for insulin, that I was able to have this last year with him. And I know he was grateful for your effort, too."

He scanned the crowd and found Diego sitting near the front, trying his best to put on a stoic face.

"I love you, Thomas. I love you so much, and I always will. Goodbye, my sweet boy."

Simone comforted her again then asked if anyone else would like to say a few words. One by one, the people of New Concord rose to speak. They told stories about Thomas and talked about how he had touched their lives.

Christopher sat in silence, observing the grief felt by so many over the loss of just one precious life.

Christopher sat with Sean at a table under the canopy. A gust of warm wind rustled the branches of the trees on the green and dried the tears of the subdued dinner crowd.

"I didn't know him real well or anything," Sean said, "but I'm gonna miss Tommy, man. He was a cool kid."

Cristopher nodded, not knowing what to say. He scanned the mournful faces of the community as they ate. The murmur of conversation was hushed.

Sean cocked his head and narrowed his eyes. "What's that?" he asked.

"What's what?"

"That sound. You don't hear that?"

He cocked his head and listened. Another gust of wind rushed through the air, stirring the leaves and flapping the canopy.

"I don't hear anything."

The breeze dissipated. The trees fell quiet.

"That!"

Then he heard it: the snarl of engines, somewhere in the distance.

"Shit, you're right," he said, his eyes growing wide.

The sound of the motors ripped through the air, getting closer.

"I've heard this before. The ATVs." He shot up from his seat. "Simone," he yelled.

Panic surged through the gathered residents. Someone gasped, and people scrambled from their seats.

"Quiet! Everyone!"

The crowd turned toward the voice. Simone stood on the crate at the end of the canopy, her arms in the air.

"Everyone, listen carefully."

The sound of the engines grew louder.

"Whatever is coming, we know we're strongest when we stick together, so that's exactly what we're gonna to do. We're gonna stay calm and stick together. And remember, it's been a minute now, but this ain't nothing we haven't done before. We're gonna be just fine." She looked over the crowd. "Jordan, where are you?"

A hand shot up. "I'm here."

"I need you to get the kids to safety."

Jordan nodded. "Kids, let's go, come with me. Quickly."

The children snaked through the crowd toward Jordan, who then led them away.

"Everyone else, to the front gate," Simone said. "Stay together, and stay calm."

Everyone filed out from under the canopy, walking quickly across the green toward the gate. Christopher hobbled toward Simone.

"Weapons," he said, his pulse quickening. "We need guns. I've seen these guys before. They're no joke."

"No time," she said, and she strode to the front of the pack.

The motors buzzed like chainsaws as the residents, over one-hundred strong, marched to the gate.

"Everyone, stand together. All together, right here," Simone said, positioning the residents on the drive, blocking the way in with a wall of humanity behind the open gate. She stood on the front line, her back straight, chin raised.

Christopher staked out a spot on the periphery of the crowd, finding a vantage point with a good view of the gate, just as three riders on ATVs came into view on the road.

"Down a few guys from last time," he said to himself.

The vehicles came to a stop just beyond the gate. Their riders were fully covered in camo shirts and pants and wore chest protectors with shoulder pads and helmets with dark lenses, hiding their eyes.

"How can we help you, gentlemen?" Simone asked.

The lead rider rose from his seat and stood on his ATV. He drew a handgun from a holster at his side.

"We want your food and your water," the rider said through his helmet.

"Anything else?"

"A woman," he said, raising the gun.

"And if we refuse?"

The two other riders, still seated, drew their weapons. Simone eyed them and took a breath. If she was nervous, she was hiding it well.

"We're happy to share with those who come in peace," Simone said, "but we cannot do so under threat. And we certainly will not turn over any of our residents."

"Lady, in case you hadn't noticed," said the lead rider, "you've got three guns on you. You'll do what we say, or your people are gonna start eating bullets."

"*You* may notice that you're greatly outnumbered. How many bullets you got in that gun?"

"We'll start with you and see how far we get," the man said, pointing the gun at Simone.

Christopher pushed forward. "I've seen you before," he said. "There were more of you then. What kind of ragtag outfit you running?"

The man took the gun off Simone and aimed at Christopher.

"Who are you?"

"Things must not be going too well out there, huh?"

"You shut the fuck up."

Simone looked at Christopher, then back at the group of riders.

"This man here," Simone said, pointing at Christopher, "came to us from the outside. Others here have as well. Any of you are welcome to join us, on the condition that you lay down your weapons and join us in peace."

The two seated riders exchanged a glance.

"We have food, water, shelter," Simone continued, "a whole functioning community. We're always willing to help those in need."

"We do not lie down for anyone," said the leader, raising his voice. "We go where we please and we take what we want. This conversation is over."

The man aimed at Simone. He put weight on the trigger.

"Captain."

The lead rider turned around.

"Maybe we should talk this over," said the rider on the left.

The leader looked at the rider on the right, who nodded in agreement. He stared down his subordinates then shook his head. He whipped back around to face the phalanx of residents.

"We are going to go have a little chat," he said, gesturing with his gun. "While we're gone, say your goodbyes to your friends. Not all of you are going to make it out of this alive."

He sat down on his ATV, revved the engine, and peeled away, his two followers in tow. The three riders disappeared from view as they rounded the corner.

"Everyone stay calm," Simone ordered, hushing the nervous chatter of the crowd. "Listen to me. It doesn't sound like this guy wants to negotiate peacefully. If they come back, we're gonna have to fight, so we need to be ready. I need our strongest and fastest people at the front, and if things get ugly we'll rush 'em. It's the best chance we have."

The crowd shifted as the most physically fit among them stepped forward.

Simone looked at Christopher and mouthed, "Thank you," then she turned to hash out strategy with the people on the front lines.

He took a breath, adrenaline surging through him. He had surprised himself by coming forward, putting himself in the line of fire, but there was no time for psychoanalysis or second-guessing. The road was quiet. He listened for the sound of engines.

There was a slight commotion in the crowd. Diego and another man stepped forward, holding guns. Simone directed Diego to one end of the front line and the second man to the other. They each settled into position, holding their weapons inconspicuously at their sides.

A sharp pop rang out from somewhere in the distance. The sound echoed off the buildings behind them, followed closely by two more loud pops. "Gunfire," Christopher said, then the ATVs came blaring down the road.

"Everyone, get ready," Simone shouted. "This is it."

"There's only two of them," Christopher yelled back to the crowd as the ATVs came into view around the corner.

The remaining ATVs came to a stop in front of the gate. The leader was missing.

The riders dismounted and held their guns up in the air as they walked through the gate toward the crowd.

Simone put her hand in the air, signaling to the crowd. Everyone held their positions.

The two riders set their weapons on the ground and took off their dark-lensed helmets. One was middle-aged, the other younger, maybe in his twenties.

"We want to take you up on your offer," the older man said. "My name is Dale. This is my son, Jim. If you'll have us, we'd like to stay."

"What happened to the other guy?" Christopher asked.

"He won't be bothering you anymore."

Christopher had been up for hours, pacing around his room in the still-dark morning, waiting for sunrise. He went to the window for what must have been the fortieth time and stuck a finger through the blinds. The soft orange glow of the sun was just beginning to bleed over the horizon. "Finally," he said.

The sharp, metallic rapping of the knocker sounded through the apartment.

He took a deep breath and looked in the mirror. He had begun to fill out, gaining back a few pounds of muscle and body fat. Dressed in a tan t-shirt, jeans, and boots, he was as ready as he could be. He exited the bedroom to find Sean had gotten out of bed to answer the door. Jordan stood in the doorway.

"Dude, did you have to use the knocker?" Sean said. "I think I pulled a muscle, I bolted out of bed so fast."

"Sorry, princess, I know you need your beauty sleep," Jordan said.

"You know it." He yawned and shuffled back into his room. "Good luck out there, man," he said sleepily, shutting the door behind him.

"Just be glad he wasn't naked," Christopher said, and Jordan raised her eyebrows. "Seriously, that guy has no shame."

Jordan smirked but quickly got down to business. She looked him directly in the eye.

"You ready for this?"

"Yes."

"You remember the rules?"

"Yes."

"If you do something stupid and cause a problem out there, this'll be your first and *last* run. You follow my lead. And Diego's. Got it?"

He nodded.

"I want to hear you say it."

"I understand."

"Good. Then I believe this belongs to you."

Jordan reached behind her back and pulled out Christopher's Glock 17. She held it out to him, and he did his best to hide his excitement behind a stone-cold expression. He nodded, wordlessly acknowledging her leap of faith. She nodded back.

He reached out and accepted the weapon. Its textured grip was instantly familiar, like reuniting with an old friend. He measured its weight in his hand. Only two months had passed since he left the bunker but, holding the Glock in his hand, it may as well have been another lifetime. The lonely yard hidden behind the pines, a distant memory.

"You got a holster for that?"

He lifted his eyes from the gun. "Yeah, I do."

"Grab it, and a couple spare mags, and let's get going."

He went back to his room and found the holster tucked away in a drawer. He put it on and holstered the weapon, pocketed two spare magazines, then went back to the door.

"Okay, soldier. Time for your first supply run," Jordan said.

"I'm ready."

They made the short trek from the apartment building to the cars parked along the loop. Diego was leaning against the side of the black SUV. Two other men stood beside him, talking and laughing. The red pickup truck was parked directly behind the SUV.

"Hey, there they are," Diego said. "You two get lost or something?"

"Just trying to delay the inevitable moment I had to see your face." Jordan shot back, and the other two men laughed.

"But I like my face," Diego said, feigning hurt feelings.

"That makes one of us," Jordan said as she and Christopher joined the group, and she winked and blew him an exaggerated kiss. Diego grabbed it from the air and held it to his heart.

Christopher stood a half step behind Jordan. Diego pushed himself off the SUV and stood upright. "Why don't you introduce the new guy to the team?" he said to Jordan, his eyes locked on Christopher.

"Christopher, you've already met Diego," Jordan said.

Diego waved an indifferent two-fingered salute over his head.

"This is Dan. Dan, Christopher."

Dan was very tall, very thin, and very pale, his blonde hair cut close on the sides but left longer on the top and styled so that it stood up on end. He reached out and shook Christopher's hand. "Pleasure."

"And this is Tyreek. Tyreek, meet Christopher."

Tyreek had light brown skin, short black hair, and a ring through the cartilage between his nostrils. "Hey, what's up, man?"

"Okay, everybody knows everybody," Jordan said impatiently. "Let's get this show on the road." She flicked Christopher with the back of her hand. "New guy, you're with me in the truck."

Tyreek and Dan piled into the SUV, and Diego went around and got in the driver's seat. Christopher followed Jordan to the truck and got in on the passenger side.

"New guy?"

A smile formed on Jordan's cheek as she turned the ignition.

"From here on out, no joking around," Jordan said. "Focus up. Stay sharp. Got it?"

He drew a long breath and hardened his face, then he turned to Jordan and nodded. "Let's roll."

Jordan rolled down the window and signaled to Diego in the SUV, and he nodded back through the side mirror. The SUV roared to life with a deep rumble and pulled out onto the loop. Jordan pressed the gas, and the engine rattled and hummed. The two vehicles moved in unison toward the gate.

They rolled along the loop, passing through New Concord as its early risers began their day. Residents headed for the showers with towels slung over their shoulders while others gathered around the well with bottles and buckets in their hands. Cathy unrolled her yoga mat under the old oak. The chickens stirred in their coop. To the east, the morning sun hung low over the tree line. Sparrows and cicadas filled the air with music.

The black SUV passed through the open gate, followed closely by the red pickup. The vehicles turned onto the road, out into the desolation of abandoned houses, gas stations, pharmacies, convenience stores, and office parks. Beyond New Concord's borders, for the first time since he had arrived, he was suddenly vulnerable, small, exposed. His stomach churned as he stared through the truck's windows at the overgrown remains of civilization as it passed by. He fingered the holstered handgun at his side.

"You okay over there?" Jordan asked.

"I'm fine," he answered without breaking his gaze through the passenger window.

"If we need to go back..."

He cocked his head slightly toward the driver. "I said I'm fine."

"Okay," she said with a nod. "Just making sure."

The vehicles passed through a stretch of road peppered with entrances to subdivisions.

"We've already canvassed most of this area," Jordan said. "All these houses. Went door to door, looking for supplies, and for anyone left alive, of course. We rescued as many people as we could in those early days... if they wanted to be rescued, that is." She gave him a knowing look, and he turned to meet her eye.

"Where are we headed?" he asked, changing the subject.

"Down the East-West Connector, toward West Hampton. Every time we go out, we push a little farther."

"So what are we looking for?"

"When we stop, it's going to be your job to stay with the cars. You're on security detail today. Leave the looking to the rest of us."

He turned to the window and scowled.

Jordan glanced over at him. "It's important," she said. "If something happens to the cars, we're stranded out there and might never make it back. Someone always keeps watch. This is your first run, so today it's you."

He nodded.

They drove for over half an hour, and the vehicles kept a tight formation even as they maneuvered around abandoned cars and debris. No sign of life was visible from the road.

Finally, they pulled into the parking lot of a supermarket then rolled to a stop along the curb near the road. The team exited the vehicles cautiously, listening carefully and watching for movement as they stepped out into the open. They quietly pressed the car doors shut.

Grass and weeds had grown through the sidewalks and the cracked asphalt of the parking lot. Most paper trash littered across the landscape had long since disintegrated into the earth, but plastic grocery bags clung like paper mâché to lamp posts and utility poles and the wheels of rusted shopping carts.

The supermarket's large windows were broken, as well as its automatic sliding doors. Shards of glass lay scattered across the pavement, reflecting the sun.

A jumbled pile of human bodies stretched from the doorway out into the parking lot, their organic tissue decomposed, leaving only bones wrapped in tattered clothing.

"Okay, let's go," Diego said, looking over the grim scene, satisfied they were not in immediate danger. He shot Christopher a stern look. "Keep your eye out. Honk if there's any trouble."

"There's a good view of the surrounding area, here by the road," Jordan said. "Stay quiet. We won't be long."

Each team member slipped an empty duffle bag over their shoulders. They drew their weapons, wordlessly acknowledged each other, then walked toward the supermarket. Tyreek and

Dan trailed closely behind Diego and Jordan, each scanning the surroundings on their side of the formation as they moved in unison. Not up to military standards, but it was clear they had developed good teamwork with practice. His four companions crossed the parking lot, stepped over the piles of bones wrapped in clothes, crunched over the broken glass of the supermarket's doors, and disappeared into the building.

An eerie quiet fell over the desolated suburban sprawl. The big-box supermarket had a familiar brick facade and thick brick columns, the company's familiar logo spelled out in large green letters on an arch above the entrance. The dingy, decaying structure was like a ruin of an ancient basilica.

He took a deep breath, trying not to let his mind wander.

The late-August sun was bright, and the air was thick with humidity. Sweat beaded on his brow and began to soak through his shirt. He rested his hand on the hilt of his Glock and turned slowly in place, surveying the landscape. The overgrown, decorative trees planted in the parking lot swayed gently in the warm breeze. A large black bird cawed from the top of a streetlamp, and the sound somehow emphasized the silence and stillness of the place.

He looked at the shattered doors of the supermarket. What was the team looking for inside? How long were they going to take? He huffed impatiently.

A blast of cool air blew through the parking lot, and the trees rustled loudly, their green leaves flickering silver. He turned into the rising wind. A dark cloud approached from the west.

"Shit, that's coming on fast," he said. "They better get a move on." He turned his eyes back to the storefront and was relieved to see the members of the scavenger team making their way through the shattered doors. First, Tyreek and Dan, several pink and purple boxes stacked precariously in their arms. Diego and Jordan followed, each carrying a load of the colorful boxes.

"Open the trunk!" Tyreek shout-whispered, and Christopher pulled the handle, opening the SUV's rear hatch. Tyreek and Dan piled their boxes into the trunk, and Diego and Jordan soon did the same.

Christopher glanced at the sky. The storm was close. He turned to help Jordan arrange the boxes.

"Tampons and pads. You guys think you got enough?" he asked sarcastically.

"Not yet," Jordan said, straight-faced. "We're going back in for more."

"Going back in? Are you fucking nuts?" Christopher asked. "That storm's gonna be on us in just a few minutes."

"Then we'll have to get wet," Jordan said. "We hit the motherload in there. The storage room in the back is practically untouched."

"Chris, you're coming in with us this time," Diego said.

"What about the cars?"

"We'll have to risk it. We need as many hands as we can get."

Christopher peeked over his shoulder at the approaching blanket of clouds and steeled himself. He turned back to the team. "Okay. Let's go."

Lightning flickered to the west. The wind rose, and the rustling leaves sounded like an ocean. The team hustled across the parking lot, dispensing with tactics and stealth. They high-stepped over the piles of bones and glass, then careened into the supermarket.

Christopher stopped in his tracks after crossing the threshold. The rest of the team continued straight to the storeroom in the back.

"Holy shit."

The interior was dark and grimy. Dirt and pollen stained the tile floor. Leaves blown in through the broken windows littered the front of the store. The shelves were stripped bare, and one was tipped over, smashed against the next, a pair of bony legs protruding from beneath. Skeletal remains lay scattered across the tile, concentrated near the entrance.

He stood still, surrounded by bones wrapped in ragged clothes, imagining a desperate struggle for the door—the pushing, the clawing, the trampling. It was like a scene out of the war.

Jordan turned back to him. "Come on!" she said, waving her arm furiously.

Dazed, he staggered forward in slow motion, trying not to step on the bodies.

"Christopher, wake up," she said, clapping her hands. "We need you." She came back to him in a huff, crunching someone's ribs as she stepped. She took his hand and yanked him forward. "Let's *go*."

His mind refocusing, he lumbered forward, one foot in front of the other, pulled by Jordan's hand.

"It's like this everywhere we go. Bodies all over the place," Jordan said as they made their way to the back. "I'd say you get used to it, but you never really do."

They pushed through the swinging doors to the storeroom. Diego, Dan, and Tyreek all held flashlights, illuminating the darkness with dancing spotlights. The walls were lined with metal warehouse shelves, stocked floor to ceiling with boxes of goods.

"How?" Christopher asked, not directing the question to anyone in particular. "How is this... *here*?"

"No clue," Dan said while scouring the shelves and putting items in his duffle. "But it is."

"Could have been the stampede," Tyreek said from a ladder, peering into the boxes on the top shelf. "Maybe something spooked 'em. Someone pulls a gun and fires a shot, everyone bolts for the door. Back of the store goes untouched. Something like that."

"Seems plausible," Diego said, chiming in from the end of the row. "And it's just blind luck no one's come across it since."

"It's not luck," Jordan said, clicking on her own flashlight. "There's just not many people left to find it. Everyone's dead. Except..." A booming roll of thunder rattled the shelves. The air pressure shifted in the building as a stiff wind blew through the broken windows at the front of the store. "...us."

The team exchanged wide-eyed looks, their sense of urgency electrifying the air. Christopher jumped into action, and everyone else quickened their pace. They stuffed loose items into their duffle bags: hand sanitizers and soaps, sticks of deodorant, toothpaste and toothbrushes, sunscreen, matches, lighter fluid, batteries, and bottles of painkillers, antihistamines, and cough syrup. They lifted whole crates of items packed in bulk from the shelves. Cans of soup, packs of ramen, boxes of rice, pasta, and cereal, oats and granola, peanut butter, and bags of flour and sugar were all stacked by the door.

Another roll of thunder rumbled the supermarket. The sound of rain began to tap on the thin roof.

The pile by the door grew. "This all gonna fit?" Christopher asked.

"We'll make it fit," Diego said, adding more to the pile.

When they decided they had enough, the team gathered around the stack and formulated a strategy to carry it to the cars as efficiently as possible.

The tapping rain turned into a roar, and Christopher's heart sank. "That's not going to make it any easier," he said, raising his eyes to the ceiling.

"Should we wait it out or make a break for it?" Dan asked.

"No way to know how long this shit is gonna last. Could be hours," Tyreek said.

Everyone exchanged anxious glances, waiting for a decision to be made.

Christopher flashed back to the night he rode out the storm in the bunker, and to the next morning, emerging from below to find everything he had built left in ruins. "Let's get the hell out of here," he said.

"I agree, I say we go now," Jordan said. "We could be waiting all day, and I don't want to get stuck so far from home after dark."

Diego looked at each member of the team in turn, then nodded. "Okay," he said. "Grab as much as you can and let's go."

They quickly decided which items could make the trip in the pickup's bed and which would go in the SUV. Leaving their duffle bags on the floor for the second trip, they each grabbed as much from the pile as they could, then pushed through the swinging doors and headed toward the front entrance. With the weight precariously balanced in their arms, they stepped carefully over bodies and debris. Tyreek followed Dan's lead through the dark, and Christopher fell in behind Tyreek. Jordan and Diego took up the rear.

Dan stopped in his tracks, and Tyreek ran straight into his back, almost dropping the load balanced in his arms. "What the hell, man?" Tyreek said, but Dan just stared straight ahead, frozen. Tyreek peeked around his stack of goods, then he froze in place, too.

"What's the holdup?" Christopher asked, stepping around the two frozen men. He turned, following their gaze.

Near the front of the store, huddled next to one of the empty shelves, stood a thin woman with olive skin. She was drenched. Long black hair clung to her face and neck. She held a small knife in her hand, arm shaking as she pointed it toward them.

Christopher dropped his stack of goods and reached for his holstered Glock as the items clattered to the floor.

"No!" Jordan yelled, and she too dropped her stack and lunged forward to grab his arm before he could aim the weapon. "She's got a kid."

Peeking out from behind the soaked woman's leg was a young boy, his arms wrapped around her thigh, a baseball glove in his hand.

"She's just protecting her kid. Put the gun away," Jordan said, calming her voice.

He slowly lowered the weapon.

"No nos haga daño," the woman said, tears mixing with the rainwater on her cheeks. "Por favor, por favor, no le haga daño a mi hijo."

Diego slowly set down the load in his arms and approached the woman with his hands up. "Está bien. No se preocupe. No vamos a dañarles. Podría volver a guardar el cuchillo." Diego stepped closer to the frightened woman.

Trembling, the woman turned to shield her son and pointed the knife at Diego's neck. Keeping his eyes on the woman, Diego instructed the team to take a step backward with a wave of his arm. Christopher kept his gun at his side while he and the others retreated a few feet.

Christopher couldn't understand what he was saying, but Diego continued to speak to the woman in Spanish, a reassuring calmness in his voice. He gestured to the team and pointed out the door. The fear in the woman's eyes began to fade. She lowered the knife and wiped the tears and rain from her face.

"Looks like he's explaining that we're just trying to go home," Jordan whispered.

The young boy peeked out from behind his mother's leg and made eye contact with Christopher, then bashfully tucked his head back out of sight. He waited for the hiding boy to take another peek, then waved when he did. The boy giggled and buried his face in his mother's leg.

Lightning lit up the room, the thunder rumbling menacingly as the downpour continued.

Diego turned to face the team.

"They're coming with us.

The two vehicles pressed through the storm. Jordan led in the red truck, its headlights illuminating the rain blowing across the road in thick horizontal bands. The cabin swayed with each powerful gust. Jordan gripped the wheel with tight fists and squinted through the rain while Christopher held the handle on the passenger door. Soaked to the bone, their clothes clung to their bodies.

The wiper blades whipped back and forth over the foggy windshield, barely keeping up with the heavy sheets of rainwater. "I can't see a damn thing," Jordan said, reaching over the wheel to wipe the glass.

The team had rushed out into the rain, packing the vehicles with all the goods from the supermarket, then Christopher and Diego went back to collect the stranded woman and her son. Diego put his arm around the woman and led her across the parking lot while Christopher picked up the child and carried him in his arms to the safety of the SUV.

A strong gust of wind blasted the truck, and the steering wheel pulled sharply to the right. Jordan gasped and yanked it back, steadying the vehicle. "Holy fuck," she said, catching her breath.

"Stay focused. Take it slow." He turned to Jordan and said with confidence, "We're gonna make it."

Jordan glanced at him, then steadied herself and focused on the road. She nodded her head. "We're gonna make it."

The pair of vehicles rolled through the gates of New Concord under a sky streaked with rose and lavender, the remnants of the storm glowing in the twilight sun. The truck and the SUV parked on the loop not far from the canopy.

"I told you we'd make it," Christopher said.

Jordan punched him in the arm, then smiled.

A cheer erupted from the green, and a few people made their way over to the vehicles. Christopher and the rest of the team stepped out of the cars, followed by the rescued woman and child. The gathering throng gasped, then cheered again.

"Step back everyone, step back. Give them some room," said Simone, emerging from the crowd. Diego whispered in her ear. She nodded then turned back to the residents. "I need someone to run and fetch Dr. Rajavi. And let's get these good folks some food. Quickly now."

Her face drained of color, the woman looked frail and exhausted. Diego whispered something in her ear and led her toward the canopy, but she turned back forcefully. "Mijo," she cried.

"No se preocupe. Aquí está. No le vamos a dañar a su hijo," Diego said in a calming tone. "Cuándo fue la última vez que comieron bien?"

The young boy held his baseball glove tightly to his chest. He was thin but seemed less weak and tired than his mother. Panic swept over his face as his mother was led away through the crowd.

Simone turned back and called out to Christopher. He met her eyes then she pointed to the child. His face curled in confusion, and he pointed to his chest and mouthed back, "Me?" Simone nodded her head then turned and continued toward the canopy with Diego, Jordan, and the boy's mother.

The child began to cry.

"Shit," he muttered, then he took a breath and knelt to the boy's level. "Uhh, hey... kid."

The boy sobbed harder.

Christopher looked at him helplessly. "Eh, hey, don't cry. Shh, shh." He raised his eyes to the heavens and took a breath, then looked the weeping boy in the eye. "My name is Christopher," he said, pointing to himself. "Uhh, mi... nombre... Christopher." He pointed at the child. "What's *your* name? Uhh, qué... es... tu nombre?" The boy stopped crying and sniffed to clear his running nose. Tears stained his dirty cheeks. "Qué es tu nombre?" he asked again more confidently as he wiped away the boy's wet cheeks with his thumb.

"Me llamo Cristóbal," the boy said meekly, wiping his eyes.

"Cristóbal? No, that's my name. *I'm* Christopher," he said, tapping his chest. "What's *your* name? Tu nombre?" he asked, tapping the boy's chest.

"Me llamo Cristóbal," the boy said again, then Christopher understood.

"We have the same name," he said mostly to himself. He smiled. "Come on, let's go find some food."

He stood and held out his hand to Cristóbal. The boy took it, and together they followed the others to the canopy.

Voices buzzed under the canopy as concerned onlookers formed a semicircle around the bench where Cristóbal's mother had just been seated. Dr. Rajavi had made his way down to the green and stood ready to examine the refugees. Simone supervised the scene, keeping people from getting too close. Diego sat on the bench beside the woman and served as translator.

Christopher and Cristóbal crossed under the canopy and approached the cluster of people, hand in hand. Dr. Rajavi had just knelt in front of the woman when she saw her son arrive. "Cristóbal," the woman said, clearly drained and exhausted. She reached out for the boy.

"Mamá!" the small child called back as he bolted for his mother. Christopher, still holding his hand, snagged him before he could get too far and scooped him into his arms.

"We have to stand back," he said. "We need to give Mama some room while she gets checked out by the doctor. We can stand over here and watch, okay?" He wasn't sure if Cristóbal could understand him, but he patted the boy on the back as he spoke, and it seemed to be working. The child relaxed and rubbed his eyes.

Simone and Diego turned and saw him standing with the child in his arms, and Diego turned back to the woman and assured her that her son was in safe hands. Simone nodded to him.

Dr. Rajavi regained the woman's attention as he put on a pair of rubber gloves. "Miss, what is your name?" the doctor said, then he nodded to Diego to translate.

"Isabella."

"Good. Isabella, are you in any pain?"

She answered, then Diego translated. "I am very tired and very hungry, and my head aches."

The doctor nodded. "Well, we're going to take good care of you and your son. Would you allow me to examine you?"

Isabella listened to Diego's translation then nodded wearily.

Dr. Rajavi took the stethoscope from his neck and put the earpieces in his ears, then placed the diaphragm over his patient's heart. He moved it over her lungs and listened, then he moved around to her back and asked to take deep breaths. He draped the stethoscope over his neck, then reached into his bag, pulled out a thermometer, and asked her to open her mouth. He placed it under her tongue, then took the thermometer from her mouth after a few moments and read the results. Next, he went back to his bag and retrieved a blood pressure meter. He wrapped it around her bicep and pumped it full of air, then took note of the reading.

"One last test, Isabella," Dr. Rajavi said. "Just a little pinch." Diego translated, and the doctor pinched the skin on her arm into a tent shape, then let go and watched it spring back into place.

Dr. Rajavi took off his gloves and sat on the bench next to Isabella. "Good news, everything looks pretty good, all things considered. I think you're suffering from dehydration and malnourishment, and you're running a bit of a fever. You need rest and nutrition, and you should be back on your feet in a few days."

Diego translated, and Isabella nodded. "Gracias," she said, her eyes half closed.

The doctor looked up at Simone. "Let's get her some food and water, and then we need to get her up to the Health Wing for some rest."

Simone directed a few bystanders to gather up plates of food for their new guests, and the doctor signaled Christopher to bring the boy forward. He plopped Cristóbal down on the bench next to the doctor.

"All right young man, let's see what's going on with you," the doctor said to the child, then Diego leaned in and translated. Dr. Rajavi began his examination of the boy, and Christopher stepped out of the way. He stood next to Simone.

"I hear you did well today," Simone said.

"News travels fast around here."

"I keep my ear to the ground."

"The storm made things more interesting than we were expecting."

"And picking up these two, as well."

"Just did what we had to."

Simone smiled. "You've come a long way, Mr. James. Perhaps further than you even realize."

Maybe she was right. Maybe he had adapted to life in New Concord better than he thought he could. Maybe this community concept wasn't so crazy after all. Maybe he had changed. Though not enough to admit it.

"He seems like he's taken a liking to you," Simone said, nodding toward the child.

He turned back to the doctor and the young boy.

"I guess so. He was scared and I just..."

"You did the kind and decent thing." Simone turned and looked up at him over the frames of her glasses. "The human thing."

"All I did was talk to him. Calmed him down."

"Exactly," Simone said. "You were there for him. Sometimes that's all any of us really need."

A group of children not too much older than Cristóbal arrived with plates of food and cups of water for Isabella and her son. Dr. Rajavi continued Cristóbal's exam with the help of Diego's translation.

Christopher turned Simone's words over in his mind. *The human thing.* They had just taken in two total strangers off the street. Those strangers were being cared for by a community doctor. Food and water were being given away with no expectation of anything in return. Several people stood by, ready to help with any need that might arise. It really was a fully functional community, its people connected, bound together in mutual service, everyone the better off for it.

"Christopher, I'm going to put you in charge of helping Isabella and Cristóbal get settled, once they're healthy and ready to move in, if that's what they decide to do."

"What? Me?" he asked. "There has to be someone better. I can't..."

"Yes. You can. I know you can."

"Why not Diego? I don't speak Spanish."

A sly smile formed at the corners of Simone's lips. "That doesn't matter."

Christopher opened the door to apartment unit 802 and invited Isabella and Cristóbal to cross the threshold with a slightly awkward gesture. "Well, uh... home sweet home."

Isabella flicked her eyes at Christopher and quickly pulled them back, then she leaned over her son and said something in Spanish that Christopher didn't understand. She patted the boy on the back, and he went charging through the doorway into the apartment, squealing with glee as he ran. She gathered herself with a breath then followed her son inside.

Christopher stepped into the unit and watched from the foyer as the mother and son explored their new home. Cristóbal tossed his baseball glove on the couch then raced from room to room, opening every door and peeking into every cabinet and drawer.

Isabella scanned the space with wide, disbelieving eyes. She moved slowly through the apartment, touching every surface gently, more like she was shopping in a store, being careful not to break anything, rather than moving into a new home.

Framed paintings were hanging on the walls, and flowers were in a vase on the table in the living room. The kitchen was stocked with utensils, plates and bowls, cups and pitchers, and water bottles for filling at the well. The linen closet was full of towels, washcloths, and spare sheets.

"This is all for you," he said, and the woman's eyes pooled with tears.

Cristóbal flew past her legs. "Ten cuidado, mi amor," Isabella said to her son, but he was already exploring the guest room before the message could reach his ears.

"They told me to let you know, everyone pitched in and donated spare supplies," he said. He dodged Cristóbal, who was pretending to be an airplane, zooming from the nook to the end of the living room. He turned back to Isabella and said, "I need to show you something," and he beckoned her with a wave.

She came through the door of the bedroom just as he was pulling open the drawers of the dresser, each stuffed with clothes. He then went to the closet and pulled open the door, revealing more clothes hanging inside.

"You should have everything you need, for you and your son."

Isabella put her hand over her mouth and shook her head. Tears slipped down her cheeks. "No lo creo. Es un milagro." She sank to the bed and put both hands over her face as she began to weep. "Es un milagro."

"Mamá, por qué lloras?" Cristóbal said as he came through the doorway. His mother held out her arms.

"Ven acá, m'ijito." The child came forward and leapt into his mother's arms, and she pulled him in tightly. "Mamá está bien. Vamos a quedarnos bien."

Christopher took a step back and leaned against the wall. He couldn't decipher the words spoken between the mother and her son, but he understood what they meant. There was a flutter in his chest and his nose tingled. Inhaling sharply, he put his hand to his face and turned away. Neither the woman nor her son would see the tear that escaped his eye.

Christopher opened his eyes. He took a deep breath of life-giving air. His mind was clear. His body was at ease, rested and refreshed. There was nowhere he needed to be, nothing specific he needed to do. If he wanted, he could spend all day under the covers, cozy and comfortable. He smiled at the thought.

He rolled over and put his arm around Wendy, still peacefully asleep beside him. Her bare shoulder and flame-kissed hair peeked out from beneath the sheet. He planted a gentle kiss on her butterfly tattoo and ran his hand through her hair. She breathed a soft "Good morning" as she woke.

"Think I'm going to go down to the green for some yoga. Wanna come?"

Still half asleep, she rolled over, stretched her arms, and arched her back. "Mmm, I could lie here all day, and I think I just might. You go ahead. I need my beauty rest before the big bash tonight."

"I certainly won't keep you from that," he said, then he kissed her champagne lips.

Yoga mat under his arm, Christopher was the first to arrive at the oak tree. He staked out a nice spot and took in the crisp September air, stretching while he waited.

Under the morning sun, people emerged from the apartment buildings that ringed the green. From his mat, he watched as they went about their routines—waiting their turn at the outhouses, heading to the showers, pulling water from the well, jogging around the loop—and it occurred to him that *he* was going about *his* daily routine. No longer an outsider, he was one of them. He was at peace, and just as free from stress and worry as everyone else in New Concord. His anxieties and fears, held so tightly within for so long, had been exorcised. Only in their absence could he feel their weight.

One by one, the yogis joined him under the oak tree. Cathy led the class, as she always did, and Christopher struggled through it as *he* always did. When it ended, he asked Cathy if she was still up for the walk she had asked him for, and she was. He tightened his knee brace then they walked the loop around New Concord.

The air passed through his lungs with a carefree ease. At that moment, he was exactly where he was meant to be, heading in exactly the right direction. Fully present, the clarity of mind was exhilarating. Would it last? Did everyone in New Concord feel this way?

As they walked, he hung on every word of Cathy's story about how she had been rescued by one of the first teams the fledgling community had sent to look for survivors. She lived in the row of high-priced townhouses just down the road, across the street from a trendy mixed-use development. Her husband was a corporate lawyer, and she had made the classic mistake of marrying for the money, against her better judgment, she explained. It was his third marriage, her second, and was loveless almost from the start. He was a workaholic. She was a free spirit, trapped in the sterile luxury of their townhome. Soon, her confinement became literal. On the day society fell, she had been home alone, as she seemingly always was. She waited for her husband to come home. For three days, she hid in the shadows and peeked out the windows, waiting, but he never came. On the fourth day, she saw a fleet of cars roll up to her row of townhouses. Friendly-looking people got out of the cars and called out for anyone who needed help, and she flew out the door to greet them. These friendly strangers helped her gather up some of her things and told her they would bring her to a community of survivors called New Concord. And that's exactly what they did. So here she was, no longer trapped and alone, but free and a valued member of the community, fulfilled, living a life of tranquility and harmony.

Cathy thanked him for the walk, and they agreed to have another sometime soon. "I'll see you tonight," she said. "Save a dance for me."

Cathy walked away, leaving Christopher alone on the loop.

He stood there for a moment, enjoying the atmosphere. The day was his to do with as he pleased. There was no reason to make a definitive decision. Not right away, anyway. Instead, he would stroll around, letting fate take the wheel until something struck his fancy.

He turned his face to the sun and basked in its warmth. Birds chirped pleasantly in the trees. Squirrels and chipmunks scurried across the grass. Children's laughter drifted through the air, coming from somewhere on the green. Behind him, something clicked along the pavement, and he turned around.

"Hey, Coco," he said with a smile. Open-mouthed, the brown dog pranced up to him, and he petted her head, her ears flopping up and down. "That's a good girl."

He knelt to Coco's level and stroked the fur on her neck.

"You know," he said, looking the dog directly in her dark brown eyes, "I never got a chance to thank you. You saved my life."

He snapped his fingers and held out his hand, and Coco raised her paw. Christopher shook it.

"Thanks," he said, and Coco licked him on the cheek. He smiled and wiped the slobber from his face. "Come on, girl. Walk with me for a while."

Coco walked by his side as he completed another loop around the community. The pair walked with an assured nonchalance, soaking in the last of the sultry summer until they came upon the path to the community's fruit and vegetable garden.

"I think I'll help out in the field today, if you don't mind," he said to Coco. He reached down and petted her head. "Thanks for the walk."

"Co-co," a young girl called out from a distance, and the dog's ears perked up. Her tongue hanging out, she looked up at him.

"Co-co."

"It's okay, girl. Go on," he said, and he smiled as Coco took off in the direction of the girl's voice.

He stepped off the loop, taking the path between the apartments. He went down the hill and opened the gate, and was pleased to find Jane right where he expected her to be.

He joined her in the field, and together they walked up and down the rows, watering the crops, then they harvested an assortment of grapes, squash, cauliflower, and broccoli. They joked and laughed as they worked. Christopher found her southern drawl and frank manner of speech endearing—a type of talk you can only get away with when you're older and quit caring what people think. The sun hung hot over the field, and they sweated through their clothes until their baskets were filled.

"It's funny," he said to Jane as they walked up the hill, "I never really had much of a green thumb. I had an apple tree in my backyard. Year after year, it refused to grow any apples. Edible ones, anyway."

"Just *one* apple tree?" Jane asked.

"Yeah, just one."

"Well, there ya go. Ya see, apple trees need a partner to bear fruit. Ya gotta plant different types'a trees 'round each other for cross-pollination. If you got a Baldwin or a Winesap you need a Whitney or a Wickson nearby. They don't do well on their own."

He shook his head, smiling to himself. Something so simple, completely overlooked.

He walked with Jane to the community kitchen. They found Anthony, Isaiah, and Jaylen inside, preparing the kitchen for the evening's meal. The crew was happy to see him and asked if he wanted to pitch in. He nodded. "Absolutely."

While they sliced and diced, chopped and stirred, the three young men regaled Christopher with restaurant war stories. He returned the favor by telling the story of the ant invasion in the bunker. The four friends laughed loudly while they worked.

To make time for the evening's festivities, they finished cooking early and rang the gong. The members of the community trickled in and got in line for food under the canopy. Christopher and his kitchen mates got their food and sat at a table, and soon they were joined by Wendy, Sean, and Jordan. The seven of them ate together. Smiles never left their faces.

Amid the laughter and stories crisscrossing the table, Christopher turned in his seat and looked out over the community gathered under the canopy. All the voices mingled in the air to create the distinct murmur of a crowd, a sound which was so disconcerting at first but was now familiar and cozy, filling him with warmth and comfort. He nodded. These were his people. He was home.

He turned back to the table and waited for a lull in the conversation.

"Anyone know where I can find a baseball?"

The residents made their way across the green from the canopy to the new library. Christopher settled on a spot by a brick retaining wall as the crowd gathered in front of the building. Everyone cheered as Simone emerged from among the people and ducked under the ribbon strung up between the columns on the patio. She turned to face the residents and raised her arms to quiet the crowd.

"Hey, y'all, I want to make this as short and sweet as I can," Simone began, and a hush fell over the audience as all eyes focused on her. "We've come a long way, don't you think? How 'bout a round of applause just... for *us*. For making it this far together."

Everyone clapped, and those who could put their fingers in their mouths and whistled. Christopher joined the sea of smiling faces in the round of applause.

"I think we'd all agree," Simone continued, "we've got a pretty good thing going here, and I hope none of y'all take that for granted. Because, you know, things didn't have to turn out this way. When things were at their worst, when it looked bleak and hopeless, when the world was literally falling apart, we didn't *have* to come together the way we did. There was nothing inevitable about it. But we stuck together, we worked hard, and we've built a place we can all be proud of."

The crowd cheered and clapped, and so did Christopher, a smile forming on his cheek.

"Because we all, each and every one of us, *chose* to be a part of something bigger than ourselves. We've sacrificed for each other, and we've built a place that's truly special. Tonight, we get to add something new to this special community. One more thing that we've worked hard for. One more thing that all will benefit from. Through these doors behind me is our new community library."

His insides fluttered as the crowd burst into an ovation. Simone let the community holler and cheer for a moment then she raised her arms again.

"This is a great day for everyone here in this place we call New Concord, but it's an especially great day for our children, who will now have a place they can go to grow their minds and explore new worlds. A place to learn, and dream, and *imagine*."

As Simone paused to allow the residents to clap, Christopher thought of the small bookcase left behind in his dark hideaway, and it occurred to him that he hadn't missed his collection of books since he had arrived in New Concord. Strange. Those books had been his only company on his small, lonely patch of land. They had reassured him, affirmed his convictions, and hardened his resolve to press on alone against the dark, terrifying void beyond his borders. And yet, he hadn't given them even the slightest passing thought since he left. Whatever wisdom he had gained from them had been rendered obsolete in this new reality.

"Let's get the children up here," Simone said enthusiastically. "Come on up, kids, I've got an important job for you."

A young girl brushed past Christopher as she snaked through the crowd, and several other children also weaved through the people and ducked under the ribbon to join Simone on the patio. Simone arranged them in a line behind the ribbon. The children waved and smiled at people in the crowd as Simone picked up a small box from the patio and reached inside.

"Now kids, I want you to be very careful with these. When we count down to zero, I want you all to cut the ribbon, okay?"

Simone went down the row and handed each child a pair of scissors. Once everyone was in position, she turned back to face the crowd.

"People of New Concord, let's help the kids out with a countdown from three. Three..."

The crowd chanted in unison, "... two... one... zero!" then each of the children snipped the ribbon, and the pieces twisted to the ground.

"Ladies and gentlemen, the New Concord Community Library is officially open," Simone declared, and the crowd's ovation soared over the green and the apartment buildings and echoed through the trees and the empty neighborhoods that surrounded their community.

Simone took the scissors from the children then opened the door to the library so they could be its first official patrons. As they ran inside the building, Simone turned back to the crowd and said with a smile, "Now let's not wreck the place on the first night, but everyone, please feel free to go in and take a look around inside." Then with a shimmy of her hips, she said, "And then I hope y'all are ready to get your groove on tonight."

The atmosphere glowed indigo as the sun was extinguished over the horizon. Christopher leaned against the retaining wall as everyone filed through the library door. He was in no rush, basking in his newfound serenity, just as he had all day. He drew a deep breath of the twilight air, perfectly content to be exactly where he was.

The last of the residents made their way into the building as those who had completed their tour made their way out. Christopher propelled himself off the wall with a nudge of his elbow, then went up the walk to the door and stepped inside.

The interior was dark despite the solar-powered lanterns scattered between the bookcases. Their pockets of white light cast long shadows onto the high ceiling. The murmur of hushed conversation and the smattering of laughter from the people still inside the library echoed through the building as he paced through the massive collection of books.

He came to one of the bookcases he had helped build and ran his hand along its sanded-smooth frame, nodding in approval. He turned in place. Row after row of bookcases were arranged in neat diagonals across the room, each filled with hundreds of books. Even under the sporadic lighting of the solar lanterns, it was impressive.

He stepped deliberately through each room of what was now the New Concord Community Library, taking his time as he marveled at the achievement. He hadn't done the work on his own. He hadn't even been the foreman on the job. He had merely been one of many whose labor had contributed to something larger than themselves. And he hadn't done it for personal gain, either. There had been no specific reward for contributing his time and energy to the project, and there would have been no punishment if he hadn't. The doing of the job had made him feel useful, engaging his body and mind. As he walked through the completed product, his heart swelled with pride. He couldn't think of a more personally fulfilling thing he had done in his life.

The library fell silent except for the sound of his steps, which echoed off the ceiling as he moved from room to book-filled room, and he realized he was the last left inside. His boots clicking against the smooth tile floor, he headed back to the front door, stopping at each island of white light to turn off the lanterns. He closed the door behind him and stepped back into the late-summer air filled with the song of crickets, cicadas, and katydids.

He headed toward the canopy across the green, knowing that's where everyone would be. Just as the white canvas came dimly into view through the dark, it was illuminated by strings of Christmas lights, splashing color through the fabric. The people gathered underneath clapped for the lights, and a small band of musicians began to play. The tables cleared away, people quickly made use of the dance floor of patchy grass and dirt, moving in time to the beat and rhythm of the music.

He stopped to take in the rare sight from a distance. Where else in the world could people gather in the hundreds and dance to live music under the magic glow of electric light? He savored the enchanted, otherworldly vision of the canopy shining red and green and blue against the darkness, the light and sound of the party dissipating into the black night.

His eyes drifted over and beyond the celebration.

The black night.

The gravity of the murky void tugged at his chest. The darkness called.

It's not too late. You can slip away into the dark. You can try again, on your own.

A figure approached, silhouetted by the kaleidoscope of light.

"Mr. James, is that you?" asked the approaching silhouette, a woman's figure becoming clearer. Recognizing the voice, he smiled in the dark. "It *is* you," Wendy said, materializing before him. "What are you doing out here, standing in the dark all by your lonesome?"

He nodded toward the oasis of light and sound radiating from the darkness.

"Just taking in the sights."

Wendy looped her arm through his and turned to face the party.

"It is quite a view, isn't it?"

They stood together in silence and watched their neighbors as they danced under the lights—a mass of bodies moving rhythmically, cohesive and interconnected, yet each part of the whole unequivocally distinct. Wendy clutched his arm tighter and rested her head on his shoulder. "Come on," she said, "let's go dance."

He let Wendy's words linger in the air. He turned his gaze away from the light, back toward the darkness, tempted by its pull, one last time.

"Okay," he said. "Let's dance."

Wendy pulled Christopher by the hand through the mass of spinning, pulsating bodies to the center of the dance floor beneath the illuminated canopy. She turned to face him and ran her hands through her wild red hair, then she lifted her arms above her head and rolled her shoulders, swaying to the beat like a flower child transported from the summer of love. He watched, spellbound, until he remembered that he was supposed to be dancing with her. Though not much of a dancer, he listened to the band—a brass band with a saxophone, trumpet, trombone, and a percussionist—and did his best to move to their New Orleans groove. With his eyes locked on Wendy's and his hands balled into loose fists, he kicked his feet, pumped his arms, and rocked in time with the music.

The brass horns blew and the drums kicked. All around them, their friends and neighbors bounced up and down and swung side to side. Natalie, the future doctor, danced without a care in the world, her eyes closed, head bobbing back and forth, arms flying over her head. Jason held Sharon close by the waist while she had her arms slung over his shoulders, the pair's hips matching each other's movements. In a contest to see who could pull off the coolest dance step, Isaiah and Jaylen mixed it up together in the middle of the crowd. Anthony danced slowly with a woman, their foreheads touching as they held each other in their arms, despite the up-tempo beat of the music. Jane found a young man to lead her in a dance, and a smile radiated from her kind face as he lifted her arm over her head and gently spun her. Diego held the hands of both Isabella and her young son Cristóbal, and the three of them danced playfully in a circle. Dr. Rajavi stood on the outskirts of the dance floor, snapping his fingers and nodding his head.

Christopher turned back to Wendy and did his best to groove to the music with a minimum of awkwardness. She smiled at his attempt, then pulled him close and gave him a light peck on the lips. She wrapped her arms around him, and they swayed together, falling out of time with the music while the party raged around them.

"Bro, mind if I cut in?"

He felt a hand on his shoulder, and he turned to see Sean's grinning face. A flash of anger coursed through him and landed in his gut. Wendy gently squeezed his arm, and he turned back to see her smiling reassuringly. "Of course he won't mind," she said with a nod as she looked Christopher in the eyes.

He took a breath and let go of Wendy, then he turned to Sean and said, "Good luck trying to follow my amazing dance skills."

Sean burst out laughing and slapped Christopher in the stomach with the back of his hand. "Shouldn't be too hard, dude, from what I saw," Sean said as he took Wendy by the hand, then they stepped into the raucous dance, whirling and twisting among the mass of humanity.

He snickered to himself. Sean was right.

The musicians' horns wailed, their drums pounded. Standing under the canopy, surrounded by his neighbors, the beat crept into his toes, then up through his legs, and soon he was tapping his feet and bobbing his head, dancing with himself as if no one was watching. His injured knee throbbed beneath the brace, but he pushed the pain to the back of his mind and moved with abandon. He bounced up and down on the dance floor and waved his arms, overtaken by a carefree joy, a cathartic cleansing of the soul. It was pure, unbridled fun, and he laughed like he was a kid again as he danced among his new friends and neighbors.

Someone bumped him from behind, and he was jostled from his state of ecstasy.

"Well, if it isn't that guy who almost blew my head off that one time," Jordan yelled over the blaring horns. She had her arms around another woman, and the two were swaying to the music.

Christopher shrugged and threw his hands up with a smile. "Sorry!" he shouted back, then he nodded toward Jordan's dancing partner and asked, "So, who's this?"

She had a slender build and was taller than Jordan by several inches. Her blonde hair was cut short, and she had a silver nose stud. She reached around Jordan and held out her hand. "Samantha," she said. "Thanks for not blowing my girlfriend's head off."

He shook her hand and, with a smile, said, "It wasn't for lack of trying, believe me. But it's nice to meet you." He turned and gave Jordan a quizzical look.

"I told you you're not my type," Jordan said with a wink, then she turned back to Samantha, and the two rejoined the dance without missing a beat.

He chuckled to himself and shook his head. With a smile on his face, he stood in the middle of the dance floor, surrounded by the people of New Concord as they whirled around him. He turned slowly in a circle and took in the celebration, watching as everyone bobbed and spun and bounced to the beat of the music.

They were a people free of stress and worry, a people filled to the brim with love for life and each other. He would make a life here, too. A *real* life, beyond existence for the sake of itself, beyond mere survival. A life with roots and relationships. A life of commitment to other people, to something larger than himself, and all the sweat and blood and tears and hard work under the golden sun that comes with it. A life filled with love.

The warmth of that feeling began to overtake him, and he let it, surrendering to its comfort.

He belonged.

Under the magic glow of the lights strung up under the canopy, Christopher helped move the last of the heavy picnic tables back into place. He held one end while Diego had the other, and they gasped for air after they set it down at the end of the row.

"Thanks, man," Diego said as he came around the table.

"No problem," he said, then the two men clasped hands, snapped each other's fingers, and bumped fists.

"So, you have a good time tonight?" Diego asked.

He nodded. "Yeah. I did," a smile spreading across his lips. "I think... I think I really needed that. To let loose."

"Absolutely. It's good to let go now and then, you know?"

"Yeah. I do now."

"Alright, man. You have a good night, okay?"

Diego turned and began to walk away.

"Yeah, you too," Christopher said.

"Hey," Diego said, turning back around. "I've been meaning to tell you, I had my doubts at first... but you're all right. I'm glad you're here."

"Thanks. That means a lot. And to tell you the truth, I wasn't so sure about you either."

Diego smiled and nodded, then Christopher watched as his new friend turned and walked away, disappearing beyond the canopy's glow.

"That was some party, wasn't it?"

Simone stood at the end of the canopy, the colors of the lights reflecting in her glasses.

"The lights were a nice touch," he said, looking up.

"I think so, too. Really sets the mood."

The music over and the partiers tucked into bed, nature's soundscape filled the crisp night air.

"But all good things must come to an end," she continued. "Would you mind pulling the plug on the lights for me?" She pointed him toward the extension cord that ran through the grass and plugged into the strings of lights. He separated the cords, and the reds and greens and blues under the canopy were extinguished, leaving them alone in the dark. "Thanks, dear. Wouldn't want to use up *all* the juice just for a party, now would we?"

"Of course not," he said, answering her rhetorical question with a chuckle as he approached her in the dark.

"If I could ask you one more favor, would you mind walking a tired old lady home?"

"Not at all."

They stepped out from underneath the canopy and walked through the green toward the loop.

"Looks like you and Diego are getting along," Simone said.

"Yeah. He's a good guy."

"I knew you two would figure it out, once you decided to give each other a chance."

"How did you know I—"

"Didn't trust him? Christopher James, haven't you learned by now? I see all."

"Apparently."

Simone smiled and looked up at him as they walked side by side.

"You've come a long way, Christopher. I knew you would. Even that very first time we spoke and you were talkin' all that individualistic, 'other people drag me down' bullshit, I knew you'd turn out all right."

"What made you so sure?"

She gestured to the apartment buildings on their left then swept her arm toward the green. "I believe in this place," she said. "Plus, remember, I saw you when you first got here. Let's face it, you were in rough shape, honey. Thin, weak, a fresh bullet wound. It didn't take a genius to see things weren't goin' too well for you out there, and that New Concord would be a big improvement. It was only a matter of time before we won you over."

"I was kind of a mess, wasn't I?"

Simone smiled. "You know how I actually knew, though?" she asked. Christopher shook his head. "You agreed to give it a chance. And even though you probably didn't *really* want to, I could see in your eyes you were ready for a change. You meant it when you agreed to try. And that's all this place needs, an honest effort. As long as you do that, you'll find yourself lifted up by the community."

He nodded. "I always believed that sort of thing was impossible," he said. "That it was our nature to just look out for ourselves, to try to 'get ahead,' like they used to say. And then I came here and saw everyone working together, as equals. At first, I couldn't believe it. How'd you do it? What is it about this place?"

Simone smiled. "I wish I could tell you there was some secret to it, but there ain't. Except that all your beliefs about human nature are dead wrong." Christopher turned, bewilderment on his face. She looked back at him over the rims of her glasses. "What? You haven't figured that out for yourself by now?"

"I can see it—how everyone gets along and works together, everyone just willingly doing their part—I just don't understand it. It didn't seem like that's how the world worked, before all this."

"Well, you're part of 'everyone,' aren't you? Now that you're here, doing your part, why do you do it?"

"I... don't know," he said, cocking his head. The question was so simple, so obvious, now that he was faced with it directly. "I never really stopped to think about it. I just— You feel... compelled, or obligated. But in a good way, if that makes sense. Everyone else is doing their part, and so you feel like you should, too. But it's not just a guilt thing, it's more than that. After a while, it feels... *good*, having something productive to do, knowing that you're contributing."

"That's exactly right. *Exactly* right," Simone said, her voice swelling with pride. "Man, I can't even begin to tell you how many times I heard that 'human nature' argument. All my life! People acting like it's somehow coded into our DNA to be selfish assholes, each and every one of us. And so of course, the argument goes, since there's nothing we can do about it, we might as well embrace it and start stepping on people's faces while we make our climb to the top, taking as much for ourselves as we can along the way. And should we feel any guilt about it? Hell no! Because it's 'natural,' you see. What a load of crap. Boy, lemme tell you, that used to make me so damn mad, every time I heard it."

"Why do you think it became such conventional wisdom, if it's all bullshit? I mean, I certainly believed it."

"Oh, that's an easy one. It was all about them Benjamins, baby. Profits!"

"What do you mean?"

"Well, think about it. Who determines the dominant ideologies and the conventional wisdoms of a society? The people with the most influence, right? And who are those people? Call 'em what you want. The one percent. The elite. The rich and powerful. If you're part of a class that controls the most wealth and has a grip on political power, it's going to be in your interest to make sure it stays that way. And what better way to keep that status quo in place than to perpetuate the idea that it's natural, that it might as well be written into the fabric of the universe, like gravity? What alternative can there possibly be if any fundamental changes people try to make are against human nature? If you can achieve that, if you can use your power and influence to convince society that this is the best and only way, well, you've successfully insulated your wealth and power and cemented your status at the top."

He walked beside Simone as the crickets chirped, processing what she said. "So, it was like a big conspiracy then?"

Simone laughed. "No, no. It wasn't a conspiracy. It's not like all them rich folks held a secret backroom meeting and hatched this plot. No need for that. It's a byproduct of their class interest, played out on an individual level through the logic of the economy. 'Work hard and you'll get ahead,' they say. But *they're* the ones benefiting the most from everyone else's labor, and it's in their interest to maintain that status quo. Over time, that prevailing ideology filters down into society, through the government, and the schools, and the media. It's not a conspiracy, it's just the way the system functions."

"That sounds like some communist propaganda if I've ever heard it."

"Well, you can call it what you want. But look around. We're doing pretty well, don't you think? Hard to argue with the results."

Simone stopped in front of the 1700 building and looked up the stairs to the breezeway. "Well, this is me," she said. "Thanks for humoring an old lady."

He smirked. "I think I caught a glimpse of you out on that dance floor tonight. You've still got it."

Simone laughed. "You flatter me, honey, but I think my dancing days are coming to an end. I'm gonna be feelin' it in the morning."

He smiled. "Goodnight, Simone," he said, and he turned toward his apartment.

"Wait, Christopher," Simone called back to him, and he stopped and came back to the stairway. "I know I said that there was no real secret to making this place tick, and I'm still mostly stickin' to that. But I need to say, I think, if there is such a thing as human nature at all, this place we've built reflects it far more than the old world did. You said it yourself. It makes you feel good to do work that you know needs to be done and is genuinely beneficial to others. It's fulfilling. It gets inside you. I think that's *actually* our natural state. That's what it really means to be a human being. To build a society that fosters creativity and problem solving, and where everyone has a valuable role to play, working for the common good. We *like* doing that stuff, you know? As long as their basic needs are secure, people don't actually *need* some selfish profit incentive to do the work that needs to be done. If work truly *needs* to be done, that's all the motivation we need, and people organize and figure out how to do it. If you ask me, I think what we're doing here is a hell of a lot more natural than it was commuting for hours to jobs that we hate just so other people can get rich from our labor while we struggle to make ends meet, always a paycheck away from disaster. Good riddance to that soul-crushing shit. Don't get me wrong, what happened to the world was a tragedy, and when I think about how many millions died... I ache inside, truly. But that old system crumbling is what allowed us to get a fresh start, on new terms, and I think we owe it to everyone we lost to build a new and better world, rather than trying to rebuild the old one. New Concord works because people were ready for a new way of doing things. They were desperate for it, even if they didn't know it."

He nodded. "I would always hear people say 'people suck' and things like that, and I looked around, and everything seemed to confirm that idea. All the violence in the world, all the ugliness people are capable of. It always felt like the bad outweighed the good, you know? I had no reason to think we could be better."

"I can understand that," Simone said. "It's easy to overlook all the good and dwell on the ugliness, especially if you don't step back and try to understand the forces that cause people to come into conflict. But you know what, when I look at people, you know what I see? I see beauty. I mean it, I think people are just so beautiful. And when you strip away all the things that keep us divided, all the things that cause hate and fear, all the things that encourage us to step on each other's throats just to get ahead, that beauty shines through, just like all the stars up there tonight. You know what I hope, Christopher? I hope we're not the only ones left who figured that out. I hope the world is dotted with New Concords, and that they'll grow and prosper, and one day they'll join together. Then civilization will truly get another shot, and we can do it right this time. Because you know what? Despite everything, I think humanity deserves a second chance. I truly do."

He looked up at Simone on the stairs as the community's chorus of crickets chirped their song, then he turned his gaze upward to the inky black sky shimmering with a blanket of stars brighter than any humankind had seen in a century.

"Yeah," Christopher replied. "Maybe we do deserve another shot."

Christopher knocked on Sharon's door and waited for the counselor to answer. She opened the door, greeted him with a warm smile, and invited him inside.

"Feel free to make yourself comfortable on the couch," she said.

"Don't mind if I do," he replied, and he sank into the cushions.

"You seem like you're in good spirits today," Sharon said, taking a seat in the chair on the other side of the coffee table. "You look good."

"Thanks, yeah. Been getting back in shape. I feel good. Lighter, somehow, even though I've actually been putting some weight back on."

"Well, that's new," the counselor said with a smile. "Tell me more about this feeling."

"I don't quite know how to describe it. It's going to sound really corny if I try."

"There's no one here but me. You don't have to worry about anyone judging you. Kick back and let it all out."

He smirked and took an exaggerated deep breath. "If you insist," he said, and he slipped off his shoes and stretched out across the couch. "I'll give it a shot."

Sharon smiled and nodded then picked up her notepad.

"Though I'm not sure if I can do it justice, to be honest with you."

"That's perfectly fine. Just talk yourself through it as best you can."

He settled in on the couch and looked at the ceiling.

"The other day, everything just... snapped into place. From first thing in the morning straight through till midnight, it was basically a perfect day."

"Which day was that? Tell me about it."

"The day of the library opening."

"Ah, yes. That was a good day. And a great night."

"I know this sounds stupid, but, all day, I felt like I was like walking on air. It was like any decision I made would be exactly right. Everywhere I went would be exactly where I was supposed to be. Everyone I talked to would be who I should be spending my time with at that moment. My mind was uncluttered. It felt like, I dunno, like a vacation, where you can put aside all your worries and just enjoy the moment. Even work didn't feel like work at all."

"Wow. I have to say, Christopher, that's great progress. Don't you think?"

"I suppose so, yeah."

"When you first arrived here, you were barely speaking, anxious around people, quick to lash out in anger. Do you remember the first time we spoke, in the hospital? And your first visit here? Surely you can see you've come a long way since then."

"Yeah. I remember." He tilted his head to look at Sharon, then looked back to the ceiling. "I do feel a lot better..."

"Something's bothering you."

"There was... a moment..."

"What kind of a moment?"

He took a breath.

"I was the last one in the library before the party. Not for any real reason, I was just taking my time, enjoying the space, and then I headed down toward the party. The sun had gone down by then and it was dark, and I stopped in the middle of the green and just watched everyone from a distance. The whole community was gathered under the canopy for the dance, and I could see all of them, under the lights, but they couldn't see me, alone, in the dark. And even though I had a great day—a perfect day—suddenly, there I was, back where I had started, on the out-side looking in."

"And then what happened?"

"I felt it calling..."

"What? What was calling?"

"The darkness."

Sharon quickly scribbled a few words down on her notepad then looked back up at him.

"For a moment, I felt the urge to leave. To just walk away. To slip into the night, find some other empty house out there, away from everyone, and start over on my own."

"Well, you're still here. So why didn't you?"

"Wendy came looking for me. She stood with me in the dark and we watched the party for a while, and then she said she wanted to dance and pulled me down to join everyone."

"And unless I'm mistaken, I think I saw you dancing. Did you have a good time at the party?"

"I did, yeah. I hadn't felt like that in a long time."

Sharon finished scribbling a note then looked up at her patient. She set the pen down on the paper.

"So, Wendy came and found you, and that kept you from giving in to your impulse to isolate yourself. That's good. A meaningful human connection. Have you been making any other friends? Any other connections with people?"

"I think so. There's Jordan, of course. She's the one who helped get me settled, even though I had tried to kill her once, before I got here. So I guess you could say she's my best friend here. God, it sounds really fucking lame to say it like that."

"You think becoming friends with someone is something to be ashamed of?"

"No, I guess not. It just sounds kinda pathetic, or something, to say it out loud like that."

"I don't think it's pathetic at all," Sharon said as she flipped back a page on her notepad. "We all need friends. And I think that's a good segue to a topic I wanted to revisit. Do you think you're ready to talk about why your time in the bunker began to feel pointless?"

He smiled. "I knew you weren't going to let me off the hook on that one."

"I think you've known the answer for a while."

He knew his next words represented the completion of a long journey. Saying them aloud, admitting the truth to himself, would allow him to close one chapter of his life and move on to the next, truly changed. He took a deep breath, giving himself a moment to reflect on who he had once been and since become, then he said the words.

"I had no one to live for."

A single tear slipped down his cheek as Sharon nodded in approval. A chill ran through him as a sense of relief flooded his body.

"Sorry," he said, wiping the tear from his face, "it's not easy to admit that everything I used to believe is total bullshit. But... I can see now how you need other people to give you purpose, to give you a reason to keep going. To have something outside of yourself to fight for. Having friends again... it's been nice."

He was quiet for a moment, still deep in thought, and Sharon allowed the silence to go uninterrupted. She rested the pen on the notepad, her eyes telling him she would wait until he was ready to speak again. He cleared his throat.

"Simone put me in charge of helping the new people settle in. Isabella and Cristóbal," he said, breaking the silence. "Just like Jordan helped me."

"That's a big responsibility."

"Yeah. I didn't understand it at first. I don't speak Spanish, you know? Why not Diego?"

"So why do you think Simone chose you?"

"I think it was a test. I don't know, maybe 'test' is the wrong word. A challenge. I think she wanted me to rise to the occasion."

"To what end, do you think?"

"To force me to break out of my comfort zone, I would guess. To help me connect with people. Since I can't really *speak* with them, I have to really *be there*, you know? Like, be present. Find ways to communicate on a deeper level, somehow."

"And how's that been going?"

"Good, I think. I'm not sure why, but that kid seemed to like me from the start. It's been nice spending time around him. Strange though, because I had always thought I didn't like kids.

Always thought they were annoying little brats, you know? But Cristóbal... it feels good looking out for him."

Sharon nodded as she finished writing.

"Well, Christopher, like I said, I think you're doing great. Sounds to me like you're forming relationships, making friends. You're communicating. You're buying in and making a real effort to build a life here. I'm really proud of you."

"But what about that... moment?"

"Well, I think it's important to remember, despite all the progress you've been making, you're still very new here. It's understandable that you'd still have some desire, or a subconscious impulse or whatever you want to call it, to retreat to the comfort of your old habits, even if those habits are unhealthy. It's not easy to rewire our brains and learn how to live all over again. It's not easy to integrate into a new community. But you're doing it."

"Do you think I'll always feel conflicted?"

"Maybe. I don't think we can know that for sure at this point. But I do think the more time you spend here, the more invested in the community you'll become, through your new relationships and your labor. I think, over time, that feeling of wanting to retreat to your old ways will probably fade. And, hey, you know, New Concord isn't a prison. If you feel like you need to see what you've been missing out there, you can always take a little trip down memory lane."

"A trip?"

"Sure, absolutely."

"Like, go back to my old house?"

"Yeah, why not? Actually, I recommend it. I think it might do you good. Now that you've been away for a while, maybe you'll see it with new eyes. You might be surprised by what you find."

Christopher opened the black SUV's passenger door and climbed inside while Jordan got in on the driver's side. Sean and Wendy piled into the backseat and strapped on their seatbelts. Jordan turned around in her seat and looked Sean and Wendy dead in the eyes.

"Okay, listen up. Neither of you have ever set foot outside New Concord since you've been here, is that right?"

They both nodded.

"That's what I thought," Jordan said. "For the record, I think this is a bad idea, but Christopher wants you both to ride along for some reason, so you're coming. Here are the rules. Stay alert at all times. Keep your eyes peeled and listen for anything you think could be trouble. Stay as quiet as you can, and we all stay together as a group at all times. And no fucking around. If either Christopher or I tell you to do something, you do it. Got it?"

With wide eyes, Wendy meekly nodded her head.

"Good," Jordan said, then she turned to Sean. "And you?"

"Dude, you are *scary*," said Sean, turning to Wendy, "Did you know she could be this scary?"

Jordan reached into the back and grabbed him by the chin. "Hey! I'm serious. No fucking around."

"Okay, okay. It's cool, man. I'll be cool."

She nodded, then let go of Sean's face and turned to Christopher. "You sure you want to do this?"

"I'm sure."

"Okay. We're off."

Jordan hit the gas, and the SUV lurched forward. They drove along the loop until they reached the main gate, then Jordan brought the vehicle to a stop. Christopher and Jordan peered through the windows. Satisfied the coast was clear, they nodded to each other, then Jordan pulled the SUV onto the road.

As they traveled down the two-lane road, Christopher's eyes were drawn to the sidewalk. He pictured himself lugging his bags, thin, weak, blood-soaked, under the anvil of the sun. A lifetime ago. The lines of the sidewalk whizzed by in a blur. In a matter of minutes, he'd be back where he started. He drew a long breath.

"You okay over there?" Jordan asked.

"I'm fine," he said, staring out the window.

Ivy had begun to snake up the trunks of trees and cover the sides of houses. Pinecones and branches littered the road, and weeds poked through the cracks in the asphalt. Jordan steered around the large impediments but plowed over the smaller debris.

The turn for his old neighborhood came into view on the horizon. He pointed toward it.

"It's there, on the left."

"How could I ever forget?" Jordan said, a smile in the corner of her mouth. She slowed the SUV to a crawl and took the turn into the subdivision.

Wendy reached forward from the backseat and put her hand on Christopher's shoulder. "I'm excited to see where you lived," she said. He put his hand on hers and smiled at her through the side mirror. His stomach fluttered as the cabin fell quiet. The SUV rolled over the residential streets, rubber pressing into the pavement.

Over the long, hot summer months since he'd left, nature had reasserted itself over the landscape. The already overgrown lawns were now wild, with tall, flowering grass that stretched several feet high. English ivy choked the trees and wound tightly around streetlamps. Long dandelions peppered the tangle of weedy overgrowth with blots of yellow.

Jordan steered onto Christopher's old street, an eerie tension in the air. Christopher's eyes locked onto his house, and Sean and Wendy followed his gaze. No one spoke as Jordan turned around in the driveway and parked along the curb, pointing the SUV back the way they had come.

"Sick house, bro," Sean said, breaking the silence, then Wendy reached over and quieted him with a touch.

"Home sweet home," Christopher said under his breath as he looked at the ivy-covered brick and the algae-covered siding through the passenger window, then he pulled the handle, opened the door, and stepped out of the vehicle. Everyone else followed his lead, and the group assembled on the driveway. Jordan's hand hovered over her holstered pistol as she surveyed the surrounding area. Christopher also scanned the background, his hand resting on his Glock. The late-summer day was clear and warm, but a gentle breeze drifted past, laced with a crispness hinting at the coming change of seasons.

"It's too overgrown on the sides," Christopher said. "We'll go through the house."

He led the group up the driveway and over the walk with solemn, purposeful strides, brushing aside the long grass and overgrown weeds as they approached the open threshold. They stood on the stoop and peered into the house. Leaves and dirt littered the foyer, and yellow pollen stained the floor.

"The door blew off in the tornado," he said. "I never bothered to rehang it."

Sean cocked his head. "Why not, man?"

"What would've been the point?"

The group stepped into the house and the debris caked into the hardwood crunched under their boots. They stayed tightly together as they passed through the foyer into the living room. The front door still lay on the floor, jammed under the couch.

Wendy gasped and covered her mouth as she pointed at the blood splatter on the wall.

"There's more over here, too," Christopher said flatly, a slight crack in his voice, nodding toward the mantle painted with his own blood. "Come on, let's keep moving. Nothing to see in here."

He stepped into the kitchen, followed by his three companions. He came to the sliding glass door and pulled on its handle. It made a gravelly sound and moved only a few inches before getting stuck in the track. He pulled again, but it wouldn't budge.

"Don't tell me we're gonna have to shoot this door open," Jordan said.

"Hang on," Christopher said, and he put his hand and his boot through the small opening and pushed from the side until the door was forced open.

They stepped through the door and onto the small cement patio, surrounded by a wall of overgrown grass and weeds.

"Come on, it's through here," he said, and he stepped into the tall grass, clearing a path for the others to follow. Wendy went next, keeping her hand on Christopher's shoulder as they pushed through the tangle, followed by Sean, then Jordan at the rear.

"This gives me the creeps, bro," Sean said.

"Keep it down," Jordan whispered.

"It's only a few feet," Christopher said quietly. "We're almost there."

He emerged from the overgrowth and stepped onto the hill, then the rest of the company joined him at the base of the slope. Strands of ivy blanketed the ground, and stalks of thick, green weeds reached from the dirt toward the sky. They marched up the hill and Christopher directed his companions through the gap in the chain-link fence. One by one, they squeezed through the opening and past the fallen evergreens, emerging on the other side, into the once secluded survival retreat.

The grass around the perimeter was waist high, and scraggly weeds had covered the bare patch in the center. The uprooted evergreens on the west side lay brown and shriveled, and the few remaining shards of the storage sheds in the southwest corner were covered with dirt and ivy, slowly being claimed by the earth. The great hickory tree, which had once stood proudly in the center of the yard, lay fallen across the east side of the grounds, the shattered remains of the greenhouse crushed beneath its colossal trunk.

"I can see why you had to bug out, man," Sean said, and Wendy came up beside Christopher and wrapped herself around his arm. Standing back, Jordan kept a watchful eye on the background, letting Christopher process the scene.

He stood silently and took in the ruin of his old life with new eyes. He wasn't angry, at least not in the way he imagined he might feel if he ever saw this place again. Instead, striking a stoic, thoughtful pose, he wondered what he had been thinking. After all the months that had passed, after becoming a resident of New Concord, after working side by side with other people, after making friends, the futility of his obsessive survivalism became obvious. The yard, once his great fortress, his brilliant oasis, was revealed to be utterly small, pathetic, fragile. How could he have ever lived in such a place? How was it ever going to last? It was suddenly clear how false it was. It was a lie and always had been. One way or another, the world was always going to find him and come crashing through his borders. He could only hide for so long.

He stepped through the overgrowth, and his three companions followed closely behind. He stopped, knelt, and searched through vines of ivy, finding the metal hatch underneath. Ripping the vines aside, he uncovered the hatch and pulled it open, revealing a dark hole in the ground and a ladder descending into it. He turned around, stepped onto the ladder, and began to climb down. Jordan, Sean, and Wendy exchanged glances.

"Uh, you sure this is safe, dude?" Sean asked.

Christopher hopped off the last rung and landed on the floor with a metallic thud that reverberated through the container.

"Come on," he said from below.

"It'll be okay," Jordan said to the others. "Sean, you first."

"Eek," Sean said as he turned and took his first step down the ladder, then he too disappeared through the hatch.

"You next," Jordan said to Wendy, who smiled nervously and followed Sean down the ladder. Once Wendy was safely at the bottom, Jordan took a look around with a swivel of her head then joined the others belowground.

A beam of sunlight streamed through the hatch, casting long shadows into the darkness. The air inside was stale and stank of mildew, dank and musty. Christopher stood in the center of the steel tube, and the others gathered around him. Jordan pulled a small flashlight from her pocket and clicked it on, then Christopher found a small battery-powered lantern in a bin and turned the dial, bathing the interior in fluorescent light.

The bunker was filthy. Empty soup cans and the discarded wrappers of survival bars littered the floor, along with tools and supplies spilled from the shelves. His old mattress lay sadly in the corner, the sheets and blankets rumpled, covered in a fine layer of dust. A cockroach scurried around their feet, and Sean yelped and jumped back.

"This place is gnarly, dude," Sean said, catching his breath. "You actually lived down here?"

"I did."

Wendy looked at him with watery eyes. "You poor thing," she said. "It must have been so lonely."

"It was," he said. "Just took me a while to realize it."

He stood silently and studied the metal cell, its corrugated walls cold and oppressive. Even with the beam of sunlight and the fluorescent glow of the lantern, it was somehow still dark in the container. He breathed the bunker's dank, stale air, feeling how cramped and uncomfortable it was in the gloom.

"You all right, Chris?" Jordan asked.

He lifted his head. "Yeah," he said with a nod, "I am now." He looked each of his friends in the eyes. "Let's gather up anything useful and get the hell out of this shithole."

They grabbed the shotgun and the rifle from the gun safe, along with all the boxes of ammunition. They picked up the night vision goggles, batteries, toilet paper, cans of soup and survival bars, the box of gold and silver coins, and all the clothes he had left behind. The salvaged goods were handed up to the surface through the hatch.

"What about these books?" Jordan asked. "Should we add these to the library?"

His old books were strewn about, spilled from the bookcase onto the floor. He took a deep breath and cleared his throat.

"We are challenged to change ourselves," he whispered, raising his gaze from the pile of dusty books. He met Jordan's eye.

"Frankl?"

"Yeah. Leave the books."

"You sure?"

"Yeah."

Jordan nodded. "Okay. Then I think we're done down here."

"Okay. I'll see you topside."

Jordan climbed the ladder with the last handful of supplies, leaving Christopher alone in the bunker.

He stood in the center of the narrow room, the battery-powered lantern in hand. He turned slowly. The dark, dreary place was both familiar and foreign, like a childhood memory. Just yesterday. A lifetime ago. His eyes fell on the calendar hanging on the wall, still on June's page. He smirked, then shifted his eyes to the mirror and nodded to himself.

There was nothing else worth salvaging. He clicked off the lantern then followed his friends into the light.

Jordan drove the SUV through the gates of New Concord and parked on the loop near the canopy. Christopher and his three companions got out and unloaded the salvaged supplies into the waiting arms of the people gathered to help.

When they finished, he leaned against the side of the SUV and watched as the last of his stockpile, items he had spent years meticulously gathering, were carried off by the residents. The food would be stored in the kitchen, the clothing cleaned, sorted, and distributed, the weapons safely secured, and the various supplies organized and put to use.

"Do you want me to come back to your room tonight?" Wendy asked.

He smiled and kissed her on the cheek.

"I think I need a night to myself."

"Alright," she said, and she stood on her toes and kissed him on the lips. "See you tonight at dinner."

"Thanks for coming with me today. I don't know if I could have—"

"I know," she said. "That's what I'm here for. What we're all here for."

Christopher arrived at his apartment and found a small box by the door. He reached down and picked it up, revealing a piece of paper tucked underneath. He brought them inside and sat at the kitchen table. Unfolding the piece of blue-lined paper, he found a handwritten note inside.

> *Christopher,*
> *I did some asking around and tracked this*
> *down for you.*
> *-Anthony*

He set the note aside and picked up the box. He shook it gently and an object tapped against the sides, then he pulled open the flaps and looked inside. A baseball. An old ball, its leather stained with dirt and grass, but a baseball nonetheless. He smiled to himself as he poured the ball into his hand.

He went to his room, tossing the ball to himself as he walked, and closed the door behind him. He sat down at the end of the bed and held the ball to his nose, breathing it in, then fell back onto the bed, his mind awash with memories of childhood games. Flat on his back, he tossed the ball toward the ceiling and caught it over his face.

He was home. Finally home.

This is where I live, he thought. This is my bed. This is my room. I am in my apartment. I am a member of this community. The people here are my friends. I belong here.

For the first time, he truly believed it.

This is where I live. I am home.

His eyes fell on the black backpack on the floor. It sat untouched, leaning against the wall. He sat up, his eyes locked on the bag. He took a breath, then reached out and grabbed it by its loop. Its contents rattled as he pulled it toward him and set it on his lap.

His hand trembled as he slowly unzipped the bag. He reached inside and grasped a smooth, thin object, then carefully extracted it.

He looked down at a photograph of a family in a cherry wood picture frame. There was a mother, a father, three sons, and a daughter. They were posed in front of a lake and wore matching green polo shirts. He stared into each of their faces and wondered what their names were and what they had been thinking at that moment.

He set the frame down on the bed, then reached into the bag and pulled out another frame, this one metallic silver. It held a picture of another family, and he studied it just as he had the first before setting it aside on the bed. He pulled another picture frame from the bag, then another, and another, until the bag was empty and over a dozen frames were laid out on the bed, each containing a portrait of a different family.

Christopher cleared a pile of clothes from the top of his dresser. One by one, he picked up each framed portrait and arranged it neatly on the dresser, filling its surface with families he had never known. They would be his family now, and he would be theirs—long-lost relatives, separated by distance and time. He would look at their smiling faces every day and do his best to make them proud.

Christopher stood outside of apartment 802 and knocked on the door. He heard voices inside followed by a quick flurry of footsteps, then Cristóbal opened the door.

"Christopher!" the child yelled.

"Cristóbal!" he yelled back, holding one hand behind his back. "I have a surprise for you."

He pulled his hand from behind his back and smiled as he held up the baseball. Excitement grew on the child's face as the boy realized what it was, and Christopher was filled with joy.

"Un béisbol! Mamá, tiene un béisbol!"

Cristóbal ran back inside, squealing with delight as he went, and quickly returned with his baseball glove. He ran out into the breezeway, clearly thrilled to play catch with a real ball.

Isabella appeared at the door and smiled. "Not too long," she said in English with a wag of her finger.

He smiled and nodded. "Si, señora," he said, then he turned and jogged after Cristóbal, who was already down the steps and on his way to the green. He caught up to the boy on the other side of the loop and staked out an open patch of grass.

Christopher held up the ball to make sure Cristóbal was ready, then lobbed it gently to the boy. Cristóbal swiped at the ball and plucked it out of the air with his glove. He pulled the ball from the pocket and held it to his face, breathing in its distinctive leathery scent with a satisfying "Ahh." Then he wound up and fired the ball back to Christopher, who caught it in his bare hands.

"You've got a cannon there, kid," he said, and he tossed the ball back to Cristóbal, a little harder than the first time. Once again, the child caught the ball with ease, then tossed a strike back to Christopher's hands.

The man and the boy with the same name stood on the green and played catch as the sun began to set and the sky glowed ruby and tangerine. They threw and caught until it was too dark to see and the boy's arm dangled from his side like a wet noodle and the man's hands were swollen and numb. They would play again soon, Christopher promised Cristóbal, before returning the boy to his mother.

Christopher opened his eyes and stretched his arms lazily over his head. Rays of sunlight slipped through the blinds, splashing the room with a golden glow. He flexed his hand, swollen and sore, and smiled. Totally worth it.

He pushed off the sheets and stood to dress, even though he could have lain in bed all day, fulfilled and at peace.

The day called to him through the window. He opened the blinds, flooding the room with morning light. First, he would head to Cathy's yoga class under the old oak. Then he would go down to the canopy and get some ripe fruit for breakfast, and scrambled eggs if they were cooking. Later he would meet Jane in the field to help with the day's harvest, and maybe take a shift in the library in the afternoon. In the evening, he would pay a visit to Cristóbal and Isabella, then have dinner with his friends under the canopy. The day was out there, waiting for him on the other side of the window, and he was ready to meet it.

He dressed. He strapped on his knee brace. He looked at his new family on the dresser, studying their faces.

"I hope I make you proud today."

He grasped the doorknob, ready to head out into the day.

A scream. A flurry of footsteps.

He went back across the room to the window. People were running. Lots of people, all headed in the same direction, concern written on their faces. The sound of the gong rang out, and rang and rang, in quick, sharp beats.

"Something's wrong."

He bolted across the room and flung open the bedroom door, then raced across the living room and pounded on Sean's door.

"Get up, man, something's happening. Something bad."

He flew out the front door before Sean could answer, out into the breezeway, leaving the door swinging open behind him. Down the steps, to the loop. Jogging, he joined the river of people alerted by the gong, flowing toward the trouble, whatever it was.

He stopped.

Black smoke. Thick and angry, it billowed above the trees, high into the pristine blue sky.

People brushed past him. Wails and shouts streaked through the air. Someone bumped him from behind and he staggered forward, then he regained his balance and jogged ahead, closer, closer, until he was upon it.

"Oh my God, building 800."

People were gathering on the loop in front of the building, and he sprinted to join them.

Simone and Jordan stood on the curb, their hands curled around their mouths, shouting orders.

"We're gonna form a bucket brigade," Simone called out. "Runners, gather as many buckets as you can carry and take them to the well. Everyone else, start forming a line."

"Come on, people, we need all the buckets we can get. Move, move!" Jordan said, and people scattered in different directions.

Christopher ran up to Jordan, breathing heavily. "Jordan, how did this happen?"

"No idea. Got here as soon as I saw the smoke."

"Did everyone get out?"

"Not sure yet. Wendy got out but she's a bit shaken up."

"Wendy, oh my God. Where is she? Is she okay?"

"The doc is taking a look at her," Jordan said, nodding in their direction.

"What about the kid? Cristóbal? And Isabella?"

Jordan shook her head. "Haven't seen them."

"Shit," he said, turning toward the burning building. Black smoke spewed from its seams. He winced, squinting at the spreading blaze, then turned and scanned the faces of the people on the street.

No Isabella. No Cristóbal.

He turned back to Jordan. She was busy shouting instructions, waving her arms to get people into line.

"I'm gonna check on Wendy," he said, getting her attention for a second.

Jordan nodded, then turned and continued to bark out orders. "Toward the well!"

He weaved through a cluster of people and found Wendy seated on the curb and Dr. Rajavi kneeling in front of her. She wore an oxygen mask over her soot-stained face. The doctor listened to her lungs through a stethoscope.

"Give me one more deep breath," the doctor said to Wendy. "Good."

Christopher got down on his knee and put his hand on her shoulder. "Thank God you made it out. Are you all right? Doc, is she going to be okay?"

Wendy nodded, a tear rolling down her cheek.

"She's going to be fine," Dr. Rajavi said. "Give her some space, okay? She just needs some air."

Christopher ran his hand through her red hair then wiped the tear from her face with his thumb.

"Okay," he said, nodding his head. "I'm going to look for Cristóbal. I'll find you later."

Wendy pulled down the mask.

"Be careful," she said, wheezing.

He turned toward the burning building. The fire was louder now, crackling and roaring, smoke erupting from the second-story windows. He ran past the human chain, stretching from the well to the building, as the first buckets of water made their way up the line from the well.

"Mijo! Cristóbal!"

Isabella was sprinting toward the building from the green, crossing over the loop, frantic, tears streaming down her face. Christopher altered course, intercepting the panicked mother as she bolted toward the stairs. "Isabella!" he yelled as he caught her.

The strength in Isabella's legs gave out and she sank to the ground, cradled in his arms. "Mi hijo. Mi niño está atrapado adentro! Cristóbal!"

Orange flames flared from the second-story windows. The fire was growing.

The anguished mother pounded the ground with her fist, sobbing.

"Stay here. I'm going to bring him back. I promise." He held Isabella's face and looked her directly in the eye. "I promise."

Christopher stood. He turned toward the burning building, flames flickering in his eyes as he took a breath, then he walked, deliberately, resolutely, up the steps to the breezeway, passing the bucket brigade.

"What are you doing?" Diego shouted as he splashed a bucket of water through a broken ground floor window. Christopher walked into the smoke-filled breezeway. "Where are you going? Are you fucking crazy?"

He pulled his shirt over his nose and mouth as he stepped into the hall. With his arm, he shielded his eyes from the smoke. The crowd of volunteers faded behind him as he approached 802 on the far side of the building.

He stood in front of the door, black smoke seeping from its seams. He placed the back of his hand on the door. It was warm. He tried the doorknob. "Shit," he said, yanking his hand away.

He took a step back from the smoking door. Sweat poured from his face. His heart pounded in his chest. He looked down the breezeway, back the way he had come. Dark smoke flowed down the hall like a river toward the daylight.

It's not too late to turn back, he thought. No one expects you to do this. You don't have to risk yourself.

Isabella's cry echoed through the breezeway. "Cristóbal!"

He turned back at the door, then closed his eyes and took a breath. He steeled himself, then yelled as he charged the door, crashing into it with his shoulder. The frame cracked, but the door held. He stepped back into the hall, then rammed the door a second time. Wood splintered, and his clavicle snapped.

He staggered back and doubled over, pain shooting through his arm. He clutched his shoulder and grimaced. Again, he looked down the hall, then back at the door.

He rose to his full height, reared back, and kicked the door with the heel of his boot. He gasped for breath as he kicked again and again until the wood shattered and the door flung open. A ball of flame ripped through the door into the hall's open air. He recoiled from the blast, falling back onto the cement.

Shoulder damaged, hair singed, blood dripping from his elbow, he picked himself off the breezeway floor. Heat radiated from the doorway, the red glow of fire flickering through the smoke.

He stood at the threshold, strangely aware that the arc of his life had brought him here, to this place, to this moment. Every person he had met, every place he had been, every decision he had made—the incalculable sum of everything—had placed him in front of this fiery abyss. A whole life, distilled to an ultimate, defining act of discretion.

He took a final look down the breezeway, through the smoke and flame, to the white light beyond, to his friends and the new life he had just begun to build with them in New Concord. Their faces flashed through his mind.

He peered into the apartment. What fate awaited him inside, he didn't know, but once the decision was made, a wave of serenity passed through him, as though it was the only possible option.

"I'm coming for you, kid."

He again covered his face with his shirt and hurled himself through the open door.

The heat was sweltering. Smoke hung in the entryway, and flames flickered on the carpet and climbed up the walls in strands. "Cristóbal!" he yelled through the smoke, "Cristóbal!" but there was no response.

He came to the bedroom off the hall and bashed through the door. The room was filled with smoke that swirled as he rushed in. He called out for Cristóbal as he dove to the floor and looked under the bed. Not there. He got back to his feet, adrenaline blocking out the pain in his shoulder, and yanked open the closet. Clear.

He stepped back into the hall. The heat scalded his skin, and smoke stung his eyes. His throat burned with every gulp of air. He crossed into the living room. The couch was burning, and flames rippled up the wall and across the ceiling. He turned toward the kitchen. An inferno raged on the other side of the bar.

Frantic, he spun in a circle, then looked under the coffee table.

"Cristóbal!"

He crossed through the living room toward the bedroom on the backside of the unit. Flames ringed the doorframe. His arm shielding his face, he kicked open the door and stepped inside. He looked under the bed. He looked in the closet. He shouted the boy's name.

"Where are you?"

Somewhere behind him, there was a loud crack, then a crash, like a tree falling in the forest. He turned and stepped out of the bedroom. "Holy shit." The overhang between the living room and the kitchen lay in a burning heap on the floor, blocking the hall to the front door.

The fire was growing larger, hotter. His face felt like it was melting, and Cristóbal was nowhere to be found. Fear coursed through his body, from his chest to his toes. He was going to die in this room, for nothing.

Then he heard a child's scream.

He spun around. The bathroom.

Flames had covered the living room's walls and ringed the entryway to the back hall. Dark smoke clouded the room.

"Hang on, Cristóbal," he yelled, then he put his arm over his face and ran through the flames. The fire nipped at his arms and legs, and he winced as he stopped in front of the bathroom door. He gathered himself then crashed through it with his good shoulder.

A cloud of smoke hung in the air. Through the haze, he made out the shape of a small boy curled up in the bathtub.

"Cristóbal, thank God. Are you okay?"

"Te quemas!" Cristóbal sputtered, pointing to Christopher's arm.

He quickly snuffed out the flames on his sleeve with his hand.

"Let's get out of here, okay buddy?"

He scooped the boy out of the tub and found he was clutching his baseball glove to his chest, the ball tucked safely in its pocket. Cristóbal wrapped his arms around Christopher's neck.

With the boy in his arms, he peeked through the bathroom door, down the hall. The fire crackled and roared through the apartment, on the carpet, up the walls, and across the ceiling. There was a loud snap overhead. Time was running out. Cristóbal coughed and wheezed.

Christopher grabbed a bath towel from a hook on the wall and soaked it with water from a jug on the sink.

"We're gonna wrap you up in this to keep you safe, then we're gonna make a run for it, okay?"

He draped the towel over Cristóbal's head and wrapped it around his body, then moved the cloth aside so he could see the boy's face.

"Don't be scared. You're gonna be alright, you hear me, kid? Now close your eyes and hold on tight."

He again stuck his head out into the hall. The fire popped, hissed, and roared. The ceiling was bowed, about to cave in. Across the apartment, through the smoke and flames, light from the breezeway was coming in through the open door. Through that doorway was a desperate mother waiting for her son. Through that doorway, his friends and neighbors were furiously fighting the fire. He pictured the expressions of joy and relief that would light up their faces when he rejoined them outside. Nothing had ever been more important to him than reaching that open door so that the child in his arms could live, so he could see the faces of his friends again.

"Here we go."

He squeezed Cristóbal tightly against this chest and stepped out into the flaming corridor. Heat flashed on his face as he tucked his head and ran through the flames, down the hall, into the living room. He cried out in pain and determination, the fire stinging his body and singeing his hair, as he approached the pile of flaming debris on the floor. He was going to have to jump. Three more steps. The door was only a few feet away on the other side. He planted his foot to jump, and his injured knee buckled under his weight. He stumbled, and his boot caught on the burning wood. Cristóbal spilled out of his arms and landed in the hall on the other side of the debris, the wet towel still wrapped around him. Christopher came crashing down on the flaming pile of wood and drywall.

"Papá!" Cristóbal screamed.

The arc of his life had brought him here, to this place, to this moment—the incalculable sum of everything. A whole life, distilled to an ultimate, defining act of discretion. This was as far as he could go, but the kid could still make it. Fire engulfing his clothes, he raised his head and reached out his arm. "Go!" he yelled, pointing to the open door.

With a sound that cracked like thunder, the ceiling broke, and an avalanche of fire poured down from the floor above, burying Christopher beneath the flames.

"Let's go, keep it moving!" Jordan yelled down the line after she passed a bucket of water to Diego.

The human chain stretched from the building engulfed in fire, down the steps, across the loop, and through the green to the well, where people frantically cranked the handle and lifted buckets of water up from the earth. Others filled buckets from the showers and sent them up the line toward the burning building. Diego was the last in the line, and he raced to a window and splashed water inside, repeating the process with every bucket that reached him.

"This is useless," he said as he sent another empty bucket back down the line. "The building is gone."

There was a loud cracking sound and a rumble. Flames burst through the roof of the second floor.

"That's it, everyone get back. Get back!" Simone shouted. "It's too dangerous. There's nothing more we can do."

Isabella's mouth fell open, her eyes wide with horror. She screamed and threw herself on the grass, pounding the ground as tears streamed down her face.

"Mamá."

Everyone looked up.

Cristóbal stood at the base of the breezeway's stairs. The boy was pale and covered in black soot and ash. He held his baseball glove in his arms.

"Cristóbal!"

Isabella sprang forward and swept up the boy in her arms, and her anguished cries transformed to tears of joy and relief.

"Mi querido, cómo es que te escapaste?"

Sean emerged from the crowd, and Wendy and Dr. Rajavi approached from across the loop. Everyone turned to Isabella and Cristóbal.

"El otro Christopher me salvó."

"He says Christopher saved him," Diego said.

Isabella stroked her son's face. "Qué le pasó a Cristóbal? Dónde está?"

Cristóbal's head dropped. "Se le cayó el fuego."

"He says the fire... fell on him," Diego said, and he pressed his eyes shut.

Wendy dropped her head into her hands and wept. Sean held her in his arms as tears rolled down his face.

Simone took off her glasses and cleared her eyes. She collected herself with a long, deep breath, then let the air out slowly. "Okay," she said, her voice cracking, "we need to keep the fire from spreading to other buildings. Let's get to work."

Jordan looked up at the building as it burned, red and hot, flames reflected in her eyes. A single tear rolled down her cheek.

Simone stood on the green, the burned-out remains of apartment building 800 at her back. The residents of New Concord were gathered before her, seated on the grass, on an unseasonably chilly day at the end of a long, hot summer. Low-hanging clouds blanketed the sky. The veiled sun painted the earth with a muted silver light.

A cool breeze gently rustled the leaves on the trees. Tiny drops of rainwater dripped from the heavens as Simone began to speak.

"My friends, there's no gettin' around it, these last few days have been hard. Maybe the hardest we've had to face since this whole mess started. We lost a building and everything in it. Homes destroyed. But much more importantly we lost a good man. I speak of Christopher James, and we're gathered here today, not so much to mourn his loss—though we surely will mourn—but to celebrate him. To celebrate his life and the impact he made in our community, though he was a part of it for far too short a time."

Jordan listened to Simone's eulogy from the back of the gathering. She sat on the ground and stared vacantly ahead, picking at the grass. Samantha reached out and rubbed Jordan's back, but she went on plucking one blade at a time, tossing them each into the wind.

"When Christopher first arrived here, he was badly injured. He had deep wounds that needed healing. And not just physical wounds. He needed a lot of help, to heal his body *and* his mind. And we gladly gave him that help. He had a lot to learn. About people. About coexisting with others. We gladly taught him. Everyone sitting here helped to demonstrate to Christopher something he didn't think was possible before he got here. The concept that people can live and work together, in peace and harmony, without being motivated exclusively by personal gain."

Sean sat cross-legged in the middle of the crowd, a solemn expression on his usually cheerful face. Wendy sat at his side, their arms laced together, her head resting on his shoulder. She clenched her lips and shut her eyes, tears running down her cheeks. Sean pulled her closer and touched his head to hers.

"And he did heal. Body and mind. He got the message. He learned. And it's not like we had to hammer it into him, no. Once he got settled in, our way of life just rubbed off on him naturally, and he grew, like a seedling that just needed some water and sunshine to help it put down some roots and blossom into a big, strong tree. It was organic. All he needed was to see there was another way. To see it in action. To see us all living for each other, working for the common good. That's what changed him. All of you."

Jason and Sharon sat hand in hand near the front of the audience. With heavy eyes, they nodded along with Simone's words. Not far from them, Dr. Rajavi rested his arms on his knees. He closed his eyes and breathed in the cool air. Natalie sat at the doctor's side, lips pursed and eyes heavy with tears as she looked to the silver sky.

"Christopher had been living a life of extreme solitude. But here, he forged genuine connections with other people. He developed relationships. He made friends. And it didn't take long for him to begin to realize that it's these connections with others that are what keep us going, in good times and bad. They're what fill us up and add meaning and purpose to our lives. Our bonds with others are what keep us sane. They're what make us... *people*, really."

Jane sat at the end of a row, her legs crossed and her back straight as she listened intently to Simone. She was flanked by Jaylen, who held his head mournfully in his hand, Isaiah, who shook his head and sniffled, and Anthony, who lay flat on his back and stared at the illuminated blanket overhead, a smattering of tiny raindrops splashing against his face.

"Christopher learned to become more in tune with the world around him. To connect his spirit or his soul or his life force—whatever you want to call it—to the earth. To nature. To the air and the trees. He learned how to breathe. To be still. To be at peace, in his own heart, so that he could then begin to care for others."

Cathy sat among the people, posed with perfect posture, her dark hair fluttering freely in the gentle breeze, her eyes red and swollen with tears.

"He made some mighty big strides in a short time. And the healing process he went through, in body and mind, that process of growth and discovery, allowed him to step up. He began volunteering for work. He asked for more responsibilities. He became someone people could trust. Someone people could follow. He became a leader."

Diego sat near the front and rocked back and forth as he stared at the grass, his baseball hat pulled low. Dan and Tyreek sat beside him, nodding along to Simone's eulogy.

"Yes, Christopher came a long way, and this community taught him a lot. But you know what? He showed *us* something, too. When that building was burning, and he found out a child was trapped inside, he didn't hesitate. He went right up those steps and straight into the blaze. This little boy, sitting up here in the front, is alive today because of Christopher's brave act. Because of his sacrifice, this mother, sitting here, still has her son. He paid the ultimate price on behalf of another, and it's a lesson in courage and selflessness we should never forget."

Isabella sat in the front row and held Cristóbal on her lap, her arms were wrapped around her son. She squeezed him tightly as she cried. With both hands, Cristóbal clutched the grass-stained baseball Christopher had given him.

"And though he may be gone, let us always look to him for inspiration, as proof that we can improve ourselves, that we can *always* be better. Even better than we think we can be. Let us never forget his journey. Let us never forget his sacrifice. If we can do that, it won't have been in vain. Be at peace now, Christopher James. Goodbye, our dear friend."

Simone's final words rang out over the green, through the air and the rustling trees, then the gathered people of New Concord rose and consoled each other with hugs and kisses while the children began to race and play, bathed in the silver light of the blanketed sky and the flecks of rain carried by the wind.

ABOUT THE AUTHOR

Alexander Fedderly was raised in Ellicott City, Maryland by parents Karen and Jeff. He is the eldest of their five children. He graduated from Waynesburg University in 2006 with a degree in Communication and has worked in the news industry for fifteen years. He currently lives in Atlanta, Georgia with his wife, Beth.

Lightning Source UK Ltd.
Milton Keynes UK
UKHW010846070922
408462UK00001B/227